SYMBIOSIS

SYMBIOSIS

GUY PORTMAN

Chapter One

A CAR HORN SOUNDS, a motorbike swerves. The twins march across the road and onto the pavement where one of the policemen, his arms stretched out in front of him, calls, 'Stop!'

'Ucki bothigo wuthiwuthi waba meme!' shriek Talulah and Taliah in unison, pulling effortlessly away from their would-be captors.

Talulah darts right and scrambles under the hedge, Taliah following closely behind.

There is a football match in progress. The twins are heading towards it. Talulah barges into a female spectator who squeals, 'Oh my god!'

Talulah and Taliah are on the pitch now. Players stop and gawk at the pair.

'Stop them!' calls out a pursuing policeman.

A spectator braces himself to grab the twins.

'UGI BOBOTHI!' shout Talulah and Taliah, swerving away from him, Taliah to the right, Talulah to the left.

The man dives at Taliah's feet, misses. The twins race onwards, watched in silence by the game's stunned spectators and participants.

'They're getting away.'

*

Eleven years earlier – six-year-old identical twins Talulah and Taliah are sitting next to each other, their hands resting on their knees, their plimsoll-clad feet dangling a few inches from the floor. Talulah, leaning into her twin, whispers, 'Nana bibta budbud abta gego derdand.'

'Eain abta gego,' replies Taliah in a hushed voice.

'Gego ramp abta,' says Talulah.

Ms Browning, the speech therapist, who has been standing with her back to the twins writing on the whiteboard, spins around. She says, 'No whispering.' Now pointing at the whiteboard with her marker pen, Ms Browning says, 'Please repeat after me … br.'

There is no response. Ms Browning taps the marker pen against the letters *br* on the whiteboard several times and then says, '*Br*,' demonstrating the r sound with a rolled tongue. Two identical, cherubic faces look back at her.

'Let's try again. *Br*.'

There is no response.

'Your mummy is not going to be pleased to hear you haven't been trying, now is she?'

Taliah and Talulah shake their curly-haired heads at exactly the same time. Ms Browning smiles at this, the first response of any kind she has had from the twins that afternoon. Pointing at the whiteboard again with the pen, she says, 'Br.'

'Br,' respond Talulah and Taliah in unison, their little voices indistinguishable from one another.

'Good,' says Ms Browning, smiling serenely. Tapping the board once more, she enunciates, 'Dr.'

'Dr,' reply Taliah and Talulah in unison.

'Louder please.'

'Dr.'

The pen taps again. 'Fr.'

'Fr,' say the twins.

'Kl.'

'Kl.'
Ms Browning, tapping the whiteboard with her pen, says, 'Pl.'
'Pl,' reply Talulah and Taliah at the same time as one another.
'Su.'
'Su.'
'Su,' says Ms Browning again, studying the twins closely.
'Su.'

Although Ms Browning saw two mouths open at the same time, she only heard sound being emitted from one. Looking from one identical pretty face to the other, she is quite unsure which is Talulah and which is Taliah. She says, 'Taliah.' The twin on Ms Browning's left raises her hand in the air. 'Taliah, repeat after me … *sun*.'

'Sun,' replies Taliah.

'Talulah, please repeat after me … *sun*.'

Talulah does not respond.

'Talulah,' says Ms Browning, raising her voice. 'Your mummy will be angry. Now repeat after me … *sun*.'

'Thun,' says Talulah.

'No. Watch me. Hold the tip of your tongue on the ridge behind your front two teeth, your incisors, or where they would be if one hadn't fallen out. Now let's try again … *sun*.'

'Thun,' repeats Talulah.

'Taliah, show your sister how to do it.'

Talulah, crossing her arms across her chest, scowls. She looks at her twin. Ms Browning, turning her back on the pair, wipes the whiteboard with a cloth. Talulah and Taliah quickly swap seats. When Ms Browning turns to face them, she looks at the twin on her right. She says, 'Talulah, repeat after me … *sun*.'

'Sun.'

Ms Browning, taking a step backwards, repeats, '*Sun*.'

'Sun,' repeats Taliah.

'Great Talulah, now repeat after me … *seashells*.'

'Seashells,' says Taliah.

'*She sells seashells* by the *seashore*.'

'She sells seashells by the seashore.'

'The *shells she sells* are *surely seashells*.'

'The shells she sells are surely seashells,' repeats Taliah, perfectly enunciating each sound.

Ms Browning, biting her lower lip, shifts her attention from one twin to the other. She says, 'Now Taliah it is your turn. Repeat after me … *sun*.'

There is no response.

'*Sun*,' says Ms Browning.

'Sun.'

'Not you, your sister.' Looking directly at the twin on her left, she says, '*Sun*.'

'Thun,' replies the barely audible voice.

'You've swapped seats haven't you?'

Two emotionless faces look back at her.

*

At school, Talulah and Taliah's teachers, who regard them as two parts of a whole, almost never refer to them by their individual names, for identical twins' names do not hold the significance of yours or mine. As no one can tell them apart they are rarely uttered. Even at home their mother is sometimes forced to think before singling Talulah or Taliah out by name, and it is not uncommon for their short-sighted father to confuse one for the other. It was decided some time back that Talulah and Taliah should wear different coloured ribbons in their hair, which is worn in pigtails. This way they can be distinguished from one another. Talulah demanded blue when their mother brought up the idea. Taliah decided on pink, her second favourite colour after blue.

For the most part Talulah and Taliah, when they are not at school, stay in the bedroom they share. They sleep in a bunk bed, Talulah on the top bunk, Taliah on the bottom. On either side of their room is a desk. One of the desks is Talulah's, the other Taliah's. As for the activities they enjoy, building Lego Architecture monuments ranks amongst their favourite pastimes. The first monument they built was the Sydney Opera House, which they keep on top of their chest of drawers. There are a number of other monuments situated throughout the room, all of which were constructed by Taliah and Talulah with no adult assistance, this despite the fact Lego Architecture is aimed at children considerably older than themselves. Talulah and Taliah have built replicas of Chicago's iconic Sears Tower, the United Nations Headquarters, Singapore's Marina Bay Sands, The Leaning Tower of Pisa and Rome's Trevi Fountain.

Talulah and Taliah also enjoy indulging in activities more in keeping with girls their age. It is not an uncommon sight for there to be a miniature round dining table in the middle of their room, covered in a white tablecloth, set with a teapot and dainty crockery. Surrounding the table are chairs, seated on which are a variety of dolls, including several Barbie Dolls, a rag doll and a nineteen-eighties Cabbage Patch Doll. There are also small felt-covered toy mice, bunnies and wild boars, each one dressed as a human. Talulah likes kneeling beside the table and pretending to pour tea from the toy teapot into the miniature teacups, while Taliah places tiny slices of plastic cake and biscuits onto the floral-patterned plates. Sometimes Talulah says, *Bagedowi ke eain nuhnuh.*

When Talulah says this, Taliah removes the piece of plastic cake from the plate she is holding and replaces it with a tiny plastic replica of a digestive biscuit. She then places the plate in front of the Cabbage Patch Doll. On the occasions Talulah says, *Ucki fa fa bagedowi – wagidowi keki ou,* then Taliah puts a second piece of cake on the rag doll's plate.

*

Talulah and Taliah's scowling mother, Bethany, sits with her arms folded across her bosom, while their father Colin rocks back and forth in his chair. Addressing Bethany and Colin is Samuel Greene, one of the school's governors. At intervals Greene stops talking and turns to face Mrs Patel, the school principal, in the chair beside him. On each occasion he does this, Mrs Patel nods gravely.

'St. Benignus is not equipped to deal with your daughters,' says Greene.

'You mean not prepared,' says Bethany, glaring at Greene with her hazel eyes.

'That much we've gathered,' adds Colin, who then runs both hands through his thinning blond hair.

As Greene continues to express what he terms *the school's concerns*, Colin rocks ever faster in his chair and a glowering Bethany emits sporadic tutting noises.

'We have become very concerned with their non–verbal communication and unresponsiveness,' remarks Greene.

'They are as we all know very bright indeed,' adds Mrs Patel. 'Brilliant at English, art and design.'

Colin, who is finding Mrs Patel's habit of putting a positive spin on everything increasingly patronising, looks up at the ceiling. Greene says, 'Our priority is to assure that your daughters' unique ongoing needs are met, and for that to be achieved it is imperative that we consider every possible angle.' Turning to Mrs Patel, he adds, 'Would you not agree headmistress?'

Mrs Patel, oblivious to the question, is remembering the school trip to the aquarium last term. During the dolphin show the children had screamed and laughed when the dolphins had leapt high into the air spraying them with water, but the twins had stood looking impassively ahead, as if staring at a wall.

'Sandhra … um … would you agree?'

Mrs Patel, looking across at Greene, says, 'Yes I would.'

Greene, having made eye contact with Bethany and then

Colin, says, 'As I was saying, your daughters' taciturn ways are worrying, and...'

'Yes,' interjects Mrs Patel. 'Several of our teaching staff have noticed your daughters whispering to each other in a secret language. This is an example of the sort of thing that is stifling their development.'

Colin stops rocking back and forth in his chair. 'Their secret language is what is termed a cryptophasia,' he says. 'It's not uncommon for twins to have their own cryptophasia. In the case of Taliah and Talulah it is a simplified, childish amalgamation of English and some Patois.'

Bethany, who is of West Indian heritage, tuts when Colin says this. Several members of her family, who have contact with Talulah and Taliah, utilise Jamaican Patois terminology in their speech. Bethany does not appreciate the suggestion that they might be partially responsible for the content of her daughters' cryptophasia.

'I'll get to the point' says Greene. Having taken a deep breath, he adds in a quiet voice, 'What we are suggesting, is that … um … a, a *special* school would be more appropriate.'

'No way!' exclaims Bethany.

'I must have heard you incorrectly,' says Colin, leaning forward in his chair, piercing green eyes fixed menacingly on Greene.

Beads of sweat are visible on Greene's rotund, bald head as he continues. 'I, we, feel that, under these difficult circumstances, that they, um Talulah and T-T-*Taliah* require um an environment that can meet their particular needs.'

Drawing his chair up close to the other man's, Colin staring directly into his eyes, says, 'Are you aware that you are wearing a fluorescent floral motif tie?'

Greene, wiggling in his seat, says, 'Well um yes.'

'Oh, you are. Okay,' replies Colin.

'Don't be so defensive Colin, it isn't helping!' shrieks Bethany, before standing up and jabbing with her finger in the direction of

Greene and then Mrs Patel. 'Dere's nothing wrong with my daughters, nothing at all.'

*

The articulated bus draws to a halt, the doors spring open and its occupants hurry out onto the street. Only when all the other passengers have disembarked, do the two girls get up from their seats. They are tall for their age, their hair is tied in pigtails, knapsacks are slung over their right shoulders. Hazel eyes fixed ahead, they set off, their legs moving in exactly the same time as one another. An old woman stares at them, a small child points, and a postman stops pushing his trolley and follows them with his eyes. At the corner of Boyle Street Talulah's left shoulder collides with a lamppost. Taliah, following behind her winces and then rubs her left shoulder with her right hand. A minute later they arrive at the entrance of Royston Park School, a co-ed establishment for eleven to eighteen-year-olds with behavioural and emotional difficulties and disorders.

In single file, Taliah following behind Talulah, they make their way down passageways and up flights of stairs, before taking a right into the science department and then a left into Room 201. Ignoring both their fellow classmates who are chattering noisily amongst themselves, and Hubert, who calls out to them, 'Morning freaks,' they head to the back of the room, where they take out red exercise books and matching pens from their knapsacks. Mr Kenton the physics teacher walks in. A number of the students say, 'Good morning Mr Kenton,' others continue with their conversations. Talulah and Taliah, motionless as statues, stare blankly ahead. Standing at the front of the class in his tweed jacket and corduroy trousers, Mr Kenton describes in intricate detail Newton's Law of Universal Gravitation. The only sounds now, other than his monotone voice, are that of fidgeting and muffled snores.

Mr Kenton stops talking, turns from the whiteboard and looks out at the near comatose class, considering as he does so that it is little wonder that the nation has such a shortage of scientists. Addressing the class, he asks, 'Newton's law of universal gravitation states that the gravitational force between two objects is proportional to the mass of each, and inversely proportional to the distance between them. It is usually written how?'

Mr Kenton's attention falls on a boy; head tilted to the side, eyes barely open, a trail of saliva hanging from the corner of his mouth. He wonders whether his appearance is merely due to boredom or a result of the anti–anxiety medication half of the school's pupils seem to be on these days. Inadvertently he finds himself drawn to the motionless twins at the back of the class. Mr Kenton, looking from one insentient face to the other, is acutely aware that the twins know the answer to his question, for it was he who had marked their meticulous exam papers. A raised hand is bobbing up and down in the air.

'Yes Malcolm?' says Mr Kenton.

'$F = Gm_1m_2/r^2$'

'That is correct.'

When the bell rings the students are instantaneously re-animated. They bundle out of the classroom. Talulah and Taliah, the last to leave the room, pass silently along the corridor, watched by a gum-chewing girl leaning against the wall. Hubert steps out into the middle of the passageway, his gangly frame blocking Talulah and Taliah's path.

'Hey it's the dumb twins,' he calls out. Throwing an arm around each of their shoulders, he pulls them to him. He shouts in Talulah's ear, 'Helloooo!' and then knocks on Taliah's head with his knuckles. 'Jesus, you even smell the same.'

Three pupils passing in the opposite direction laugh. A small, hunched boy is shuffling along the passageway. Hubert shouts out jubilantly, 'It's the autistic kid!' And then, 'Waauu wauu waaauuuu.' Hubert roars with laughter.

A diminutive girl with plaited hair is scampering down the corridor, calling out in a meek voice, 'Taliah, Talulah wait for me.'

Hubert blocks her path. Bending forward he pinches her cheeks and utters in a baby voice, 'Meeeeeeeeeee.' He then calls out to a boy striding down the corridor, 'Yo wait up *bitch*.' And then in a quieter voice as he walks after him, 'You got any more of that shit?'

The girl, Veronica is her name, scampers down the corridor towards Taliah and Talulah, clasping her books in front of her in tiny hands. She calls out, 'Taliah Talulah, please come to the library and play scrabble with me.'

Taliah nods, Talulah does not. Talulah and Taliah follow Veronica down the passageway to the library. The three girls sit down at one of the library's tables, Talulah and Taliah next to each other, Veronica opposite them. A game of scrabble ensues. Talulah withdraws from the game soon after, but remains next to Taliah, watching the game unfold semi-attentively. When Veronica attains fifteen points by spelling out the word flaccid, Taliah says, 'Well done Veronica.'

Taliah is smiling as she places her tiles on the board.

'Sizzles,' says Veronica. 'That's so clever.'

*

Both Talulah and Taliah excel in their studies, with the exception of French due to the oral component. They do not partake in drama class. In classes in which the seating takes the form of benches, Talulah and Taliah sit next to each other, but in classes that utilise desks, Taliah sits at the desk directly behind Talulah's.

One day in English class when Ms Thomas asks if anyone knows who wrote *Animal Farm*, Taliah raises her hand timidly in the air. Neither Taliah nor Talulah have ever volunteered to answer a question in class before. Taliah scribbles down the correct answer on a piece of paper and then passes it to Ms

Thomas. No sooner has Ms Thomas asked another question than Talulah's hand shoots up in the air. Just as Taliah before her, Talulah scribbles down her answer on a piece of paper. Talulah's answer is incorrect.

In the staff room during breaks conversations about *The Silent Twins*, as the school's staff generally refer to them, are as common as the sound of clinking mugs. Mr Kenton often comments on their impassive appearances, Ms Philpot of the maths department frequently marvels at their sponge-like ability to consume knowledge, and on several occasions Mrs Fofana remarks that though *they are odd*, they have constructed *some quite exquisite items* in her design class, including most recently, desk tidies. It is generally only Ms Thomas who refers to Talulah and Taliah by their individual names.

As for Talulah and Taliah's home life, their father Colin no longer sees them on a daily basis, as he is now living in a friend's apartment nearby. On the weekends when Colin does spend time with them, he often observes his silent, blank-faced daughters playing peculiar, introverted games. Sometimes he notices them whispering to one another in their cryptophasia when they think no one is watching. Colin's mother endlessly offers her advice as to how to solve *the problem*, as does his father and his brother too, on the rare occasions Colin speaks to them on the telephone. And there are all kinds of other experts – his daughters' school with their endless suggestions, a psychiatrist, learning development counsellors, speech therapists, and even the wife of a friend, who offers advice uninvited. Colin's world is full of opinions but short on solutions.

It is not uncommon that when Colin visits his former home the sound of Bethany shouting can be heard emanating from the kitchen. On more than one occasion a plate is heard to smash, forcing Colin's hasty retreat.

*

February 14th 2009 – *Physics class in room 201 is like a vacuum - a black hole where time is suspended. A single physics class can last a whole day. Maybe Malcolm could write an equation to explain how this is possible. I really like Veronica's hair - it's so pretty and sweet, just like Meme's when Meme was young...*

February 14th 2009 – Ms Papin said in biology class today that there'd be loads more twins in the future. This is some thing to do with artificial ~~incemation~~ insemeination. One day there'll be twins everywhere and people won't stare at Meme anymore, but at single (non twins) instead. And crytophasias will be spoken everywhere, and teachers and parents won't send twins who speak them to speech therapists and psyciatrists. And lots of singles will be gealous of twins because they can speak 2 languages when they can only speak 1...

Every evening after they finish their homework Talulah and Taliah write their diary entry for the day, in their idiosyncratic handwriting, at their desks, on opposite sides of their bedroom. They started their diaries two years ago when they were eleven. Talulah's diary is blue, Taliah's pink. Talulah and Taliah have promised each other that they will never look in each other's diaries. Neither has broken this promise.

March 21st 2009 – In physics Mr Kenton explained the theory of ~~relavity~~ relativity ($E = mc2$) for like the 100th time this year. Why - Because only Meme and Malcolm understand it, that's why. It is really very easy ... Spaghetti ~~bolonese~~

Bolognezsse for lunch, speech therapy in afternoon. Hubert is an idiot.

March 21st 2009 – *Spaghetti Bolognese for lunch was quite yummy by school standards. Speech therapy in the afternoon. Hubert bullying Veronica, Meme and some of the small children from year below again ... Meme was playing scrabble in the library before home time. Ms Thomas came over and said she wanted to speak 'to me alone' outside the room. In the corridor she told me about next year's reading list. When went back in library scrabble board and pieces scattered on floor. Talulah said Hubert did it, but he was nowhere to be seen...*

Taliah feels a presence looming over her. She stops writing, closes her diary and spins around in her chair. On the other side of the room Talulah is watching her, a scowl creasing her attractive features.

'Dinner's ready,' calls Bethany from downstairs.

Talulah stands up.

'See you down there,' says Taliah.

Talulah does not move.

'Outh oun eain,' says Taliah.

A glimmer of a smile flashes across Talulah's face. She leaves the room.

*

The next day – 'Yo dumb twins!' exclaims Hubert, entering the classroom and striding up to Taliah and Talulah. 'We just saw your mummy waiting outside Pendergast's office.'

'She's fit yo, I'd smash it,' interjects Asif.

Some of the class laugh.

'Shut up you moron,' says Hubert.

Hubert grabs one of Taliah and Talulah's pigtails in each hand and pulls them towards him, crouching down as he does so.

'I know you can speak, I've heard one of you say stuff to your little friend, *Veronica.*'

Hubert, pulling tighter on the pigtail tied in a pink hairband belonging to Taliah, inspects her pretty face, which shows only the faintest hint of discomfort. Turning his head he looks into Talulah's hazel eyes. Hubert releases the pigtails. He recoils several feet across the floor.

'Look Hubert's scared.' It is Malcolm who says this.

A few of the students laugh.

'Shut up Malcolm you geek,' says Hubert in a faltering voice. 'You're a freak. That's why you were sent to a special school.' Hubert then takes a seat at his usual desk near the front of the class.

'Why are you at a special school then Hubert?' asks Emma from the other side of the aisle.

'Because fatty, I was too cool and crazy for my last school.'

'My neighbour Edward Tolbury used to go to your old school,' says Emma. 'He told me a very different story.'

Taliah and Talulah observe Hubert gulp. They notice too that his pale complexion turns cadaverous.

At this very moment in the headmaster's office, Bethany is perched on the corner of an armchair.

'How are Talulah and Taliah getting on at Hunter-Thornton Integrated Counselling Services,' enquires Pendergast, the headmaster, removing his spectacles and carefully placing them on the desk.

'George is wonderful, just *amazing*,' says Bethany.

'George is a quite remarkable young therapist,' says Pendergast, nodding his large head.

'But Hunter-Thornton, he is terrible.'

'A pompous old sod,' mutters Pendergast.

'Excuse me?'

'Nothing,' replies Pendergast, who then looks down at some papers on his desk before continuing. 'The results of Talulah and Taliah's intelligence tests are fairly similar. But, and I believe this is significant.' He fixes his gaze on Bethany. 'There are differences in Talulah and Taliah's perception tests.'

'I know, they've done dese tests before, so what?' replies Bethany somewhat defensively.

Pendergast opens his mouth to speak, then closes it again. He takes a piece of paper from his desk drawer, glances at it momentarily and then says, 'Now we know from the medical tests that your daughters lack of speech is not due to a congenital defect.'

'Tell me something I don't know. They speak a little, sometimes.'

Pendergast, leaning his elbows on the desk, adopts a steepling gesture, the fingertips of each hand touching the other. He says, 'Very little if at all here at school. Dorothy, the speech therapist, tells me both continue to have problems pronouncing s's.'

'Excuse me,' says Bethany. 'Talulah has de problem with s not Taliah.'

Pendergast blushes. He inspects the piece of paper again, exhales, and then says, 'No they both do.'

Bethany, her arms now folded across her bosom, opens her mouth to contest this, but closes it again. Holding a pink-varnished fingernail to her lips she looks pensively up at the ceiling. Pendergast studies her inquisitively, and then leaning back in his chair says in a quiet voice, 'What we need to do is move forward, find a solution.'

'Solution,' says Bethany, now giving the headmaster her full attention.

'Now please just hear me out on this,' continues Pendergast, holding his palms out in front of him. 'Now what I'm suggesting is er, um, er, well, brief, very brief, periods of separation.'

'No way!' shouts Bethany rising to her feet.

'Merely for an afternoon activity on a Tuesday and Thursday.'

Bethany glares at Pendergast, who, holding his palms out in front of him again, chuckles uneasily, and says, 'Okay just a Tuesday.'

Bethany plunks herself down in her chair and shakes her head. Pendergast rummages through his desk drawer and removes a sheet of paper. 'Now let's look at what's available on a Tuesday afternoon. Oh yes, there's design, gymnastics and creative writing class.'

Bethany, now twirling strands of curly hair in her fingers, is unable to hear Pendergast outlining the benefits of the various activities, for she is remembering prior separations of her daughters. An unresponsive, catatonic two-year-old Talulah lying on the sitting room floor, and a year later a frantic Colin phoning to say Taliah had gone into a hysterical state in the shopping mall, outlining exactly the same symptoms as Talulah was exhibiting that very moment in the kitchen. After that they had hardly been separated at all, and on the couple of occasions they had, the results had not been good.

'Team sports are great for developing social skills, don't you agree … Mrs Taylor.'

'Well maybe,' says Bethany doubtfully.

'Listen,' says Pendergast in a reassuring tone. 'I'm not sure what happened before, but they're thirteen-years-old now, and, well it's about time for, you know, some degree of separation.' Looking across the desk at Bethany biting on her lower lip, he adds, 'Come on separation is no big deal, they're not Siamese twins.'

CHAPTER TWO

T HE FOLLOWING TUESDAY: 'Janice calm down, I don't understand, please…'

'She's hardly breathing she's unresponsive and she's, she's collapsed on the floor, she's just lying there. She's had a stroke or a, a brain aneurism or something,' jabbers Mrs Fofana.

'I'll be right down,' says Mr Francis the PE teacher, hanging up, picking up the first aid kit from the table and heading off at a stride through the basement towards the design department. He opens the door. 'Move aside,' he orders. The circle of boys and girls part.

'She's dying!' shrieks Mrs Fofana.

Mr Francis, kneeling down beside the prostrate girl, notices the blue hairbands securing her hair. He pries open her mouth to make sure that she hasn't swallowed her tongue and then checks her pulse. 'Move back guys,' he orders. The circle of pupils step back.

'This can't be happening!' screams a hysterical Mrs Fofana.

'Looks like *rigor mortis* to me,' utters a male voice.

'Get away from here Hubert!' screams Mrs Fofana, tears streaming down her cheeks.

'Have you phoned an ambulance?' asks Mr Francis.

'Yes,' replies a girl's voice from somewhere behind him.

'Good,' says Mr Francis, and then, pointing at the weeping

Mrs Fofana, he adds sternly, 'Janice this isn't helping. Now let's put her in the recovery position … Yes, like that. Stand back please; I'm not asking again.'

The pupils take a step back. Mr Francis, ignoring Mrs Fofana's pleas of, 'Do something Henry,' scans the circle of adolescents. 'Where is she?' he asks.

There is no response.

'Where is she?' he asks again.

'They were separated innit,' says Asif.

'It was Mr Pendergast's idea,' says the now sobbing Mrs Fofana. 'Starting today, every Tuesday.'

'Well where is she now?' asks Mr Francis.

Mrs Fofana shrugs, as do some of the boys and girls gathered around.

'Go find her,' says Mr Francis.

Several of the boys and girls depart at haste. Mr Francis, placing his hand on Talulah's head, views her barely moving breast and fluttering eyelids. 'She'll be fine,' he says in a trembling voice.

*

Taliah's diary entry – August 8th 2009 – *Meme finished making the Rockefeller Centre this morning. The Rockefeller Centre is a National Historic Landmark in Midtown Manhattan with shopping & dining. It is our 5th Lego Architecture monument. It was very easy to make. Meme wants to go there when we are older. I want to make the Louvre next. Mene wants to make The White House…*

Talulah's diary entry – October 2nd 2009 – Biology, english and design in morning. In design Meme felt a little bit dizzy and sick. It is the medecine the new doctor gives us that makes us feel like this. Meme's complained to our parents about it 2 or 3 times already. Lunch was a chicken thing. It was yucki. After lunch Meme ate a Toblerone. Then double physics with Kenton in afternoon. Double physics lasts for a really really long time and is v.boring. It's the weekend ~~tomorow~~ tomorrow...

Taliah's diary entry – January 2nd 2010 – *Meme made our 6th Lego Architecture monument today – The White House. It took nearly all day to make as it has 560 pieces. Meme is going back to school on Monday for the start of the spring term. Actually most of the spring term is in wintertime, only the last bit is in the spring. And whilst I'm on this topic – lots of the summer term is in springtime not summer. Only the autumn term is correct. It is nearly all in the autumn apart from the end, which is in wintertime...*

*

One month later – Hunter-Thornton Integrated Counselling Services – framed watercolour landscapes adorn the white walls of the spacious, brightly lit room – furnished with colourful settees and chairs, polka dot beanbags and a large glass desk. Spread out on the polished wooden floor is a large gridded mat with different coloured squares. Taliah is crouched over the mat, each of her limbs resting on separate squares.

George, the young psychiatrist sitting cross-legged beside the mat, says, 'You ready Taliah.' He then runs a hand through his long jet-black hair. Taliah, smiling faintly, looks across at her sister, who is kneeling next to George. George begins to clap slowly. Talulah claps in time with George. Taliah, extending a long, slender arm to her left, brings her hand down on a square.

'Good job Taliah we're impressed,' says George. He starts clapping again. This time Talulah does not join him. Taliah braces herself. She reaches out in front of her with her right arm. Her body is trembling. Taliah giggles when she collapses to the mat, and Talulah claps enthusiastically. George says, 'Nice job Taliah.' And then, 'It's your turn madam, are you ready?'

Talulah stands up, drags her prostrate sister off the mat by her arms, and then, having released her, kneels in front of the mat, focusing on the mat's grid, her thin lips forming a perfect horizontal line across her pretty face. George starts clapping slowly, as does Taliah.

From outside comes the sound of a car screeching to a halt, followed by a door slamming shut. A moment later the eminent psychiatrist Doctor Hunter-Thornton storms into the building, his jowls quivering, eyes bloodshot, the grey strands of hair on the side of his head sticking out frenziedly in all directions, his cheeks and bald pate ablaze with anger, a result of having had his advances towards a young nurse unceremoniously rejected during his visit to a mental health facility earlier that afternoon. Uttering a tirade of pomposities he stomps down the hallway and into the reception room, where he asks in a loud voice, '*Avez-vous réservé La Trompette pour huit heures pour deux personnes?*'

The blonde receptionist, Agneska, looking up, says, 'What this mean?'

'La Trompette this evening at eight for two – has it been booked?' demands Hunter-Thornton, staring menacingly at Angeska with his bloodshot eyes.

'No.'

'And why the hell not woman?'

'The girl she phone earlier, she cancel,' replies Agneska.

Hunter-Thornton slams his fist on the desk and screams, 'These words are razors to my wounded heart!' He then collapses into a chair and exudes several desultory sighs. A short time later Agneska says, 'Doctor Hunter-Thornton.'

Hunter-Thornton does not reply.

'The Silent Twins have their monthly appointment with you in ten minutes, after they finish with George.'

'Oh you invidious creature!' exclaims Hunter-Thornton, scowling at Agneska as he marches out of the room.

He storms down the passageway, barges open the door of George's room, clicks his fingers and says, 'They are to be delivered to my office forthwith.'

'Dr Hunter-Thornton, if you could hold off dispensing your unmatched expertise to these two young ladies for just two minutes,' replies George, holding two fingers aloft to illustrate the point.

'I am in no mood to be inveigled, you have been warned,' responds Hunter-Thornton, casting a malevolent glance at Talulah and Taliah, who seemingly oblivious to his presence, kneel silently beside each other, carefully inspecting the matted floor game in front of them.

Five minutes later – Talulah and Taliah are sitting next to each other, their backs held straight, hands clasped in their laps. On the other side of the antique mahogany desk Hunter-Thornton reclines in a leather revolving chair, chewing on the base of the Montblanc fountain pen as if it were a cigar. He inspects the pair glumly. Having placed a pair of *pince-nez* spectacles on the end of his nose, he peruses the papers on his desk, then looks up solemnly at Talulah and Taliah, exhales forcefully, removes the *pince-nez* and stands up and walks over to the filing cabinet.

As he rummages through the cabinet with his back to the twins he hears a creaking noise. He stops rummaging and listens. All is silent. He is sifting through the papers in Talulah and Taliah's file when he thinks he hears whispering. Turning around abruptly he views the two insentient, mannequin-like figures staring straight ahead with disdain. Having pulled several sheets of paper from the file he heads back to the desk, collapses into his chair, places the *pince-nez* on the end of his nose and studies the papers. Looking up he examines the attractive, expressionless girls, scrunching up his face as he does so. Reclining back in the chair he says, 'Your continual disregard for oral communication is infantile and erroneous.'

His attention shifts from one blank face to the other and then back again. He grits his teeth, grabs a piece of paper from the desk, glances at it momentarily and then says in a mocking voice, 'Those puerile games you evidently so relish playing with George are nugatory.'

He looks at the paper again and then adds in a stern voice, 'The pair of you are asinine and base.' Hunter-Thornton, holding a stubby finger aloft, adds, 'You are however quite capable of the primitive oral communication sufficient for your lowly station.' He inspects a piece of paper on the desk and then bellows pompously, slapping his ample girth with one hand as he does so. 'It states here you created some rather exceptional desk tidies in Ms Fofana's design class. Remarkable that this is what passes as excellence in that establishment you attend.'

Leaning forward, staring at Talulah and Taliah with bloodshot, heavily-bagged eyes, he adds, 'At your age I was a Latin scholar of exceptional note at one of the nation's premier schools.' Grinning widely he adds in a sanctimonious voice, '*Vos autem stulti nigra.*' Then chuckles.

'Bobothi ucki bigi ugi beri beri,' says Talulah.

'How dare you cryptophasia me!' exclaims Hunter-Thornton, lunging forward toward Talulah.

'Bothi ugi beri beri waba,' says Taliah.

'You will not regress to cryptophasias, not here!' shouts Hunter-Thornton, pointing a finger at Taliah. The scarlet-cheeked psychiatrist views with consternation the two expressionless faces staring back at him. 'Here at Hunter-Thornton Integrated Counselling Services we accept cognitive disorders in all their manifestations, but insolence we will not.' Pointing a trembling finger at each of them in turn he adds in a quieter voice, 'You have been warned.'

'Ugi derriii bothi baldi.' It is Talulah who says this.

Hunter-Thornton lunges towards Talulah, jowls quivering. A pink tongue darts out in his direction.

'Ugi bothibothi fatti berri,' says Taliah.

Hunter-Thornton lurches left towards Taliah.

Talulah says, 'Ugi ugi fatti bothi baldi.'

'I'll have you separated and incarcerated in the nation's most debased psychiatric facilities where you'll languish permanently narcotised on a profusion of anti–psychotics,' blurts out Hunter-Thornton.

'Waxiwaxi ugi bothi baldi,' says Talulah.

'Bothi ucki ucki eddi fatti,' says Taliah.

'Impertinent nigresses!' exclaims Hunter-Thornton, now towering over the twins, his red face bearing down upon them. Accosted by defiant, staccato bursts of cryptophasia, interspersed with darting tongues, Hunter-Thornton, shaking his fists frenziedly in the air, cries out, 'That it should come to this!'

The eminent psychiatrist, his rabid attention flitting from one twin to the other, falls silent, his bloodshot, vein-riddled eyes open wide, the only sound now emanating from his mouth are harried gasps. Drawn unwittingly to the pair of vacuous eyes on his right, the wheezing doctor reaches out to the desk with one hand, his scarlet face glistening with sweat. After a hoarse, lengthy rasp, he collapses forward and crashes noisily to the floor.

Seconds later there is knocking at the door, followed by, 'Is everything okay in there?' George opens the door. He peers tentatively inside and says, 'Oh my god.'

He hurries over and bends over the spluttering, purpurescent-faced, convulsing figure on the floor. A tall, pleated-skirted woman, clasping the hand of a small blonde girl, appears at the door. She emits a squeal and pulls the girl to her. Turning to the impassive, identical faces staring straight ahead, she starts screaming. Agneska hurries into the room.

'Phone an ambulance,' says George.

Agneska leaves the room at a leisurely pace.

'Everyone out please,' orders George.

The now whimpering mother and her daughter leave the room, followed by Talulah and Taliah. In the reception area the mother, gawking at the identical, emotionless girls standing in the doorway, screeches, 'Get them away from my daughter!'

'Come this way girls,' says Agneska, ushering the twins out into the hallway. The doorbell rings. Agneska opens the door. Bethany walks in.

Two hours later – Bethany's mobile is vibrating. She takes it out of her apron pocket and answers it. Moments later she says, 'Well dat is great.' She then hangs up. 'Girls,' says Bethany. Talulah and Taliah look up at exactly the same time. 'Good news, Dr Hunter-Thornton is going to live.'

'Mummy,' say Talulah and Taliah in unison.

'Yes,' replies Bethany.

'Can we have a Petits-Filous?'

'Of course.' As Bethany heads to the fridge to get the Petits-Filous yoghurts, she is pleased with her daughters' vocal response, the first words she has heard from them in several days, which she concludes must be a good sign.

*

Talulah and Taliah are now fifteen-years-old. Though half-an-hour younger than Taliah, Talulah, at five-foot-ten inches, is a quarter of an inch taller than her five-foot-nine and three quarters twin. This minute difference in height is about the only physical difference between them. They can however be distinguished from one another by their hairbands. Talulah continues to wear blue hairbands and Taliah pink. One might also be able to tell them apart by their clothes, for although they wear the same outfits each and every day, they more often than not wear either a blouse, jumper, skirt or pair of socks that is a marginally different shade of colour than the other is wearing.

Taliah follows Talulah into the school's sports hall. A number of the boys stop chattering amongst themselves and ogle the twins' tight-fitting T-shirt and short clad frames. Several girls make tutting noises when they observe the boys do this.

In PE class, Talulah and Taliah are always placed on the same team, whether it be volleyball or basketball. They always appear uninterested and listless, lingering on the periphery of the game. But today Mr Francis puts Taliah and Talulah on opposing teams. Whilst the boys partake in fitness training at one end of the sports hall, the girls commence their volleyball game. Emma serves half-heartedly. A meek, double-handed return from Veronica just makes it over the net. Taliah, who is standing at the net, reaches out with her right hand – the ball travels over the net towards a tall, raven-haired girl. Talulah barges the girl out of the way and smashes the ball back over the net, winning her team the point.

Several minutes have passed when Emma says, 'Taliah, it's your turn to serve.'

Taliah makes her way to the end line at the back of the court, where she places her left foot in front of her right, holds the ball up to eye-level, left hand resting under the ball, right hand placed on top of it. She tosses the ball up in the air, pulls her right arm back and then forward. The ball sails over the net in the direction of the raven-haired girl, who, waiting for the ball's descent, bites on her lower lip. Talulah is racing across the floor.

'Excuse *me*,' says the girl as Talulah barges her out of the way. The ball is returned from whence it came with a vigorous sweep of Talulah's right hand.

A girl on the other team returns the ball deftly with a double-handed drive. The ball is heading towards Talulah, but she ignores it, and it is left to Veronica to make the return shot. Taliah casually returns Veronica's effort one-handed. Here comes Talulah, sprinting across the court, now jumping through the air, returning the ball with her outstretched right hand, oblivious to the inevitable bruises impact with the floor will cause. Taliah exhales sharply as she enthusiastically hits the ball back over the net. Talulah races across the floor, knocking over Veronica in the process, then dives through the air to return the shot. Talulah and Taliah are smashing the ball to and fro. The other girls leave the court and watch the competing twins from the sidelines.

Taliah, jumping high at the net, smashes the ball with the palm of her hand. Talulah, leaping agilely to her left, returns the ball. The boys abandon their fitness training and watch Talulah and Taliah competing, something they have never witnessed before.

'Ahhh!' shrieks Taliah, leaping high at the net once more and smashing the ball downwards.

Talulah, dropping to her knees returns the ball two-handed. Taliah returns. Talulah smashes the ball with her fist. It hits Taliah in the stomach, knocking her to the ground.

'EAAAAAA!' screams Talulah.

The spectators hold their hands to their ears. A panting Taliah, her clothes wet with sweat, hauls herself off the floor.

Talulah and Taliah arrive at their next class, physics, in customary fashion: Taliah following behind Talulah. They sit down, unpack their stationary items from their bags and wait silently for the class to begin, ignoring the scrutiny of their classmates, who had all witnessed the pair's outpouring of competitiveness.

*

As she regally flicks a pigtail off her shoulder with a slender finger, a faint smile appears on her pretty face, and for the fleetest of moments she emits a barely audible giggle. One of the four boys gathered around Talulah on the athletics track stand's concrete step, runs a thumb and index finger slowly up and down one of her blue hairband adorned pigtails, whilst another boy rests his head on her shoulder, and the other two boys perform a series of puerile antics on the step below, in an effort to impress her. Talulah cannot see her twin for Taliah is sitting a few rows behind her in the stand, conversing with their classmate, Samson. As the boys continue with their antics, Talulah yearning for her twin, wills Taliah to come and join her. A cloud passes across the sky from left to right, but still Taliah does not come. Talulah's eyes draw closer together and her hands form clenched fists at her side. Having grabbed the wrist of the hand that is now gradually edging up her denim clad thigh, Talulah deposits it in its proprietor's lap. She stands up and strides up the steps, ignoring the complaining boys behind her.

Taliah is sitting on the step, leaning towards the burly Samson beside her. When Samson whispers in Taliah's ear, she giggles coquettishly. Talulah, watching her twin, feels certain that Taliah has been whispering words in Samson's ear, each and every *s* sound perfectly enunciated. When Talulah plunks herself down on the step next to Taliah, Taliah's back remains turned to her. Talulah sits with her arms across her chest, her gaze fixed directly ahead, whilst Taliah's hazel eyes stay fixed on Samson. Several minutes have elapsed when Talulah tugs at Taliah's sleeve. Taliah ignores her. Talulah tugs at the sleeve again.

'Hat kloki bibta – wedi treki,' whispers Talulah in Taliah's ear.

'Not now, I'm busy,' replies Taliah, swivelling to face her twin.

*

Two hours later – Bethany is upstairs when she hears the front door open and close. When it opens and closes again nearly a minute later, she knows that her daughters have arrived home at different times, and therefore must have had a disagreement.

During dinner that evening Talulah and Taliah's cutlery does not move in unison with one another, and when they reach for their glasses of water, they do so at different times. Their unsynchronised actions continue into dessert, with Talulah rapidly consuming her Petits-Filous yoghurt, whilst Taliah eats hers at a leisurely pace, each time her teaspoon emerges from the pot, only the front end is covered in yoghurt. That evening Taliah does her homework in the sitting room while Talulah completes hers as usual upstairs in their bedroom.

When Talulah and Taliah walk from the bus stop to school the next morning there is a twenty metre gap between them. In their first class, English, they open their satchels and take out first their notepad then their exercise book, followed by a pencil honed to a fine point, an eraser, and finally a sharpener, before aligning these objects horizontally across their desks, just as they do every class, only on this occasion they do so at different times to one another.

'Please take out your homework,' says Ms Thomas, scanning the class. She then walks slowly down the aisles, looking left and right, checking that her students have completed their homework. Ms Thomas says, 'Very neat handwriting' to one student, and to another, 'Oh, that looks much better.' When she reaches Veronica she places a hand on her shoulder, and inspecting the little drawings of bunnies and mice in the margin of Veronica's exercise book, remarks, 'I love the illustrations.' Ms Thomas continues along the aisle. 'Asif, where is your homework?'

'Dunno innit,' responds Asif.

Some of the students laugh.

'Is that all you've written Samson?' asks Ms Thomas in a quiet voice.

Samson nods sombrely.

'Good Taliah,' says Ms Thomas, spending marginally longer looking over Taliah's shoulder than she did with the others. Ms Thomas approaches Talulah's desk, looks down, sees that the answer to her first question is wrong, which surprises her, as

Talulah like her twin, very rarely makes mistakes in her homework. Having walked to the front of the class, Ms Thomas asks, 'Does Lady Russell think Charles Musgrove would make a suitable husband for Anne Elliot?' After scanning the room of blank faces, she says, 'Does anyone know the answer?'

No hands are raised. Ms Thomas looks at Malcolm at the back of the class. She knows that he has studied Jane Austen's *Persuasion* fastidiously, but he appears disinterested – fiddling with a Rubik's Cube in his lap. The serene smile that has been a permanent feature on Ms Thomas's face all morning evaporates when she sees Hubert raise his hand. She ignores him. The room is quiet, the only sound the faint ticking of the wall clock. Out of the corner of her eye Ms Thomas notices Taliah glance furtively to her left, in the direction of Samson on the other side of the classroom. Samson nods. Taliah raises her hand.

'Yes Taliah,' says Ms Thomas, preparing to walk over to her, to read the answer she will invariably scribble out on a scrap of paper.

'Lady Russell thinks Charles Musgrove is not suitable when Anne is nineteen, but when she is still unmarried aged twenty-two, her opinion changes.'

Pupils gasp. Several clap.

'Yes,' says Ms Thomas, who despite being as astonished as the rest of the class by Taliah's vocal response, does not want to draw too much attention to it. She asks, 'How does *Persuasion* challenge the status of class culture in early nineteenth-century British society?'

Talulah raises her hand.

'Yes Talulah,' says Ms Thomas.

'By u, uzing irony and c, catire,' says Talulah.

There are more gasps and a couple of claps.

'Yes, very good,' says Ms Thomas.

'C, catire, it's called *satire*,' says a smirking Hubert. And then a moment later, 'HELP,' as Talulah having leapt from her seat, jumps on him, grabs his throat and proceeds to throttle him with both hands.

'Stop Talulah!' shrieks Ms Thomas, rushing over and trying to pry Talulah from on top of the wailing Hubert.

A thrashing Hubert utters a stifled 'help' as Samson and Asif hurry over and join Ms Thomas in her efforts to pull Talulah away. And then Talulah's hands go limp, and she is back in her seat, looking ahead impassively, as the whole of the class watch her, including Taliah.

Ms Thomas orders Talulah to the headmaster's office, along with Taliah, for she is wary of sending Talulah alone, having heard about the incident. Pendergast sends Talulah home for the day, and Taliah too, for the school will not accept responsibility for seperating them. Bethany comes and collects her daughters from the school.

When they get home, Talulah storms upstairs to the bedroom that she shares with Taliah. Taliah remains downstairs in the sitting room, where perched on the sofa, she rereads the final few chapters of *Persuasion*. Upstairs Talulah scribbles in her diary, before pacing up and down the room.

Talulah is now on the top bunk, where she sits cross-legged, hazel eyes focusing on the far wall, faint frown lines visible across her forehead, as she pines for her twin. Downstairs in the sitting room Taliah fidgets with various ornaments, and then flicks through the television channels, before picking up books from the bookshelf, only to put them back down again. Upstairs Talulah remains on the top bunk, focusing all her concentration on Taliah.

When Taliah finally makes her way upstairs she feels guilty about answering the question in English class, for she knows that Talulah would have felt obligated to follow her. Now Taliah feels the humiliation that her twin experienced over her speech impediment, as if this humiliation belongs to her too. On opening the bedroom door, Taliah sees Talulah sitting cross-legged on the top bunk. In no time Taliah and Talulah are chattering in their cryptophasia, and giggling too.

Chapter Three

TALULAH'S DIARY ENTRY – November 14th 2012 – Pendergast spoke to Meme in his office today. He said Meme's grades were mostly really good, but Meme needs to comunicate and socialize more. And Royston Park School was a big chance for us that we had to 'make the most of'. He said 'Carpe Diem,' – he often says this – it means seize the day in Latin. Maybe ucki bigi ugi bossi Hunter-Thornton taught him it. When Pendergast asked if Meme understood, Meme nodded and said 'Yes sir' or so he thought. He clapped and said 'Well done'. He didn't notice that although I opened my mouth I made no sound – only my twin did. After school Meme went to the doctor – more pills – always more pills...

Taliah's diary entry – November 16th 2012 – *Ms Thomas read from Persuasion again today. Her voice is so enchanting, evocative and rife with emotion, it is as if she has been transformed into its protagonist, Anne Elliot. Ms Thomas asked the class – Do you think the author has an opinion about marriage? There is no doubt that Austen* felt marriage should be for love. She was condemning the upper echelons of society for marrying to improve their social status and financial position. Most of the class don't know this. When Ms Thomas asked Samson, he shrugged and shook his big head. He looked so sad. I could have answered this and every other question asked in class, but Ms Thomas said she won't accept my answers written on paper anymore, and I shan't speak them, not after what happened last time...

November 22nd 2012 – It was cold but sunny today. The class went down to the athletics track and hung out in the stand. Meme stayed a little way away from the others. Veronica joined Meme. She shared her packet of Gummy Bears with Meme. Samson was sitting alone. Our eyes met for the fleetest of moments. Hubert ran over to the front of the stand with a large sports bag. He said he had something that would make our forthcoming physics class with Mr Kenton better. From the bag he took out tiny canisters of laughing gas (nitrous oxide, N2O). Most of the class ran cheering down the steps to Hubert. They proceeded to inhale the gas. Meme hasn't experienced gas before. I was nervous about taking gas, but I could feel Mene's excitement at the prospect. I thought Hubert wouldn't give her any gas after what happened in English class that day, but he did and with a big smile on his face too. I couldn't let her go through an experience like that without me. And besides as she often says, 'mene ry nuhnuh meou abtary.'

This translates as Talulah hasn't experienced it until Taliah has...

November 22nd 2012 – ... I could sense Meou was scared of the gas. I tried it first of course. Meme's ~~euforia~~ euphoria was instant. Veronica didn't want to take the gas. Hubert, holding gas kanistars in each hand chased Veronica round and round in circles, but she was saved from a gasing by Ben and S-a-m-s-o-n, who else – my twin's ~~nite~~ ~~nighte~~ (wait I'm checking the dictionary) knight (its a silent k – Meme learnt all about silent K's when she was small in speech therapy). Samson – Meou's knight in shining armor – his IQ is like so low, he can't do his 12 times tables. ... In physics Meme floated above the class on gas – together – as we'll always be. Mr Kenton was talking about Newton's Second Law of Motion again – boring!!!

December 5th 2012 – ... *Meme sits at her respective desks in Meme's room, surrounded by the Lego Architecture monuments, the dolls and the Sylvanian Families on the shelves. Will life always be like this?*

December 11th 2012 – *Samson and I sit next to each other in the library, our legs touching, I whispering in his ear, being careful to be quiet – Talulah can get waba derriii derriii when hears me speaking...*

December 14th 2012 – ... Meme wishes she had Calvin Klein jeans like Emma's, in a much smaller size

*

One month later – Veronica and her mummy walk through the front garden and approach the door. Veronica rings on the doorbell. An aproned Bethany, on opening the door, says, 'Hi Audrey, hi Veronica.' And then, 'Would you like to come in for tea Audrey?'

Audrey looks up at Talulah and Taliah, who are standing at the top of the stairs. She steps back, glances at her watch, and then says, 'I have to go to the dry cleaners.' Audrey heads off at pace towards the front gate.

Veronica scampers up the stairs and follows Talulah and Taliah into the bedroom. The blinds are drawn, a legion of dots of dust and tiny threads of fluff cascade slowly downwards, visible only as they pass the narrow rays of sunlight around the sides of the blinds. Veronica blinks, her eyes adjusting to the dusky light. Circling around she sees the faces of the dolls on the shelves watching her. Having taken a small velvet-covered toy mouse from the bookshelf, Veronica crawls over to the two figures whispering in their secret language and sits down on the floor next to Taliah. Veronica sighs contentedly. The years of abuse at the hands of her mother's now former husband have resulted in Veronica being left in a state of suspended childhood. With the onset of adolescence all the other girls at school have left their toys behind, and Talulah and Taliah's room with its dolls and toy animals, is Veronica's last refuge of childhood.

Talulah and Taliah, lying on their stomachs on the floor, flick through a magazine while Veronica, the velvet covered toy mouse still clasped in her hand, wanders around the room inspecting the Lego Architecture monuments.

'Have you two now built all the Lego Architecture monuments?' she asks, peering down at the replica of The White House on the floor next to Talulah's desk.

Taliah looks up from the magazine, Talulah does not.

'There are loads more Veronica,' says Taliah.

'Which one do you want to make next?'

'Maybe the Louvre,' replies Taliah. Talulah nudges Taliah. 'Well we haven't decided yet.'

When Taliah and Veronica start a game of scrabble, Talulah moves to her desk and sits there, arms crossed across her chest, observing the game. On the few occasions that Taliah speaks to Veronica she does so in a whisper. The game of scrabble is still in progress when Talulah leaves the room and goes downstairs. After Talulah has left the room Taliah stops whispering to Veronica and talks to her in a normal tone of voice.

*

February 3rd 2013 – *This morning's mock physics exam was so easy. Meme had revised thoroughly and there were no surprises. There was French oral in the afternoon. It was my turn first – (Ms Rainer's choice – not Meme's). Talulah waited outside the classroom, looking at me through the glass pane in the door. Sometimes I looked back at her. From the look on Ms Rainer's face she was really surprised when I answered her first question, as I am sure she'd never heard me speak before. Ms Rainier asked many questions, including 'Comment allez-vous?', 'Ou habitez-vous?' And 'Quel est votre passe-temps favori?' And I replied in a quiet voice – Je suis bien, Je reside a Londres, and Mon passe-temps favori est la lecture. I could have answered all of her later questions too, but when I opened my mouth the words didn't come out, and I had to try really hard just to say a single word or two. My final two answers were comptabilite and tennis de table, after that I was mute...*

February 3rd 2013 – Physics exam = easy. The school are trying to use speech to separate Meme. My twin did her French oral first. I could see her answering questions. This is so unfair. I conscentrated all my energy to stop her and after a while I saw through the glass pane in the door she wasn't replying to the questions anymore. When it was my turn Rainier asked many questions. First she asked me my name in French and I replied very quietly je m'appelle Talulah. Then she asked more including 'Comment allez-vous?', 'Aimez-vous voyager' and 'Quel est votre passe-temps favori?' All these responses needed s sounds so I said nothing at all. Still she asked questions. After some time I became angry and jumped up from my seat and screamed in a fault less French accent, 'HAT DERRIII ENCHI DUNCI DERRIII MENE WABA.' That was the end of the test.

Meme has no need for spoken French anyway. When Meme books the hôtel in Cannes or gay Paris, it will be done on the internet. Meme's tickets for the train will be bought from a machine. In la patisserie Plaisir Sucres and Choux Cremes will be ordered by pointing at them. When Meme is asked in French at the ticket desk in the Musee du Louvre, 'Combien de personnes?', I will hold up two fingers. When the young, handsom French porter appears breathless in Meme's room with Meme's luggage, I will give him five Euros and he will leave...

While Talulah and Taliah write in their diaries, Bethany downstairs in the sitting room, is inattentive to the programme playing on the television for she is worrying about her daughters' future. Twirling a lock of her curly hair in her fingers, Bethany reflects on the plethora of advice offered by their school and the multitude of specialists they have seen down the years. Peering out of one of the sitting room's bay windows into the darkness, she contemplates the competitiveness between Talulah and Taliah, which though present from their earliest years, has escalated in recent times.

Then, in a more nostalgic frame of mind, she remembers her daughters squeaking merrily in their prams, crawling on the sitting room floor and standing alone at the rear of the nursery school playground, facing each other, hands placed on each other's shoulders, as taunting children danced around them hand in hand. Now Bethany reflects on Talulah and Taliah's visit aged six to the screaming and writhing children-crammed health clinic. The nurse and doctor's pale faces on witnessing Taliah and Talulah's non–reaction to their jabs appear in Bethany's mind's eye, as clearly as if it had occurred only yesterday.

Talulah and Taliah finish writing their February third diary entry within a couple of seconds of each other. They stand up and go down to the kitchen, Taliah following behind Talulah. In the kitchen they each help themselves to a Petits-Filous yoghurt from the fridge and then sit down at the table, where they eat their yoghurts at a leisurely pace. Taliah goes over to the sink and pours herself a drink of water. She says, 'Oter dinki.'

'Ea.'

Taliah pours a second glass of water and gives it to Talulah.

The pair go through to the sitting room soon after.

'Evening,' greets Bethany.

The girls plant themselves on the sofa. *The BBC News* is on the television. There is a broadcast in progress, live from Copenhagen.

'I forget where Copenhagen is?' says Bethany.

'*Norway,*' says Talulah.

'Denmark,' says Taliah.

*

The following month – it is lunch break and Talulah is sitting at a table in the school library, an open book held out in front of her. Talulah is not reading the book, but instead peeking over the top of it at Taliah, at the table opposite her. Taliah, one arm draped around Samson, leans into him and whispers into his ear. Samson chuckles. As Talulah continues to watch their antics, she grasps the book in one hand and nibbles on the fingernails of her other. A tall boy with an acne-ridden face approaches Talulah, gestures with his head in the direction of Taliah and Samson, and says, 'Get your own boyfriend.' He grins and points at himself.

Talulah flicks a middle finger in his direction. The boy departs. Samson strokes Taliah's ear before kissing her on the lips. Talulah, observing this, exudes a huffing noise.

At the twins' next class, English, Talulah is already sitting at her desk when Taliah enters the classroom alongside Samson. Taliah is smiling and there is a sparkle in her eyes. On occasion during the class Taliah looks in Samson's direction. When this happens Talulah clenches her fists beneath her desk.

After afternoon classes end, prior to the commencement of activities, a number of students notice one of the twins walking down the basement corridor with Samson. A short while later they see one of the twins traipsing along the corridor, alone.

The door of the broom cupboard at the end of the basement

corridor creaks open. Samson's large head peeps out through the opening. The only person in the corridor is Ben, who is leaning against a wall bouncing a rubber ball. Samson emerges into the corridor doing up his flies as he does so. One of the twins follows Samson out of the broom cupboard. Ben laughs. He points at Samson, who gives him a thumbs-up gesture. On the opposite side of the corridor to the broom cupboard, the girls changing room door springs open. The other twin storms out of it.

'Yo Talulah,' says Samson.

The twin who has just emerged from the girls changing room is actually Taliah. Taliah launches herself at her sister, grabs a pigtail with one hand and punches Talulah in the face. Talulah, emitting a piercing, high-pitched yell that reverberates through the corridor, retaliates by clawing at Taliah's face. Samson calls out, 'Taliah Talulah stop!'

Screaming fills the air as Talulah and Taliah, each gripping one of her twin's pigtails delivers a frenzied flurry of uppercuts to the other's face.

'Ben, get over here!' yells Samson.

Samson, grabbing a screeching, scratching Taliah by the waist, hoists her up in the air and attempts to drag her away from a shrieking Talulah, who still has a grip of Taliah's hair and is now frenetically punching and kicking her.

'Do something,' orders Samson.

'What do I do!' shouts Ben, in order to be heard over the cacophony of screams.

'Pull the other one off.'

Ben grabs Talulah by both arms. Talulah shakes him to the ground just as Taliah breaks free from Samson's powerful grip and jumps two-footed at her sister, knocking her to the floor.

'Jesus Christ!' shouts Ben, as Taliah descends on her prostrate sister, banging Talulah's head against the floor, whilst Talulah, pinned to her back, claws at Taliah's face.

Samson and Ben gawk at the writhing mass of malignant

energy, now venting a ghastly, piercing shrieking. Then Samson, seizing one of Taliah's squirming legs, shouts, 'Get the other leg!' And then, 'Ben get the leg!'

Ben, waking from his stupor, clutches onto one of Taliah's legs with both hands and tugs at it. Stampeding feet are rushing down the corridor. A melee of students descend and gape as Taliah, who is bleeding profusely from a cut on her head, is dragged away by both legs, lashing out with flailing arms at Talulah, who delivers a flurry of kicks to Taliah's arms and head.

'Pull the other one away!' shouts Ben.

Asif and two girls pounce on Talulah. Asif and one of the girls are shaken off. The remaining girl clings on, screaming for assistance. The other girl and Asif dive on top of Talulah again. All four crash to the ground.

'Get the legs,' orders Samson, desperately struggling to hold onto Taliah's writhing leg by the ankle, his face now soaked with sweat.

Two girls grab one of Talulah's legs, and a girl and boy the other. Talulah and Taliah claw at the floor in their efforts to reach each other, screaming all the while, as those holding their legs struggle to drag them further apart.

The crowd watch Asif clamber around to the front of Talulah. Kneeling next to her angst-ridden face, he pleads, 'Calm down innit.' And then, 'She's got my thumb nooooo!'

There is a collective gasp from the watching congregation as Asif struggles to free his thumb from Talulah's mouth. 'Do someink,' he implores the spectators. And then, 'Help,' as he struggles to free his thumb from the vice-like grip.

A girl says, 'Punch her face.'

'Nah she's a g…'

Talulah releases. Asif falls back against the wall. Talulah returns her attention to Taliah.

Ben collapses to the floor, clutching onto Taliah's ankle, which is threatening to escape his grasp.

'Help Ben,' orders Samson.

Emma hurries over to assist Ben as the expanding crowd look on. Talulah and Taliah fall silent and go limp at the exact same moment.

High-pitched wailing comes from the end of the corridor. Mrs Fofana is rushing down the corridor, arms flailing wildly, tears streaming down her cheeks.

'Oh just what we need,' says Emma.

'Get her away from here,' says a breathless Ben.

'She'll start em off again,' whimpers Asif, sitting with his back to the wall, holding a matted length of tissue to his bleeding thumb.

Samson, still holding resolutely to one of Taliah's legs with both hands, looks from one prostrate, motionless twin to the other, and then up at the wailing teacher, weaving her way through the circle of pupils. He shouts, 'SHUT UP!'

Mrs Fofana collapses whimpering to her knees. Mr Francis is hurrying down the corridor. He is holding a first aid kit. He pushes his way through the circle of students, who are now chattering amongst themselves. Mr Francis shudders as he peers down at the bloodied, listless sisters, lying on the floor in their torn clothes.

Soon after a flushed Pendergast pushes his way through the circle. Addressing Mr Francis, he orders, 'You take Taliah to the staff room and dispense first aid.' He then asks, 'Where's another first aider?'

Heads turn to the whimpering Mrs Fofana. Pendergast looks her up and down. He spits out, *Pathetic.* And then pointing at two girls, he says, 'You and you find Ms Thomas. Emma help T-T-Talulah to my office.'

The group watch the limp, lifeless sisters being led away. Talulah and Taliah's apathetic eyes give not the slightest hint to the titanic struggle their scratched and bloodied faces bear testimony to. Samson, wiping sweat from his face with his sleeve, makes eye contact with Ben and motions with his head towards the exit at the end of the corridor. As the two teenagers stagger towards the door, the crowd of adolescents descend upon them, demanding to know the exact course of events that led to the incident.

'Nah later,' says Samson sternly, closing the door behind him. Ben and Samson take a seat on the steps that lead up to the pavement.

'Jesus Christ,' says Ben, rubbing the back of his head.

'Listen up,' says Samson. 'If Pendergast asks what happened and that, tell him, but leave out the stuff about seeing me and her coming out the broom cupboard, alright.'

'Like I'd mention that,' replies Ben, who then adds, 'that was crazy, they were so strong, like they had supernatural powers or something.'

Samson, shaking his head, mutters, 'They were both wearing pink hairbands.'

'Hairbands, what are you talking about?'

'Think about it,' responds Samson tapping his head with the knuckles of his right hand. 'How did the whole thing kick off?'

'Cause one of em, T-T-T, whichever one it is, was jealous of her sister.'

'Do you want me to spell it out?' says Samson gruffly. 'If they were both wearing pink hairbands, what's that mean?'

Ben looks down at the ground for quite some time. Then, holding a finger aloft triumphantly, he exclaims, 'Okay okay I get it, the one in the broom cupboard was tricking you into thinking she was the other twin!'

*

Colin is in his office sipping tea, looking through the window at the car park four storeys below, where a gleaming, red Ferrari F430 is sliding effortlessly into one of the spaces. Colin groans when the driver door opens, and Gerald, one of the firm's senior partners clambers out. As far back as Colin can remember he has been led to believe that ownership of a Ferrari offers the prospect of redemption, but now as he looks down upon its metallic, inanimate form, and its balding proprietor Gerald, heaving his corpulent carcass towards the office entrance, it occurs to Colin that redemption is merely an illusion. Colin's mobile is vibrating in his trouser pocket. He takes it out, looks at the screen, sees that it is the number of his daughters' school. Having muttered a quick prayer he answers the call. Pendergast tells Colin that there has been an incident involving his daughters, and that he or Bethany are required at the school immediately. After several failed attempts to reach Bethany on her mobile, Colin makes his way over to the school.

In Pendergast's office, Colin is so distraught at the sight of his bedraggled, bloodied and bruised daughters that he walks out of the office, his excuse that he has to take a quick call.

Colin is now leaning against one of the sinks at the far end of the men's toilets on the ground floor, trying to compose himself. Two teenage boys enter the room and make their way to the urinals. One is pale and gangly with shoulder length greasy black hair, the other stocky and handsome. Neither boy appears to notice Colin.

'That was some crazy shit bro,' remarks the shorter of the two.

'Ben, exactly what happened?' asks the gangly one.

Colin listens attentively as Ben describes the fight earlier that afternoon involving his daughters. He is upset by what Ben has to say, and is incensed by his gangly companion's exuberant manner, which entails laughing hysterically and cheering at regular intervals.

At the conclusion of Ben's synopsis, Colin hears the gangly youth say, 'That's crazy, I wish I'd been there.'

The pair pull up the zips of their respective trousers, and then turning to each other, continue their conversation, oblivious to

Colin's presence. Colin, looking at his reflection in the mirror above the sink, sighs.

'Oh wait I forgot something, check this out!' exclaims Ben.

'What?' says the gangly youth.

'They were both wearing the same coloured hairbands when it kicked off.'

'What're you talking about dick head?'

'The twins, they were both wearing pink hairbands.'

'So.'

'You want me to spell it out to you?'

Colin sees the gangly one shrug his shoulders.

'They were both wearing pink hairbands, pink being um T-T-Taliah's colour I think,' says Ben a moment later.

'Dun know, can't remember which wears which colour. And what's it got to do with anything anyway.'

'Cause, Huby, one came out from the broom cupboard with Samson, and...'

'You never said nothing about no broom cupboard,' intrudes Hubert.

Colin grips the taps on the sink so hard his knuckles whiten.

'HOOO!' screams Hubert. 'She was sucking him off, ha ha ha hahaha.' And then leaning towards Ben, he adds in quiet voice, 'Whose that dude over there?'

'Where?'

Ben turns and looks at Colin. The pair walk towards the sink.

'Yo,' says Ben. 'Are you a replacement teacher?'

'No.'

Ben quickly rinses his hands. As the pair depart Colin hears Hubert say, 'Must be a toilet fag.'

Ben laughs. The door closes behind them. Colin hits his head against the mirror several times and screams, 'NOOOO!' He then splashes cold water on his face, stands up to his full height, breathes in, then exhales, wipes his face with a paper towel and walks out into the corridor.

'There you are,' says Pendergast when Colin returns to his study.

Talulah and Taliah are standing on opposite sides of the room. Colin's attention falls on Taliah, who is flanked by an attractive blonde woman, he has never seen before. Colin swallows as he examines the nasty gash on Taliah's head, scratch marks down her cheeks, swelled lip and matted hair hanging in strands. He does not even glance at Talulah, whose bedraggled hair is tied in blue hairbands once more.

'I don't want to see you until next Monday, 08:45 here in my office, you are suspended,' says Pendergast. 'Do you understand?'

Talulah and Taliah nod, though not at the same time. No further words are spoken. Colin, Talulah and Taliah leave the office. Several of the first year pupils mingling in the entrance hall stare as Colin marches towards the door, pulling one of The Silent Twins by the hand and the other by a pigtail.

When they arrive at the house Bethany, on opening the front door, appears poised for a lengthy tirade, but seeing her battered, listless daughters in their torn clothes, she merely holds a hand to her mouth and looks at her husband, who emits a desultory sigh. The four of them go through to the kitchen, where Talulah and Taliah take seats at opposite ends of the table. As Bethany looks from one bruised daughter to the other, Colin opens his mouth to speak, but is at a loss as to what to say, so closes it again. The room is silent. Colin feels eyes watching him. He turns his head. He sees Talulah gazing pleadingly at him with her hazel eyes, one of which is swollen, her mouth forming a horizontal line across her face. Turning abruptly away from Talulah, Colin examines Taliah's swelled lip, matted hair, scratch marks down her cheeks and the plaster covering the gash on her forehead. He gulps, then looks across the table at Bethany. Seeing the tears welling in Bethany's eyes, Colin longs to reach out to her. Still no words are spoken. Colin, loosening the tie around his neck, comes to the conclusion that it would be best if Bethany were left alone with her daughters. He leaves soon after.

In the car, Colin remembers all those years ago when Bethany had told him she was pregnant. He had slammed on the brakes of his Vauxhall Tigra and stared at her ashen-faced. When Bethany announced a moment later it was twins, he had hardly had time to push open the car door before violently throwing up. Colin has never once wished he has only one daughter, this despite the seemingly endless trials and tribulations, but now as he drives along the road, he allows the thought to linger.

Back at the house that evening, Talulah eats her dinner in the kitchen, while Taliah has hers in the sitting room. Bethany does not serve them Petits-Filous yoghurts. Both know better than to try and secure one.

As always in the aftermath of the occasional serious disagreement between Talulah and Taliah, Taliah sleeps in the tiny alcove at the far end of the corridor that serves as a spare bedroom while Talulah remains in the bedroom they usually share. However, unlike after previous serious disagreements between the twins, Taliah does not return to the bedroom they both share the following night, and she will not for many nights to come. On the occasions that Bethany peeks through the doorway of her daughters' respective rooms, she notices that Talulah and Taliah are not only partaking in different activities, but that they have adopted different postures from one another. To Bethany this emphasises the severity of their falling out, to no lesser a degree than the bruised faces and torn clothes. Not once over the next few days do Talulah and Taliah ever cross paths on their forays to the kitchen, sitting room, bathroom, or the back garden.

In the evening, three days removed from the incident, Bethany sees Taliah sitting cross-legged in the sitting room, leaning on the glass coffee table, writing at a frenetic pace in her diary, a single tear dribbling down her cheek. Bethany is determined to find out the cause of the rift between her daughters, a rift more serious than any that she can remember previously. But despite trying to ascertain information from both Talulah and Taliah separately in the following days, she is none the wiser. Talulah manages a few short statements, including, *It won't happen again.* Taliah is also not forthcoming, a five word response consisting of *Don't worry about it Mum* being as much as she says on the matter. On one occasion Taliah opens her mouth, and Bethany feels quite certain she is poised to elaborate on her *It's nothing really* statement, but she closes her mouth again without adding any additional words. For despite the severity of the rift between Talulah and Taliah, their bond of secrecy remains unaffected. Five days removed from the incident and still Talulah and Taliah remain apart, not merely physically, but also in their actions and postures.

On Monday Talulah and Taliah return to school. Although in their customary fashion Talulah leaves the house first and Taliah follows, she does not do so for a full two minutes after her twin. And when Taliah does leave the house, she is wearing a skirt, this in contrast to Talulah who is wearing trousers. Bethany is quite certain that her daughters have never worn completely different outfits before.

Although Talulah and Taliah travel to school on the same bus, Talulah sits near the front whilst Taliah sits in the very last row, on the other side of the bus. And when they got off the bus and walk to school, the gap between Talulah and Taliah is nearly thirty metres.

At school they report to Pendergast's office together as he had instructed them to do so, and stand side by side for the short time it takes Pendergast to reprimand them, and for them to offer short, scarcely audible apologies, uttered at different times. In English class Talulah sits at her normal desk, but Taliah is not to be found at the desk immediately behind, nor the desk behind that. Taliah selects a desk that is five behind Talulah's. During the class Taliah glances in Samson's direction several times. In physics class, where the seating is in the form of raised benches, Talulah and Taliah do not sit next to each other. Talulah remains in her normal place and Taliah finds a seat on the other side of the room.

March 18th 2013 – *Today Meme returned to school. I could feel students watching Meme as if we were an exhibit, or an animal in a zoo. Some seem nervous now, which is probably not surprising considering the violence of last week. Hubert was grinning from ear to ear when he bounded over to Meme this morning. He seemed to know quite a bit about what had happened. When I walked into English Samson was cowering at his desk. Who would have thought such a big boy could look so small. For the briefest of moments we exchanged glances. My face felt so flushed that I might combust at any moment. If it were not for my dark complexion I would have been beetroot red – thank God for small mercies.*

Is it a coincidence that both twin and tumour start with the letter t, or Talulah and tumour for that matter, to say nothing of Taliah and tragedy.

Talulah is getting no help with her homework from now on, no assistance with exam revision, and as for any future speech therapy sessions, I will be singing all s sounds in an operatic style. Answering questions in class are in, as is volunteering to read aloud. Oh, and I won't be making any more modern Lego Architecture structures. From this moment forth it is historical sites only, starting with The Louvre. ... If I got a big sword and cut Meme in half, would I be left with Me?

At home Bethany insists that Talulah and Taliah eat their meals together in the kitchen as normal. During mealtimes not only do Talulah and Taliah's cutlery not move in unison with one another, but they never once reach for the jug of water at the same time, or go to the fridge to get their Petits-Filous together, and when they collect their toast from the toaster, they do so separately. Neither Talulah nor Taliah make any conscious effort to do this, for each instinctively knows what the other is going to do.

It is not until breakfast, a full two weeks after the fight that Talulah and Taliah raise their glasses of orange juice to their mouths at the same moment as one another, before taking bites from their pieces of toast at exactly the same time. Although on several occasions during the remainder of breakfast and later at dinner, Taliah sporadically staggers the raising of her glass, spoon or fork so it is not synchronised with that of her twin, their actions invariably become synchronised again soon after. That evening Bethany insists that Taliah return to the bedroom she shares with Talulah. Taliah makes no objection to this, though she does so morosely, her head hung as she traipses into the bedroom, her floral patterned duvet and pillow held in her arms.

When they depart for school each day the time elapsing between the closing of the front door draws closer together, and there is less distance between them on the bus and on the walk to school from the bus station. In their classes at school Taliah moves a desk closer to her twin each day, and the usual incumbent of that desk is forced to find another. Each day Talulah and Taliah's classmates watch this happen in silence, as if it is the first time it has occurred, for although most of them have been classmates with Talulah and Taliah for several years, all continue to be amazed by the twins' peculiarities, so alien are they to their own experience of the world.

Talulah and Taliah are in their bedroom. Both are leaning forwards, their left elbows placed on the surfaces of their desks, their heads resting in their left palms. Talulah is playing a game on her mobile telephone. Taliah is doing her biology homework. Talulah stops playing the game, twists her head and watches Taliah. Although Taliah can feel her twin's scrutiny, she ignores her. Several minutes have passed when Talulah says, 'Meou mathi klathi dehabta wedi.'

'Meou wedi mene wedi.'

'Ea crible bibta mathi klathi teti meme.'

'Ea.'

These are the first words Talulah and Taliah have said to each other since their fight eighteen days previously.

*

The next day – Colin is waiting in the sitting room while Bethany finishes a telephone conversation in the kitchen. As Colin peers out into the room he remembers Taliah and Talulah lying in their cots here, then his younger self assisting them attach decorations to the Christmas tree, and then his daughters busily constructing Lego Architecture monuments on the floor. These memories so vivid, it is as if in the stillness of the room, the echoes of the past continue to reverberate.

The smile vanishes from Bethany's face the moment Colin tells her that he believes that Talulah was responsible for the fight and resulting suspension. Colin had made the decision not to tell Bethany this when he came to the house the day of the incident for fear of upsetting her further, and has waited until today to bring it up. He is careful to omit any mention of the broom cupboard. When Bethany grabs a ceramic ashtray from the coffee table and hurls it at the wall, Colin concludes that blaming Talulah was ill-advised. He departs the house soon after, adamant that Bethany's stubborn refusal to view Taliah and Talulah as anything but two parts of a whole, means that trying to change her mind is futile.

*

Summer term – English Literature GCSE Examination – Taliah is frenetically writing out her answer to the question – *Discuss how Mercutio's attitude towards Tybalt, and others influences events in Romeo and Juliet?* Taliah raises her head and rubs her eyes, before returning to the question. She has written only a couple of lines when she lifts her head again. Sensing Talulah pining for assistance from the desk in front, Taliah ignoring her, proceeds to write at a furious pace, line after line, concentrating all her focus on the exam paper. Taliah feels Talulah's relentless pining growing ever more clamorous. Adamant that she will not surrender to her twin, Taliah takes a big breath and continues writing at a frantic pace.

The pen drops to the desk, Taliah clasps her hands to her ears. She can feel Talulah's craving for assistance reverberating in her mind as clearly as if Talulah were screaming to her in cryptophasia. Taliah picks up her essay plan from the desk, checks no exam invigilators are watching, crumples up the piece of paper, and then throws it surreptitiously under Talulah's chair. Taliah repeats this action on a further two occasions during the exam.

*

Much to the surprise of most of the teaching staff at Royston Park, there is a considerable disparity in Talulah and Taliah's GCSE examination results. It had been the general consensus that as the twins always achieve near identical marks to one another in their assignments, the same would hold true under examination conditions. Taliah performs as expected, achieving A grades for the most part, with a couple of B's, including in French, due to a poor performance in the oral examination. Talulah does not fare so well. Although she outperforms her twin by a couple of percent in maths and gets almost identical marks in the three science subjects, the arts and humanities are disappointing. Other than a B in English Literature and Language, it is D grades, with an E in French, this largely due to the fact that Talulah had uttered barely a word in the oral component.

CHAPTER FOUR

ROYSTON PARK SCHOOL – first day of Autumn Term – a deluge of students enter the hall, their voices a cacophony of noise. Near the back of the hall a group of Year Twelve students, consisting of Ben, Malcolm, Emma, Veronica and Samson are in conversation. As they talk they lean towards each other to be heard above the din. A little way to their left sit Talulah and Taliah, who stare impassively ahead, their hands clasped in their laps. A number of the first year pupils, having never seen Talulah and Taliah before, stare at them. Several mention how the twins look exactly the same as each other, another asks a student from the year above how teachers tell them apart, whilst several new girls remark on how pretty they are.

As Ben, Malcolm, Emma and Veronica converse about their GCSE grades and summer holidays, Samson, leaning forward in his seat, peers down the aisle at Taliah. Her hair is longer than it was last term. It is now like Talulah's worn in braids. Some of the braids are tied in bright pink ribbons. The twins' marginally fuller figures accentuate a graceful maturity that was not present last year. Noticing these changes in Taliah, Samson knows that the girl that he first laid eyes on aged thirteen has completed her transformation into a young woman. When Taliah meets his gaze, Samson finds himself drawn into the alluring depths of her hazel eyes. A second pair of hazel eyes are watching Samson. He sighs and looks away. Emma is tugging at Samson's sleeve.

'Yo,' says Samson.

Emma points at a tall youth with a mohawk striding down the aisle to their right.

Samson says, 'What the…'

'That's Siegfried,' intrudes Emma. 'He's a German anarchist from Dresden.'

'You couldn't make that up.' It is Malcolm who says this.

'How do you know all this?' asks Ben.

'I was a school representative at the new pupils' day,' says Emma, flicking a lock of auburn hair from her face. 'Siegfried is in our year.'

Malcolm, polishing the lenses of his glasses with his sleeve, says, 'This is terrible news.'

'Doesn't he know punks went out of fashion in the eighties?' says Veronica.

'He's German,' says Ben.

'He's good looking,' says Emma.

'Whatever,' says Samson.

Talulah and Taliah are approaching along the line of seats towards their classmates. Heads swivel towards them. Talulah sits down next to Veronica and Taliah takes a seat next to Talulah. Talulah's gaze is fixed on Siegfried, this in contrast to Taliah, who glances fleetingly in his direction before looking away.

Emma smiles, revealing braced teeth. She says, 'Look Talulah likes him.'

Only now does Talulah look away from Siegfried. Samson, holding his large hands behind his head, sighs and says, 'Tell us all about him then?'

In a loud voice so as to be heard above the commotion, Emma says, 'His old school in Germany couldn't cope with him because he's an anarchist you see. He's really, really rebellious and opinionated, and his old school didn't like the hair.'

'Neither do we,' says Malcolm.

'Anyway,' continues Emma. 'His parents used to be like

hippies and they are cool about him being alternative. His dad is um an industrialist working over here, so he got sent to our school.'

'He's not like Hubert is he?' asks Veronica, tugging at Emma's sleeve.

'No sweetie, why would you think that?' replies Emma, placing her hand on Veronica's head. 'He's much better, you'll see.'

Talulah is watching Siegfried again, this in contrast to Taliah, who is looking up at the ceiling. Pendergast is striding into the hall, a column of teachers following in his wake.

After assembly Talulah and Taliah make their way to Room 201 for their first class of the new school year, physics. They enter the classroom in the same manner they always have, Taliah following behind Talulah. Then they sit down next to each other on the bench where they have always sat, except in the aftermath of their argument last year. Although their cheeks are now dabbed with rouge, their eyelashes tinted and identical shades of lipstick adorn their lips, their postures remain unchanged – upright, heads held straight, mouths fixed in a horizontal line. Despite Talulah exhibiting no outward sign of emotion, Taliah can feel her twin's anticipation. When Mr Kenton enters the room the anticipation deflates as if it were air from a balloon, as Talulah realises that the new German student is not taking physics.

Mr Kenton gives an overview of Unit One of the A Level curriculum – *Particles, Quantum Phenomena and Electricity*. To Taliah, listening to Mr Kenton's monotone voice and the muffled snores of her fellow classmates, it seems that everything is as it always has been. Were it not for Talulah's fascination in the new German student, she would no doubt feel the same.

When the bell for the end of class rings there is a rush for the exit. Only after the others have departed do Talulah and Taliah file out and head down the corridors, destination English, one of the four subjects that they are studying at A Level, along with physics, maths and biology.

Talulah and Taliah are now waiting for the commencement of English, a subject Taliah is grateful that she has been able to continue with, due to her love of literature and the fact Ms Thomas is her favourite teacher. Colin had been adamant that Taliah continue to study English, this despite the protestations of Talulah, who had initially protested the decision. That was until Colin had suggested Talulah choose a different subject, and allow Taliah to continue studying English alone.

As prior to the start of their physics class, Taliah senses her twin's anticipation. Siegfried strides into the room a full five minutes after the class has begun. During the class Talulah frequently looks to her left in the direction of Siegfried, and on several occasions Taliah glances at Samson.

September 22nd 2013 – *Ms Thomas asked lots of questions in English today. When she asked, 'What is the name of the longest major poem written by Samuel Taylor Coleridge?' I couldn't contain myself any longer even though I knew that Talulah wouldn't like it. I put up my hand. 'The Rime of the Ancient Mariner' I replied in a quiet voice. 'Yes,' she said. Then she asked when The Rime of the Ancient Mariner was first published. Talulah quickly looked up the answer under her desk on her iPhone then put her hand up. Ms Thomas selected Malcolm to answer the question.*

September 22nd – Ms Prim, Pretty, I'm so Perfect Ms Thomas talks about modern poetry and British romantic literature, as Siegfried, with his peiercing blue eyes and purple tinted Mohawk, one arm drapped over the back of his chair, looks at his watch and yawns. Even his teeth are perfect.

September 24th – Meme went to the school doctor today. He gave Meme more Zyprexa. Meme has been on medication like forever – since we were really really small. Sometimes I feel dizzy when I stand up, this is because of Zyprexa – I read about it on the internet. Meme thinks ugi bothi baldi Hunter-Thornton told the school doctor to make us take it because it will make us fat. Meme thinks he is laughing and joking about it in Latin. Meme has put on weight. Meme doesn't want to be fat like Emma and not fit into her new clothes. My twin was 1 kg more than me when we went on the scales in the bathroom yesterday. Meou says this is because she had more dinner and did less exercise than me that day. 'Are you sure Meou?' I said, looking her up and down. 'You look a teeny weeny bit fatter than me.' (I said this in our ~~erptopasia~~ secret language of course). She stomped out and went downstairs to mummy after I said it. ... What medication do they give Siegfried?

September 24th – *Samson beat an U18 bench-pressing record. His name was mentioned in the local newspaper and Pendergast congratulated him in school assembly. Samson looked so happy. Lots of girls wanted to feel his muscles afterwards, this made me feel jealous. Talulah whispered to me he was just showing off. For once the new German was not the centre of attention. In English and biology I looked across at Samson. Although he was only a few metres away it seemed like a whole ocean separated us. Is this how Anne felt in Persuasion when she was* compelled to cancel her engagement to Captain Wentworth, and he left the country?

September 29th – Siegfried stands on his desk and tells us about 'Individual Anarchy'. It's the only way to live he says. The school, just like all types of authoritey is trying to control us with medication and other things to make us obedient – I just so knew this was true but my twin didn't believe me. Everyone listens. Some cheer and clap. I clap too. Meou doesn't. Then Ms Thomas skips into the room in her floral dress. She says 'Please get down from the desk Siegfried.' Siegfried still standing on the desk says that it is simbolic of his individuality being greater than authority. This makes Ms Thomas giggle in a really silly girley way.

September 30th – *Maybe if Talulah was Siegfried's girlfriend, Samson and I could be together. Talulah and Siegfried could do individual anarchist stuff while I could help Samson with Coleridge's poetry, Jane Austen, George Orwell and all the other books we have to read. Samson could become a famous bench presser, and I could be Me, not Meme. Even though I still have a twin, but not a twin I was with all day every day, just sometimes – for afternoon tea during the week for instance, or to do some clothes shopping on a Saturday, that's if Mene doesn't call me fat just because I weighed less than 1kg more than her, like one time.*

Taliah is leaning against one of the library's bookshelves reading *Mansfield Park* by Jane Austen while Talulah peruses the shelves, running her fingers along the spines of the books as she does so. Several minutes have passed when Talulah approaches her twin. Taliah sees the name Benjamin R. Tucker on the cover of the book Talulah is holding. She recognises the name from Siegfried's frequent exhortations on the subject of anarchism. It occurs to Taliah that Talulah should instead be reading the required texts for English A Level. When Talulah looks into her eyes a moment later, Taliah feels certain that Talulah knows what she was thinking. They walk out of the library.

Ben, Emma and Veronica are approaching from the opposite direction.

Veronica says, 'Hi Taliah.'

Taliah waves at her. Hubert is hurrying towards the trio. Talulah and Taliah hear him say, 'Yo what's up bitches?' And then having expanded and deflated his cheeks, he adds, 'Let's do gas.'

A squealing Veronica scampers into the library.

'Not today bro,' says Ben, who ignoring Hubert's shout of 'Pussy!' follows Veronica into the library.

'Emma, come on ho let's go,' implores Hubert.

'No I don't think so, I've got to study for the history test later,' says Emma, who then turning to Talulah and Taliah says, 'hi twins,' before walking into the library.

Hubert, flicking a lock of long, greasy black hair from his face turns to Talulah and Taliah. The corners of Hubert's mouth turn downwards, his mouth forming the shape of a half moon. Siegfried is striding up the stairs.

'Yo Siegfried,' says Hubert, his expression of disdain dissipating instantaneously. And then leaning into the tall mohawk-haired teenager, he adds in a quieter voice, 'Want to do gas?'

'*Ja*,' says Siegfried nonchalantly. He is looking in the direction of Talulah and Taliah when he says this.

'I know you Germans like the gas, *ja*?' remarks a grinning Hubert.

'English humour iz so very funny,' says Siegfried, still looking at Talulah and Taliah, standing a few metres away on the landing. Siegfried, nudging Hubert, says, 'Let'z invite them to join us?'

'They're freaks dude,' says Hubert, casting a despairing glance in the twins' direction.

'I like freaks,' says Siegfried, looking Talulah and Taliah up and down approvingly.

Talulah smiles, Taliah does not.

'Whatever, let's go,' says Hubert, ushering Talulah and Taliah with an outstretched hand.

The quartet go outside and make their way to the nearby athletics track, Siegfried and Hubert leading the way, Talulah at their heels, Taliah bringing up the rear. An unseasonably warm October sun beams down on them as they park themselves on one of the stand's stone steps. Hubert rummages through his gym bag, takes out four small silver canisters and starts preparing the balloons.

'So you chooze not to speak,' says Siegfried.

Talulah nods and Taliah opens her mouth, then closes it again.

'I like,' replies Siegfried approvingly. 'Zere is too much verbalizing, yes Hubert?' Hubert has not stopped talking since the chance meeting on the landing, every word of which has been directed at Siegfried.

'Compulsive verbalising, okay, whatever,' says Hubert. 'Here take it,' he adds, passing Siegfried a blue balloon, his thumb and index finger pressed against the balloon's opening.

Taliah eyes the balloon nervously. Siegfried, gripping the balloon in the same way Hubert did, puts his mouth over the opening and then releases his grip.

'Ha ha ha haha *ja*,' emits a jubilant Siegfried, having inhaled the gas.

Taliah notices not for the first time, that in Siegfried's presence, her and her twin are not treated as outcasts, although Hubert does cast the occasional uneasy glance in Talulah's direction as he prepares the next balloon. Talulah, taking the balloon in the same manner as Siegfried, places the opening between her teeth and releases her grip. Taliah feels the euphoria emanating from Talulah when she inhales the gas. This soothes Taliah's apprehension about taking the gas.

All four of them are laughing. Taliah notices that the malignancy that seems to permanently envelop Hubert has abandoned him, and that he is laughing merely for joy, just as she and her twin are.

'You smoke skunk?' asks Siegfried, having composed himself.

'Hell ya,' replies Hubert.

Taliah is about to say no when Talulah nods her head, this despite the fact neither of them has tried it before, or any drug for that matter, other than the nitrous oxide they have just inhaled.

Siegfried reaches into his trouser pocket, removes a packet of cigarettes and extracts a joint. He then takes a lighter from another pocket. Talulah and Taliah watch Siegfried ogling the flickering flame as if mesmerised. Quite some time has passed when he holds the flame to the joint. He inhales on it a few times and then passes it to Hubert. Taliah notes the enthusiasm with which Talulah seizes the joint from Hubert's grasp. Talulah inhales strongly. She splutters. Siegfried and Hubert laugh. Talulah composes herself, and then inhales again. This time she does not splutter.

Even in her euphoric state Taliah is loath to put something in her mouth that has been in Hubert's. When she takes the joint from Talulah, Taliah purses her lips to the end and inhales meekly. She inhales again, coughs once, and then inhales a third time, holding the smoke in her lungs before spluttering forces its exit. Siegfried, Hubert and Talulah laugh as the joint is circulated once more, but Taliah does not. When her turn comes again, she waves the joint away with a trembling hand, her breathing now harried, her heart pounding in her chest. She closes her eyes. The panic gradually subsides. When Taliah opens her eyes Talulah is smiling at her.

October 21st 2013 – ... a fact as ~~irefuteable~~ irrefutable as Newton's Law of Universal Gravitation - physics with gas is > physics without gas. If only its affects lasted longer.

October 21st – *Now more than ever I must study for the two of us. I read A level texts by Jane Austen, George Orwell and poetry by Coleridge and Plath, whilst Talulah reads about individual anarchism and fills out her diary. Has she already forgotten what happened in our GCSE examinations? Alas, why does experience only teach the teachable? ... Love is indeed blind.*

October 24th – Is Royston Park School a leper coloney? Meme and the other pupils have been labeled by psyciatrists, doctors and teachers as disfuntional - ADHD, autistics, depressives, psycotics. Only now are we realising that the labels that have been stuck on us are not illnesses but praises. It is these 'illnesses' that make us individuals and not like everyone else out there who are all the same.

October 24th – *Mene was complaining about taking medication again today. I also don't like having to take it, but, and I'd never mention it to her, I believe the pills the school doctor gives us are good for Mene. They help keep her calm. I'm prepared to keep taking them even though I don't think I need them, because if I stop taking them, so will she. I finished reading The Bell Jar by Sylvia Plath today. It is one of the best books I've ever read. One of the themes is mental health, which is not surprising considering Plath committed suicide when she was still really young. This is really sad.*

October 27th – After lessons Meme went to the athletics track with Siegfried. He looked amazing. With his lithe physique and chiselled features he could be an Armani or Calvin Klein model. He tells Meme all about individual anarchism. About Benjamin R. Tucker, who said, 'If the individual has the right to govern himself, all external government is tyranny.' He tells us about William Godwin who avocated extreme individualism and Pierre-Joseph Proudhon – the first philosopher to lable himself an anarchist, and also about Johann Kaspar Schmidt's Einzige und sein Eigentum (this means The Ego and His Own in English). Siegfried says Meme's silence is a defence against the corruption of society and this is a good thing.

October 27th – *Our eyes met for the fleetest of moments in the hall, mine a little bloodshot due to what Meme was doing at the athletics track with Siegfried after afternoon classes. Samson's shoulders were slumped and his head lolled forward as he traipsed away towards the door, a gym bag held in one hand. He must have been going to the gym to do weight training. I*

*

At school no further attempts are made to separate Talulah and Taliah, as the teaching staff have not forgotten what happened. With the exception of Ms Thomas, the teachers are not particularly interested in persuading the twins to increase their oral communication, although Talulah and Taliah still have the occasional session with the school's speech therapist. The general consensus amongst the staff is that as long as the twins achieve some academic success, and that there are no more serious incidents such as the fight last term, then Royston Park can be deemed to have successfully managed the reticent but unpredictable pair.

When Ms Thomas speaks to Pendergast about the twins, she quickly realises that how Taliah and Talulah are likely to fare in the world once their school days are over is not a pressing concern. Pendergast, a big grin adorning his pudgy face, merely says one word when Ms Thomas asks him if he is concerned about another falling out between the pair. The word is Zyprexa. To Ms Thomas it seems that Pendergast utters it as if it were abracadabra, a magical word that could solve any problem. Ms Thomas has been hearing Zyprexa and Risperdal too mentioned increasingly regularly since the arrival of the new school doctor, who has been prescribing these antipsychotic medications to students with anything from pervasive development disorders and Tourette's syndrome, to ADHD and disruptive behavioural disorders. It occurs to Ms Thomas that the doctor probably prescribes these drugs for common colds and hay fever too.

As for Talulah and Taliah, taking their daily medication has been part of their lives for as far back as either can care to remember, and it is as much a part of their routine as having a Petits Filous yogurt for dessert at dinner or writing their diary entries at night. A multitude of different specialists have prescribed the pair a multitude of different medications down the years, depending on what was in vogue at the time.

Talulah and Taliah had for a short period of time some years back been prescribed the older antipsychotics, Haldol and Orap. They had both experienced side effects from these, including drowsiness, dizzy spells, and even tics and tremors. Despite all this the twins never stopped taking their pills. But now when Taliah gulps down her daily five milligram dose of Zyprexa, she often sees Talulah examining the pill lying in the palm of her hand. When Taliah sees her twin doing this she is fearful for the future. Taliah remains convinced that the pills are beneficial for her twin, and despite Talulah's vehemence that the small dose that they are currently being prescribed has resulted in weight gain, Taliah is unconvinced.

*

Taliah has just completed her diary entry. She is watching Talulah writing at her desk. In the past Talulah and Taliah always completed their diary entries, if not at the exact same moment as each other, then normally within a minute or so. Recently however Taliah has been finishing her diary entry before Talulah. When Taliah sees her twin writing in her diary, she knows that

Talulah is mostly writing about Siegfried and her newfound obsession with the anarchist cause. These changes in Talulah concern Taliah, and this concern is not only for her twin, for she knows that any consequences will be hers too.

Taliah sighs and looks up at the ceiling, twirling her pen in the fingertips of her right hand as she does so. Her mind flits back to being at the athletics track that afternoon, where she and her twin had smoked cannabis with Siegfried, a regular occurrence in recent weeks. Sat on the steps beside Talulah, Taliah experienced the strange, but mercifully brief sensation of merging with her twin. Taliah closed her eyes until the panic began to subside. When she opened them Talulah was simpering at her.

Talulah is now watching Taliah. It is quite some time before Taliah feels the scrutiny of her twin. She empties her mind and then returns Talulah's gaze.

'Ea,' says Taliah.

Talulah smiles. She says nothing. Taliah sighs, turns to face her desk, rips a piece of A4 paper from her pad and writes out a detailed essay plan for their English homework question – *How does Coleridge portray the natural world before and after the Ancient Mariner shoots the Albatross? (Use evidence pertaining to symbolism, metaphor, and rhyme scheme to support your thesis).* Taliah includes references and supporting arguments, so all her twin need do is write it out in her own words. Taliah scrunches up the piece of paper containing the plan and throws it. It lands under Talulah's chair. Talulah, remembering the same occurring in their GCSE English Literature examination, giggles. Taliah frowns, stands up, scrunches up another piece of paper and hurls it at Talulah, who laughing louder now throws the ball of paper back. Soon paper is being thrown back and forth, and Taliah, finding her twin's mirth contagious, forgets her concerns and laughs too. Talulah and Taliah collapse onto their seats at the exact same moment. Taliah, wiping tears of mirth from her cheeks with her sleeve feels love for her twin.

'Bobothi papin ogi outhe tudi,' says Talulah.

Taliah picks up the completed biology assignment from the shelf above her desk, walks over to Talulah, puts the assignment on her desk, gently places the palm of her hand on Talulah's head and says, 'Nuhnuh crible oun.'

'*Ea.*'

CHAPTER FIVE

ROYSTON PARK SCHOOL – Room 3A. In the middle of the room is a desk. Siegfried is standing on the desk. His feet are shoulder width apart. His arms gesture assuredly and his head turns from side to side, as he addresses the students who are gathered around him.

'Ve are individuals, free to make our own choices,' proclaims Siegfried, scanning the audience. 'Ze authorities are controlling us.'

The audience cheers.

'Zey label our individuality *Behavioural Problemz*,' adds Siegfried, placing his hands on his hips. Then thrusting his hips forward, he exclaims, 'How do zey control us!'

A voice at the back of the room calls out, 'Behavioural therapy.'

'*Ja*,' responds Siegried.

'Psychodynamic therapy,' calls out Ben.

'Don't even get me started on psychodynamic therapy.' It is Emma who says this.

A girl near the door says, 'Family therapy.'

Malcolm sticks two fingers down his throat.

Siegfried yells, '*JA!*'

The students cheer.

Talulah, who is standing at the front of the group next to Taliah, her gaze fixed on the piercing blue eyes of Siegfried, claps vigorously. Taliah claps softly.

Siegfried, standing up to his full height, arms outstretched, asks, 'How else do zey control us?'

'Religion innit,' says Asif.

Cheering and clapping fills the room. Siegfried holds a finger to his lips. The room falls silent. Siegfried says, 'Zey call it religion, ve call it a …'

'DISEASE!' shout the audience, with the exception of Talulah who merely mouths the words, and Taliah, whose mouth stays closed.

'*JA!*' shouts Siegfried, before adopting his hands-on-hips posture once more. Several of the students jump up and down as they await Siegfried's next utterance. Nearly thirty seconds have elapsed when Siegfried, bending down to scour the faces of his disciples, asks in a gentler tone, 'How else do zey control us?'

'By forcing uz to communicate,' says Talulah.

The audience gasp. Faces turn to Talulah. Taliah holds a hand to her mouth. Leaning forward, looking directly at Talulah and Taliah, Siegfried says, 'Zey desire to control Meme, to destroy Meme's perfect individuality.'

Several of the audience make whispered enquiries to their neighbour as to what Meme is. Having winked at Taliah and Talulah, Siegfried, standing up to his full height, says, 'Zere is one more vay ze authorities control us?'

An arm shoots up in the air.

'*Veronica,*' says Siegfried.

'Medication,' squeals Veronica.

'*JA!*' shouts Siegfried. And then, 'Vhat medication?'

'RITALIN!' calls out a girl, standing at the back of the room.

A boy calls out, 'Metadate.'

'Sertraline, brand name Zoloft, chemical formula $C17H17C12N$.' It is Malcolm who says this.

'Risperdal,' says Asif.

'Concerta,' says Ben.

A tall girl by the door cries out, 'Metadate.'

'We've so had Metadate already,' says Emma,

'Oh we have, *sorry*,' says the girl.

And then comes a deluge of voices that call out, 'Zyprexa,' 'Cylert,' 'Wellbutrin,' 'Depo Provera,' 'Dexedrine,' 'Dextrosta' and 'Prozac.'

All are silent. Faces turn to Siegfried, who bending forward, pointing at his audience, says, 'From now on, ve take only ze drugz ve want to.'

'*JA!*' scream the audience, including Talulah, but not Taliah.

Siegfried leaps down from the desk. He grabs a wastepaper basket from the floor and strides towards the door, the students parting before him. The crowd follow their leader to the male changing room in the basement. Siegfried slams the bin down in the middle of the floor. Having run a hand through his purple-streaked mohawk, Siegfried reaches into his pocket, takes out a packet of Risperdal, scrunches it up, hurls it into the bin, and shouts, '*FREIHEIT!*'

The students file out of the room and stampede down the corridor. On reaching the lockers, they fumble with keys, unlock their lockers, rummage through the contents, and pull out packets, bottles and paper bags with green crosses printed on them. Meanwhile Taliah trudges slowly along the corridor behind Talulah towards the lockers.

Back in the changing rooms the girls and boys gather around the bin with their packets, bottles and papers bags. A girl steps forward. She exclaims '*Freiheit!*' and then drops a packet of Ritalin in the bin. Siegfried leans towards her, clasps her by the ears, looks into her eyes and kisses her on the top of her head.

More students are coming forward and dropping their packages into the bin, others hurling them. Veronica, on throwing her packet of the antidepressant Wellbutrin into the bin, emits a high-pitched, '*Freiheit!*' Many of the boys and girls hold their hands to their ears when she does this. Siegfried roars with laughter. A red-haired boy drops a packet in the bin. Asif says, 'Dat's Xanax innit?'

'Yeah,' says the boy.

Looking up at Siegfried, Asif says, 'Can I ave it man?'

'*Ja*,' replies Siegfried.

Asif removes the Xanax from the bin and puts it in his pocket. Ben steps forward with an armful of packets.

'What's all that Ben!' shouts a male voice. 'Has your mum got you on the homeopathic alternatives again?'

Laughter fills the room. Ben drops his armful of packets. A bin liner appears. The bin is emptied and set down again.

'Oh my god that's Adderall!' exclaims the new American girl, Helen, in a high-pitched voice, when another girl discards a packet in the bin. Helen, dashing over to the bin and removing the packet of Adderall, says, 'This is like the most amazing appetite suppressant *ever*.'

'Give me some, please please,' pleads Emma. Looking up at Siegfried she asks, 'Can we share?'

'*Ja*,' replies Siegfried.

'Where's Hubert?' says Ben, looking around.

'Hubi's got a rucksack of prescription gear in his locker innit,' remarks Asif.

'It doesn't seem to be working very well,' says Veronica.

Everyone laughs. The door opens. Talulah walks in, followed by Taliah. Talulah walks up to the bin. The room falls silent. Talulah holds two packets over the bin; one is the antipsychotic medication Zyprexa and the other, the anticonvulsant Depakote. She drops the packets in the bin. Some of the students clap. Siegfried points at Talulah and winks. Taliah takes a hesitant step forward, then another. She holds out her two packets of drugs over the bin with trembling hands. Taliah looks down into the bin, her breath coming in harried gasps. She releases the packets. Siegfried claps, students cheer. Still Taliah looks down into the bin. Talulah grabs Taliah by the waist and drags her away.

*

Three weeks later – as the class complete the written exercise, for the most part in silence, Ms Thomas, standing at the front of the class, surveys her students. Taliah sees Ms Thomas smile when she looks at the empty desk where Hubert usually sits. Ms Thomas shifts her attention to Siegfried, who reclining back in his chair, winks at her. Both Talulah and Taliah observe this, and they notice too that Ms Thomas's cheeks redden. Turning her back on the class, Ms Thomas proceeds to wipe the whiteboard, this despite the fact that it is already clean. Talulah is glaring at Ms Thomas. Ms Thomas, spinning around and meeting the intense, unblinking stare of Talulah's hazel eyes, reaches out with one hand to support her weight against the desk.

The bell rings soon after and the students file out of the class. As today is a half-day Talulah and Taliah head for home, Taliah walking behind Talulah to the bus stop in customary fashion. When they arrive home Talulah goes upstairs and takes a left into the bathroom. Taliah is about to turn right into the bedroom when Talulah grabs her sleeve and pulls her into the bathroom. In the bathroom Talulah removes her shoes, jumper and trousers, then stands on the bathroom scales. Talulah and Taliah look down in unison at the scales. Talulah shrieks jubilantly when the electronic display shows sixty-one point three kilograms. She says, 'Zyprexa mene fa zyprexa nuhnuh tin.'

Taliah shrugs her shoulders.

'Meou wei,' says Talulah, pointing at the scales beneath her feet.

Taliah removes her shoes, jumper and trousers and steps onto the scales. The electronic display blinks several times before showing sixty-one point one kilograms. Talulah grimaces.

'Meou tin mene nuhuh tin,' says Taliah.

Talulah makes a huffing sound and storms out of the bathroom. Taliah puts her clothes back on, splashes some cold water on her face and inspects her reflection in the mirror above the sink. As she gazes at her reflection she wonders what it would be like to not have a twin and only brothers and sisters, or even to be an only child like Veronica and Emma. For quite some time Taliah thinks about this. On entering the bedroom she sees Talulah is doing her homework, which is unusual. Taliah knows that Talulah is only doing her homework because she is feeling defensive about weighing more than her, and for now at least is unwilling to ask to copy hers.

Nearly an hour has passed when Taliah feels her twin looking at her. Taliah closes *Jacob's Room* by Virginia Woolf, one of the books from the English Literature A Level reading list, and places it on the table. She revolves around in her chair to face her twin. Talulah, wearing a faint smile, waves a joint in the air with one hand. Taliah, inspecting her twin's healthy complexion, lustrous eyes and high cheekbones, considers that she is extremely pretty. A moment later she admonishes herself for such a vain thought. Still the joint waves in the air.

'Wedi gogo,' says Talulah.

Taliah looks up at the clock on the wall. She notes that her mother is not due back for nearly half an hour. She stands up and walks over to the door, where a scowling Talulah is now waiting.

Taliah follows Talulah out to the back garden, where they sit next to each other on the brick wall that surrounds the lawn. They pass the joint back and forth, for the most part in silence, Talulah uttering a few words in their cryptophasia.

They re-enter the house through the glass door at the back of the kitchen. Upstairs in their bedroom, Talulah plays a game on her mobile telephone while Taliah picks up her copy of *Jacob's Room* and starts to read, but unable to concentrate on the words, she puts the book down, yawns and rubs her eyes. Her attention falls inadvertently on the Lego Architecture replica of The Leaning Tower of Pisa beside her desk. Taliah imagines a miniature version of herself traipsing up to the monument behind a miniature Talulah. Now, peering down at the replica of Rome's Trevi Fountain on the other side of her desk, Taliah imagines

Talulah standing beside the fountain, hands on hips, waiting impatiently for her to catch up. Taliah realises that if she ever gets to visit these, or any sites, it will be with her twin. She is still pondering this when the sound of the doorbell reverberates through the house. This is followed by the front door being opened. The recently returned Bethany calls up from downstairs, '*Talulah*, Taliah, your fatha is here.'

Talulah and Taliah stand up and go downstairs to the kitchen. Colin and Bethany are in the kitchen. Although Talulah is the first to enter the room it is Taliah who approaches her father and wraps her arms him, her head pressing against his chest. Colin places an arm around his daughter's shoulders and hugs her to him. When Taliah steps back, Talulah steps forward. As Taliah before her she places her arms around her father's neck, but limply, her head only momentarily touching his chest. Colin does not put his arm around Talulah's shoulders. Bethany, seeing this, bites on her lower lip. Colin, noticing that the whites of his daughters' eyes are a reddish colour, is suspicious as to why.

The four of them sit down at the table. Colin and Bethany on one side, Taliah and Talulah on the other. They sip tea and nibble on chocolate *éclairs* that Colin had bought from a local *patisserie*. The room is silent, save for the sporadic clinking of teacups against saucers and the barely perceptible sound of tea being sipped. Minutes pass. Colin swallows a mouthful of *éclair*, looks across the table at his daughters and says, 'Parents' Day was interesting, wasn't it girls? I got to chat with your teachers. Ms Thomas is great.'

A faint smile flickers across Taliah's face, but not Talulah's.

'Ms Thomas is very nice,' says Bethany before taking a sip from the cup held delicately in her fingertips. She then adds, 'Dat new German boy is so … charismatic.'

A smile appears on Talulah's face. Taliah stares up at the ceiling. Colin, looking up from the remnants of the *éclair* on his plate, says, 'Ah the kraut with the mohawk, how could I forget.'

Talulah glares across the table at her father, who leaning forward towards her, his elbows placed on the table top, a sullen expression upon his countenance, asks, 'Do you know why mohawks went out of fashion in the eighties?'

Taliah and Talulah shake their heads, as does Bethany.

'Because they suck,' says Colin.

'Itz an emblem of individuality,' blurts out Talulah.

Colin jerks back with such force that the front two legs of his chair come off the floor. His arms shoot up from his sides and flap wildly in the air, as he fights to prevent himself from toppling to the floor.

'Is everything okay?' asks Bethany when the chair is resting on four legs again.

'Yes, um fine,' says Colin.

The room is silent. Colin picks up his teacup and peers down at the tea leaf residue at the bottom of the cup. Minutes pass. Having pulled down the sleeve of his shirt and looked at his watch, Colin says, 'It's nearly five-thirty, I must be going.' He stands up and walks out into the hallway. Bethany beckons her daughters with an outstretched hand. Taliah stands up abruptly while Talulah rises slowly to her feet. The sisters file out into the hallway. Colin, who is now standing by the coat rack in the hall, says, 'Taliah, a quick word?'

Taliah nods. Talulah goes back into the kitchen, where Bethany is now clearing the table.

'Listen,' says Colin in a quiet voice. 'It's not too late to throw in the maths or biology and do design instead, or another subject of your choosing.'

'Yes Dad,' replies Taliah.

'You don't have to study what your sister wants you to. It is about time you started doing your own thing. Your headmaster tells me the end of this week is the deadline for any subject changes.'

Taliah opens her mouth then closes it again.

'Anyway, think about it,' says Colin. He calls out, 'Bye,' and then walks to the door and opens it. Taliah follows him. Colin places a hand on her head and strokes her hair. He says, 'See you soon.'

'Bye Dad.'

The door closes. Leaning against the wall, contemplating her father's words, Taliah wonders what Talulah's reaction would be if she announced that she was changing subjects. She concludes that Talulah would either persuade her not to, or failing that would change subject too. Taliah, sensing her sister's presence, spins around. Talulah is watching her from the kitchen doorway.

*

The following week – 'Why are half the school following Siegfried around all the time?' asks Pendergast, straightening his tie with one hand, prodding with his other in the direction of the mass of pupils at the other end of the corridor. Ms Thomas is poised to answer when Mr Francis approaches and says, 'Good morning.'

'We were discussing the students' obsession with the mohawked German,' says Pendergast.

Mr Francis says, 'Well he's certainly made an impression, hasn't he. He …'

'Why is Laticia doing that?' interrupts Pendergast. He is watching a tall, brown-haired girl pacing in circles by the stairs to the basement. 'One can only presume she hasn't been taking her Risperdal, Zyprexa, Wellbutrin, whatever it is she's on.'

Mr Francis shrugs, and Ms Thomas says, 'Perhaps, or maybe she's just having a difficult day.'

'Don't be so trite Sophia,' replies Pendergast. 'That girl was removed from her last school in a strait jacket, you can understand my concern.'

'At least The Antichrist's gone,' remarks Mr Francis, alluding to Hubert's recent absence from school.

Pendergast, throwing his rotund head back, laughs heartily. Having slapped Mr Francis on the back, he says, 'We'll have to crack open a bottle of bubbly to celebrate.'

Mr Francis glances at his watch and says, 'Is that the time, better get going, got Year Eleven for PE, see you at lunch.' The tracksuited PE teacher then jogs away.

'They really do seem pretty interested in the German, don't they?' says Pendergast, prodding with one of his pudgy fingers in the direction of the twins.

At this moment Talulah is pulling Taliah by the sleeve towards the front of the students surrounding Siegfried, who, holding a lit lighter above his head, scans the circle of onlookers. He says, 'Fire iz power, fire iz freedom, fire cannot be controlled.'

'You're a firomaniac.' It is Samson who says this as he strides up to the group, a gym bag slung over a burly shoulder.

'They're called pyromaniacs dickwad,' says Helen, the new American girl.

Siegfried, bellowing with laughter, runs his fingers through his purple-tinted mohawk.

'Whatever,' says Samson.

Samson and Taliah's eyes meet. Taliah, smiling faintly, waves meekly at him with one hand. Samson turns his back on her and walks away. Taliah watches him traipse down the corridor.

That evening – the key turns in the lock. The front door opens. Talulah enters the house followed by Taliah. In the kitchen Bethany gasps when Talulah and Taliah walk into the room. Having felt behind her, Bethany pulls up a chair and collapses into it. Talulah does a pirouette on the kitchen floor. Bethany, shaking her head, is at a loss as to what to say, so says nothing, and merely stares with her large hazel eyes at her daughters' hair, which earlier that afternoon at the hairdresser's had been shaved with an electric razor at the sides and back, and is now approximately one centimetre in length, whilst the long, soft, highlighted hair on the tops of their heads is styled in what

Bethany considers to be a floppy mohawk. Several ribbons have been braided into the long hair on the top of Talulah and Taliah's heads. Talulah's ribbons are blue, Taliah's pink. Bethany, who is not averse to perusing fashion magazines, is aware that these mohawk-type hairstyles are popular with young females, but not once has she ever envisaged such a hairstyle adorning the heads of her beloved daughters. She manages an unenthusiastic, 'That will take some getting used to.'

Talulah exhales sharply, turns her back on her mother and heads upstairs, followed by Taliah. In the bedroom Taliah sits at her desk while Talulah, inspecting her reflection in the wall mirror, adopts a variety of different postures. Taliah, finding the pride and confidence emanating from her twin stifling, undoes the top button of her shirt. Only when Talulah goes to her desk does Taliah make her way over to the mirror and cautiously examine her reflection. 'It will take some getting used to,' she mutters to herself.

Taliah has known for a while that her days of plaited hair were numbered. Recently she has taken to gazing at her hair in the mirror, running her thumb and index finger down the plaits, already experiencing a sense of nostalgia at their impending demise. Taliah was initially resistant to the hairstyle Talulah proposed. Taliah even considered keeping her hair as it was, but knew Talulah would never tolerate this, and she also wondered how her mother would react to the two of them looking different from one another.

But now as she looks at her reflection in the mirror, first front on and then from the side, a hint of a smile is visible, for despite the style being too rebellious for Taliah's tastes, she takes some satisfaction from the fact that it is fashionable and not altogether unattractive. She accepts that it could be worse. In the hairdresser that afternoon Taliah noticed Talulah frequently glancing in the direction of the bottles of hair dyes, one of which was purple. She was relieved when Talulah's interest was drawn elsewhere. Taliah now takes to wondering if Samson will like her new hair. So engrossed does she become with this thought that she does not hear Talulah say, 'Kloki wuthiwuthi outhe nana.'

When Talulah repeats her words a second time at a louder volume, gesturing with her mohawked head in the direction of the wall clock, Taliah returns to her desk. Taking her diary from the shelf and a pen from the desk tidy she made in Mrs Fofana's design class, she opens her diary and starts writing.

Meme has new a new hairstyle, it is like a mohawk, but floppy, not like you know who. (photograph to follow). I think I might want something girlier in future but it is okay and I might even grow to like it - just maybe. On another subject, Hubert has not been at school for a long time. Today Mr Pendergast announced in assembly that Hubert would not be returning to school. He did not outline why, other than to say he was 'very very sick mentally,' and that Royston Park 'could no longer meet his needs.' Veronica shrieked jubilantly and jumped up and down like a little kid at Christmas. Many of the first year students held hands and danced around in circles. Meme is apathetic. He didn't tease Meme anymore, not since Talulah accosted him. Also he knew Siegfried liked Meme so he wouldn't have dared tease us. Maybe Hubert even respected Meme a little because of the gas.

Meanwhile Talulah, writing in her diary at her desk, describes her hair at great length. All she writes about Hubert's departure is: *Hubert will not be returning to school, Meme will find gas elsewhere.*

Talulah closes her diary, stands up, goes over to the wardrobe, puts on her silver Puffa coat, places her wallet in the right hand side pocket, and then admires her reflection in the wall mirror again, pirouetting in front of it several times, ruffling the long soft hair on the top of her head. She then steps over to the door and waits silently. Taliah, sitting at her desk, with her back to the door can feel Talulah watching her. The copy of *Jacob's Room* Taliah has just picked up begins to tremble. She puts one of her perfectly manicured fingernails in her mouth, clamps down on it with her teeth, then relieves the pressure and extracts the unharmed fingernail from her mouth. She places the book on the desk and holds her trembling hands in her lap. Still Talulah waits by the door, watching her twin. Taliah stands up. She takes her Puffa coat out of wardrobe, which is identical to Talulah's, only khaki not silver. Having put it on, she places her purse in the right hand side pocket. She then approaches her twin. Taliah can sense Talulah's excitement as they descend the stairs.

'Where are you going?' asks Bethany in the hallway.

'Going to see friends from school,' utter Talulah and Taliah in unison, though Talulah merely mouths the s sounds.

'Be back by eleven-thirty,' says Bethany, wagging a finger in their direction.

'We will,' say Talulah and Taliah as they head down the hallway towards the front door. They walk to Bainbridge Road, where they take a westbound Number 723 bus. Sitting in the back row, they travel in silence, Talulah staring impassively ahead, Taliah on occasion looking wistfully out of the window.

Bustling streets and rows of terraced houses give way to tree-lined roads with spacious front-gardened detached houses. At the Paisley Park stop, the sisters get off the bus. Talulah takes her iPhone from her pocket and presses the map icon on its screen. Taliah, putting her hands in the pockets of her coat, observes the puffs of mist being exhaled from her twin's nose. A pizza delivery moped churns out murky plumes of exhaust as it whizzes past.

Talulah returns the iPhone to her coat pocket and crosses the road. Taliah follows her. They turn right onto a narrow asphalt path, which, unadorned with street lighting, is immersed in near darkness, the only illumination the half moon that hangs suspended in a star studded, near cloudless sky. Taliah stops walking and peers out into the gloom of the expansive playing fields that lie on either side of the path. When Taliah proceeds up the path, her steps are soon synchronised with that of her twin, who has disappeared into the darkness ahead of her.

Animated voices emanating from further up the path are followed by the sound of heavy footsteps. Talulah and Taliah step off the path and crouch down by the hedge. A horde of boisterous young men are approaching. Even in the dim light Taliah can see that they are wearing shorts and rugby shirts, sports bags slung over their shoulders. Only when the commotion subsides do Talulah and Taliah emerge onto the path. A timorous Taliah, her hands held in the pockets of her Puffa coat, jogs up the path. She feels relief when she catches up with her twin.

The pair have walked but a short way when Talulah takes the iPhone out of her pocket and inspects the screen. She takes a right turn down a narrow footpath. Taliah stops at the entrance to the footpath, looks left and right, takes a deep breath, and then follows the faint figure of her twin. The leafless branches that protrude from the trees on either side of the path seem to Taliah to resemble skeletal fingers. Talulah breaks into a jog. No longer able to see her twin, Taliah follows the sound of her feet. Then the footsteps stop and all Taliah can hear is the wind whistling in the branches of the trees. She stops and listens.

'Here.'

Taliah inhales sharply.

'Over here.'

Taliah shuffles towards the voice. She finds Talulah and Siegfried crouching at the base of a horse chestnut tree. They tug on Taliah's coat sleeves. She lowers herself to a crouching position. Siegfried points at Talulah and Taliah with the index finger of each hand, and then at his eyes. He says, 'Follow me, do as I do.' And then, 'Nice hair, very nice.'

Taliah senses Talulah's satisfaction when Siegfried says this. Siegfried smiles widely, revealing perfectly aligned teeth, as white as ivory. The three stand up and head off down the pathway in single file, Siegfried leading the way, followed by Talulah, with Taliah bringing up the rear. To Taliah, hearing her reverberating heartbeat, it seems that her twin's heart is also beating within her, that their two hearts have formed a single, pounding organ. Having turned off the path the trio enter an expanse of grass. Siegfried starts to run. The twins follow in single file. Taliah sees the outlines of rugby posts and football goals. Ahead is a small, single storey brick building. Siegfried draws to a halt at the front of the building. He takes a box of long matches from one of his black trench coat's pockets, lights one and holds it up. Above the building's door, Taliah sees the words *Paisley Parish Church Community Centre*.

'Ha ha ha, *ja!*' exclaims Siegfried before blowing out the match.

Talulah and Taliah watch as Siegfried takes a can from a pocket, then holds it out in front of him. This is followed by a loud and prolonged hissing. Talulah hurries over to Siegfried. Taliah takes a tentative step towards them, then another. Siegfried returns the can to his pocket. From another pocket he takes out a small tin. There is a letterbox in the door. Siegfried opens the letterbox, pushes the tin through the opening, tips it and shakes it vigorously. Talulah and Taliah watch Siegfried put the tin back in his pocket, take out the matches from the same pocket, strike a match against the side of the box, and then hold the match up – lighting up his handsome face, which Taliah notices is etched in glee.

Siegfried drops the match through the letterbox. He laughs aloud and then dashes around to the side of the building. Talulah rushes after him. Taliah, following slowly behind hears glass shatter, then sees the outline of Siegfried's arm leaning through a window. Taliah gasps. She steps forward towards the window. Talulah's slender arm reaches into the side pocket of Siegfried's trench coat and emerges with the box of matches. Talulah strikes a match. When she turns to her sister, the flickering flame illuminates her face. Talulah approaches the broken window and drops the match through it. Then, standing on tiptoes, peers down through the window at the flames licking at the carpet.

'To ze front,' orders Siegfried, striding towards the door, Talulah clutching at his arm. Siegfried takes out the tin and turns it upside down. Its contents trickle down the wooden door. Talulah lights a match. She holds the match out to Taliah who is now standing behind her. Taliah's hands remain in the pockets of her coat. Still Talulah holds out the match. Taliah feels her hands rising from her pockets, sees her right hand reaching towards the match. She plunges her hands back into the pockets of her coat and grips the lining at their base. An expressionless Talulah spins around and reaches out with the match. Taliah gulps as the flames engulf the door.

'Hahaha *ja*,' says Siegfried jubilantly, punching the air with his fist.

Siegfried and Talulah, taking a step back, stand besides Taliah, listening to the woodwork's paint hiss. The intensifying flames reveal a large spray-painted circle with a capital A in the middle of it. Talulah and Taliah watch mesmerised as the orange and yellow flames dance alluringly.

The sound of shouting fills the night air. Neither Taliah nor Talulah hear Siegfried say, 'Letz go.'

The shouting intensifies. Siegfried pulls on the collars of Talulah and Taliah's coats. Taliah, looking away from the flames, hears the shouting.

'Ve leave now,' says Siegfried, pulling harder on the collars.

'Wuthiwuthi mene,' says Taliah to Talulah, who is still staring transfixed at the flames. 'Wuthiwuthi, quick quick,' she implores, tugging at Talulah's arm.

Talulah, awakening from her trance, blinks, spins around and runs after the fleeing Siegfried towards the path, Taliah following close behind her, the sound of shouting echoing in their ears. At the edge of the playing fields they collapse to the ground breathing heavily. They watch in silence as the fire engulfs the building, then listen to the sirens in the distance. They even stay to watch the firemen fight the inferno.

CHAPTER SIX

TALULAH AND TALIAH are in biology class. Talulah is nibbling at her pink-varnished fingernails with her porcelain white teeth, whilst Taliah sits as motionless as one of the potted cacti that reside on the classroom's window ledges. Taliah's perfectly manicured pink nails are embellished with silver glitter, but Talulah's nails, though also painted pink and embellished with silver glitter, are shorter and more uneven. Ms Papin, the biology teacher, having noticed this difference in the state of the twins' nails, inquisitively inspects one pair of hands and then the other. Talulah glares at Ms Papin, who recoils in fright and then scurries back to the front of the class, her hip colliding with a desk en route.

In their next class, physics, Talulah nibbles at her fingernails and twirls the long stands of highlighted hair on the top of her head in her long, slender fingers. Sensing her twin's agitation, Taliah twirls her own hair in her fingertips, and now inserts the fingernail of her little finger into her mouth and grips it between her teeth, only to take it out again, undamaged. Taliah slides a few centimetres along the bench, away from her twin.

In English, Taliah, her hands clasped in her lap, smiles faintly as she listens to Ms Thomas's enchanting, gentrified voice reading aloud from *Mansfield Park*. At the desk in front Talulah is nibbling at her fingernails, at the same time fiddling with the mobile telephone in her other hand. Taliah, sensing her twin's restlessness, bites on her pink-glossed lower lip as she erects an imaginary wall in her mind, many metres high with rolls of barbed wire atop of it. She then re–focuses on her English teacher's reassuring voice. Soon she is no longer aware of her twin's discomfort.

The new American girl, Helen, sitting in the row of desks adjacent to the twins, has also noticed the less than pristine state of Talulah's nails. Taliah observes Helen, fluttering her fingers in Talulah's direction, showing off her own perfectly manicured hands, emits noises that Taliah considers would not be out of place at an English ladies' tea party. The blonde-haired Helen who, though usually delightful, will not tolerate any girl she perceives to be as pretty as her, continues to mock Talulah with her ceaselessly fluttering fingers. Sensing her twin's escalating wrath, Taliah wiggles in her seat, then grips the base of it with both hands and holds her breath. Still Helen flutters her fingers. Talulah holds out a middle finger towards Helen, who now stops fluttering her fingers and looks abruptly away from Talulah. Taliah, releasing her grip of the chair, is relieved that her twin did not react more assertively.

On the journey home from school, Taliah feels her twin's craving as clearly as the late afternoon sun shining through the window of the bus. She edges across her seat, away from Talulah, but still the craving permeates her. The wall that Taliah constructed in her mind earlier is now a pile of rubble, leaving her naked and exposed. Taliah holds a perfectly manicured fingernail to her mouth, places it between her teeth and exerts downward pressure. She extracts the nail, examines it, is relieved there is no damage, returns her hand to her lap, the other unwittingly moving to her head, where it twirls the highlighted strands of hair in its fingertips, in the exact same manner as Talulah beside her. Talulah leans constantly into Taliah, whispering incessant, hushed but harried bursts of cryptophasia into her ear. Taliah wishes she were alone. The bus draws to a halt. Talulah and Taliah get off, Taliah purposefully lagging behind, grateful for the modest respite the additional space between them provides.

Trudging towards home, she yawns then rubs her eyes. She is weary from Talulah's relentless craving for drugs, her insatiable anarchist desires, resentment at society and recent appetite for arson. Taliah is unhappy that Talulah is not taking her medication, which they continue to be prescribed, but which Talulah has been discarding in the bin for several weeks now. Sometimes when alone in the bathroom at home Taliah rolls a Zyprexa pill in her fingertips, inspecting it closely, before swallowing it, vainly hoping as she does so that Talulah will do the same.

Talulah is waiting on the pavement ahead, her feet shoulder width apart, her hands placed on her hips, her mouth forming a scowl, frown lines visible on her forehead. Taliah, trudging slowly towards her, feels Talulah's craving growing stronger with each step. The twins have smoked cannabis, consumed alcohol, gas, and even shared several ecstasy pills in recent weeks, but now they have spent all their pocket money. Talulah has even sold her old textbooks on *eBay* and persuaded Taliah to sell a few of her own.

The craving emanating from Talulah is so overpowering that Taliah slows her pace to allow for a bigger gap between them. Ahead on the pavement outside The Flag pub a group of men are gathered, pint glasses and cigarettes in hand. Lascivious attentions turn to Talulah and Taliah – eyes creep up their legs, several men whistle, a heavyset man in an orange vest gestures obscenely with a protruding tongue. Taliah quickens her pace. Lifting her head she gazes at Talulah's back. Knowing that Talulah is deep in thought, Taliah focuses on her.

Holding her hand to her mouth to prevent herself from screaming out in protestation, she slows her pace again, allowing Talulah to get still further ahead. Taliah, believing that Talulah was just contemplating how the two of them might be able extract money from the men outside the pub, hopes she is mistaken.

Her sister is waiting at their home's front gate. Taliah, viewing her suspiciously, approaches hesitantly. There is no sign of the vile thought or the craving. Talulah puts a slender arm around Taliah's neck, squeezes her to her breast and ruffles the long, highlighted hair on the top of her head. Talulah unlocks the door, and then clasping her twin by the wrist, pulls her upstairs to their mother's bedroom, where she ushers Taliah to the dressing table. Talulah brushes Taliah's hair, as Taliah peers into the silver-rimmed mirror at the reflection of herself and the person closest to her in the world.

It is now evening and Talulah and Taliah are still in their bedroom, at their respective desks, busily writing in their diaries. Bethany calls from downstairs, '*Twins*, wata or aringe juice?'

Taliah stands up, walks out onto the landing and looks down the stairs, where Bethany, her arms folded across her bosom, is standing.

'Water please.'

'*Talulah*,' calls Bethany.

Upstairs, Talulah remains at her desk. A short while later Bethany walks into the twins' bedroom. She places a glass of water on Taliah's desk and then plonks a glass of water down on Talulah's desk. Several drops of water spill from the glass. Bethany leaves the room. Talulah and Taliah continue writing in their diaries.

At night in my dreams and in the daytime too when I close my eyes I can see fire – a raging infurno of orange, red and yellow burning away everything that is wrong with the world – authority, church, state, psychiatrists and the places where they store the drugs to control people that want to be individuals and not like everyone else. Individuals like Meme that they force to take Zyprexa, ~~Rispedel~~, ~~Rispardal~~.

Talulah stops writing. She takes the dictionary from the shelf above her desk, locates the letter R, flicks through the pages until she gets to *Ris*, then scans the page. She closes the dictionary, takes her iPhone from the pocket of her jeans, opens the internet browser and types in *google.com*. The page does not load. After expiring forcefully, Talulah says, 'Medi riperdal ow crible?'

'R-i-s-p-e-r-d-a-l,' says Taliah.

Talulah crosses out the two incorrect spellings and then continues writing.

Risperdal, Wellbutrin, Cylert, Depo Provera, Prozac, Dexedrine, the other one that starts with D and has an x in it.

Talulah stops writing and glances over her shoulder at Taliah before continuing with her diary entry.

The authorities force Meme and other victims to take these drugs but stop us taking the ones we want, the drugs that help us relax, have fun and bring Meme closer together. This is because 'they vant to control our minds' as they think 've' are a threat and also because they are making lots and lots of money out of these drugs. At school in the library this afternoon when Meou was playing scrabble with Veronica I read lots about the individual anarchist cause on the library computer. There is so much to learn and so little time. The teachings of individual anarchist exponants John Henry McKay and Max Stirner, as well as Josiah Warren's teachings about sexual freedom and free love, all just theory now, but fingers crossed will be put into practice really soon. Meme's messiah has awakeЯned Meme. The purple plumed Mohawk is an emblem that Meme will follow to the end of the world. Siegfried was wearing this really tight cashmere Lacoste V neck gray jumper today. He looked amazing. Underneath he had this T-Shirt with the anarchist logo on it – the circle with the big capital A in the middle.

Talulah stops writing. She closes her diary and then looks over her shoulder at Taliah, whose back is turned to her, as she sits, bent forward over her desk, writing in her diary.

In English class Ms Thomas read from Mansfield Park, which is fast becoming my favourite book along with Pride and Prejudice and Persuasion. There was also a class discussion on themes in The Rime of the Ancient Mariner. I listened attentively, Talulah didn't. I caught glimpses of Samson, his head resting in his large hands – he yawned several times. Never did he look across at me. What is love if not pain? Sometimes Talulah looked in the direction of Siegfried who was reclining in his chair, wearing his Lacoste jumper. He seemed not to have a care in the world, which is surprising under the circumstances. (I would never have guessed anarchists love Lacoste so much until Meme met Siegfried – he's got jumpers, belts, trainers, shirts, even a bag). I wonder who'll make all his Lacoste gear if and when the world turns to anarchy like he says it will. In midmorning break I played scrabble with Veronica. I got the word agreeable, one of Jane Austen's favourite words.

Jelly for dessert at lunch today. Talulah didn't finish hers even though she loves jelly - umi umi jewi budud.

I just know there's going to be another trip to the bathroom scales really really soon. After lunch Siegfried invited Meme to join him, Ben and Asif at the athletics track. We stayed at the track until it started raining. The rain ruined Meme's hair (Meme's mohawks look desultory when wet. Siegfried's spiky mohawk has so much gel that the rain just ran off it).

Afterwards we had physics. It was hard to concentrate after our post lunch activities but I did learn that the positron, the antiproton, the antineutron and the antineutrino are the antiparticles of the electron, the proton, the neutron and the neutrino - respectively.

I still feel naked and exposed without my faithful shield Zyprexa. Am I to go the way of the dinosaurs? Is my destiny to be a conjoined, Siamese twin? Recently I have been dreaming about this at nights and waking up in a panic, listening to my beating heart, staring out into the darkness of the room, wondering what the future holds for Meme, fearful that our lives are spiralling out of control. For all the excitement this year has brought, especially for Talulah, I feel fear. I bear this fear for the both of us, a burden too heavy for my slender frame and fragile heart.

Taliah, pouring out her heart onto the page, has not noticed her grimacing twin, who continues to watch her from her desk, her eyes drawn close together, as she focuses all her concentration on Taliah.

Compared to fate, free will seems but mere dust in the wind. Am I a bird without wings?

Taliah stops writing, the pen falls to the desk, she spins around in her chair and stares into the hostile depths of the hazel eyes glowering at her from the other side of the room. Taliah's fumbling hand reaches for her diary. She shuts it and then places her physics textbook on top it. As Talulah's unflinching stare remains fixed on her, she forbids any thought of her diary entry to enter her mind.

'Dinner's ready,' calls Bethany from the bottom of the stairs.

Still an unblinking Talulah glares at her twin. Taliah looks away. Talulah stands up and strides over to the door, where she waits silently.

'Oun nana eain nuhnuh kloki,' says Taliah in a faltering voice.

Talulah strides out of the room. Taliah is trembling when she picks up her diary and places it on the bookshelf. There is a strand of hair lying on the desk. Taliah looks at the strand of hair for quite some time, biting on her lower lip as she does so. Taliah opens her diary. A solitary tear trickles down her cheek when she places the strand of hair between its front cover and first page.

*

Over the course of the next six weeks two further nocturnal escapades culminate in infernos that engulf a church hall and a building used as a polling station at election time. On both occasions Siegfried spray paints a circle with a capital A in the middle of it on the building. Although Taliah is in attendance at these arson attacks, she is not involved in the setting of the fires, this despite the pressure she feels from Talulah to incriminate herself. But her lack of involvement does not prevent Taliah feeling guilty about the fires, and this guilt weighs so heavily upon her, it seems that she is also burdened with the guilt that her twin has eluded. And there is also fear. In the days following the infernos, every time Taliah hears the blare of a siren, her heartbeat quickens. This also happens when the doorbell rings at home, and when Pendergast walks into a classroom Taliah happens to be in. This is in contrast to Talulah, who feels no concern at all.

At school Ms Thomas is only too aware that Talulah is getting assistance from Taliah with assignments. She suspects Talulah is also cheating in tests, and is fairly certain that Taliah does not speak in class because she does not want to anger her twin. Ms Thomas is concerned for Taliah's future, and she feels a deep sense of unease about the inexplicable, malignant binary system that makes Taliah dependent on Talulah.

Were Ms Thomas to see Talulah's diary entries she would no doubt be surprised by the increasingly detailed and evocative descriptions, something Ms Thomas views as being a characteristic of her more artistic twin. With Talulah's newfound obsession with the individual anarchist cause, her writing continues to be enriched by the literary style of the early individual anarchists, though spelling remains an issue.

Talulah and Taliah continue to write their diaries entries every evening at their desks in their bedroom, only Taliah's entries are more reserved than before and no more torrents of emotion pour onto the page. The events of the day are summarised for the most part in a matter of fact way – the content of lessons, the weather and meals eaten. For Taliah remains concerned about Talulah's interest in her diary, and is no longer confident in releasing her emotions in what has been her one private domain for so many years. Unable to unburden her feelings, she feels pressure building within her, for there is no one she can confine in. Only in the deepest recesses of her mind does she hold her real thoughts. As for the arson attacks Talulah is involved in and that Taliah has witnessed, they are merely hinted at in Taliah's diary. There are still occasions however when the object of her heart's desire is mentioned. One evening Taliah writes – *for the fleetest of moments our eyes meet across the crowded hall.* And on another occasion – *though we stand facing each other on opposite sides of the corridor, it feels that a continent divides us.* Last Wednesday Taliah wrote – *he fidgets with a pen then compliments me on my hair, I smile faintly.* Each time Taliah completes her daily diary entry she places the strand of hair between the front cover and first page. And she makes sure never to dwell on it.

*

It is Friday evening and the twins are at their desks writing. Taliah stops writing, quickly reinserts the strand of hair between the front cover and first page, and then puts her diary in its usual position, lying flat on the shelf above the desk. She then fidgets with a biro pen, before putting the pen down and clasping her trembling hands in her lap. Her right hand raises to her mouth, a pink-varnished nail decorated with silver hearts is inserted into her mouth, porcelain white incisors exert downward pressure. The pressure is released, the nail removed from her mouth, undamaged. Taliah clasps her trembling hands in her lap again.

Talulah stops writing in her diary, closes it, places it on the shelf above her desk, stands up, goes over to the wardrobe, takes out her silver Puffa coat, puts the coat on, places her purse in one of the coat's side pockets and her mobile phone in the other, and then walks over to the door, where she stands waiting. Taliah, her back to the door, senses Talulah watching her.

'Wedi treki gogo,' says Talulah.

Taliah does not move. Still Talulah waits. Every impulse screams at Taliah to get up and follow her twin, as she has always done. Taliah feels herself rising slowly upwards. Having lowered herself back down into her chair, she grips the rim of the desk with both hands.

'UCKI MEOU DERRIII WABA MENE OUTHE GO!' shouts Talulah, who then abruptly departs the room, goes downstairs, strides through the hallway and out through the front door.

Upstairs Taliah releases her grip on the desk and slumps back in her chair.

*

The next day Bethany is at the kitchen table having breakfast when Taliah enters the kitchen alone.

'Mawnin Taliah,' greets Bethany.

'Good morning,' says Taliah.

When a few minutes later a dishevelled looking Talulah enters the kitchen, Bethany says nothing. Taliah, who is now spreading marmalade on a piece of toast, watches Talulah out of the corner of her eye. Bethany picks up the local newspaper from the kitchen top behind her, opens it and holds it up, blocking the view of her two daughters. Taliah takes a sip from her glass of orange juice and then a large bite of toast. Meanwhile Talulah nibbles unenthusiastically on a piece of toast, her head cradled in one hand.

All that morning Talulah ignores Taliah. After lunch Taliah observes Talulah through the bedroom window, smoking a joint in the back garden whilst watching the flickering flame of the lighter she is holding. Taliah sighs, then returns to her desk, where she works on an assignment, trying not to contemplate the fire she is certain that her twin and Siegfried started last night.

That afternoon Taliah is in her room alone, Talulah having gone downstairs to watch television. Ignored by her twin and with her mother having gone out for the day, Taliah feeling lonely, lays down on her bed and reads *Jacob's Room*. But even indulging in this, her favourite activity, fails to alleviate her melancholy. Taliah wishes Veronica would come and visit her. Talulah enters the bedroom soon after and parks herself at her desk, where she reads *Walden* by Henry David Thoreau, the nineteenth-century author, naturalist and early influence on individualist anarchist thought. To Taliah, casting occasional glances in her twin's direction, it seems that Talulah has erected a wall between them.

Taliah leaves the room soon after. When she returns a minute later she is clutching a nail file, a bottle of pink nail gloss, cotton wool pads, a little pot of nail glitter and a bottle of nail varnish remover. She draws her chair up alongside Talulah's, gently clasps her sister's hands in hers and places them in her lap. Having soaked a cotton wool pad with the nail varnish remover, Taliah proceeds to scrub Talulah's chipped and uneven nails. When Taliah finishes manicuring the nails of her twin's right hand, Talulah holds the hand up and waves it in the air, inspecting the glossy, glittered finish, a glimmer of a smile visible on her face. Taliah then scrubs, files and varnishes the nails of Talulah's left hand before sprinkling them with heart-shaped silver glitter. Feeling the delight radiating from Talulah when she examines the nails of her left hand, Taliah is certain that her twin is no longer angry about her refusal to go out with her last night.

The iPhone is vibrating on Talulah's desk. Talulah picks it up, looks at the screen and then shows the message to Taliah. It reads:

Dearest Meme,
You are cordially invited for drinks at mine this evening
from 7p.m. No fires, promise.
Your humble anarchist

Siegfried. Ⓐ

'Meme,' says Taliah.

Talulah shrugs her shoulders.

Taliah's eyes narrow as she studies her twin. She says, 'No fires.'

'Nuhnuh nana fia,' replies Talulah emphatically.

'Moda waba,' says Taliah. 'Mene moda hat.'

Talulah nods. Taliah leaves the room and goes downstairs to speak to Bethany.

*

6:59 p.m. – the front door of the mansion opens. Siegfried is standing in the open doorway. He is wearing a black double-breasted dinner suit, bow tie, a pleated scarlet cummerbund around his waist, his impeccably groomed, gelled, purple-highlighted mohawk, a flawless crescent running to the nape of his neck.

'*Guten Abend Fräulein* Meme,' greets Siegfried, bowing down on one knee and kissing Talulah and Taliah's hands in turn. 'Velcome to my humble abode.'

Talulah and Taliah, familiar with Siegfried's customary, carefully cultivated wealthy teenage skateboarder meets socialist revolutionary look, are surprised and impressed by his attire. Taliah feels very underdressed.

A minute later Talulah and Taliah, champagne flutes clasped demurely in immaculately manicured hands, are following Siegfried through the expansive open-planned ground floor. Gesturing towards a pair of ornate vases decorated with pictures of Highland cattle on a table to their left, Siegfried says, 'Original nineteen-twenties Royal Worcester varzes.' And then winking at Talulah and Taliah he adds, 'But you English already know all about Royal Worcester porcelain.'

Talulah and Taliah look at each other and then at Siegfried. They nod in unison, though neither of them knows anything about Royal Worcester porcelain. As the tour continues, Taliah marvels at the black marble floor beneath her feet.

99

'Do you know who painted it? Any idea Meme?' enquires Siegfried, gesturing with his champagne flute at a portrait of a seated, curly-haired lady in white, looking to her right, that Taliah considers could have come straight from a Jane Austen novel. Taliah and Talulah shake their heads.

'Anton Graff, ze neoclassical portrait painter and native of my hometown.'

Talulah and Taliah take a sip of champagne. Taliah, in awe of the portrait, keeps looking at it for quite some time, before scampering in her trainer-clad feet across the marble floor to catch up with her twin and Siegfried.

'Oh what's that!' shrieks Taliah, pointing with a quivering finger at an enormous wild boar head mounted on the wall.

Siegfried, nearly dropping his champagne flute, takes a step back.

'That, *Mademoiselle* Verboze, iz my first wild boar. Slain in the Ardennes last winter.'

Standing in front of the head, Talulah and Taliah closely inspect its large, yellowed tusks.

'A freezing vinter morning, and I am standing in a high seat, outlining the imbecility of capitalism to the chairman of a Belgian bank, who vas, how do you say in English … guffawing. He had zese red, vein-riddled cheeks and numerous … trembling chinz.'

As Siegfried tells the story, Talulah and Taliah gaze at him, Taliah acknowledging how beautiful Siegfried is, if rather ludicrous.

'Out of the corner of my eye I spy a spectacular specimen stride out of ze forest,' continues Siegfried. 'Through the telescope I saw a kindred spirit – bold, beautiful, proud, strong and vith a mohawk, ha, hahaha.' Having stroked the long, black bristles on the back of the boar's neck, he says, 'Like indigenous Americans I believe when you take a creature's life you take itz soul.' Siegfried reaches out with his left hand grabs the air when he says this.

Talulah nods her head vigorously, her pink lip-sticked mouth breaking into a smile. Taliah's expression remains unchanged.

'*Fräulein* Meme let us sojourn to the lounge,' says Siegfried in theatrical fashion.

In the lounge Talulah and Taliah recline on a white sofa, their left legs crossed coyly over their right, champagne flutes clasped in their right hands. There is a Bang and Olufsen music system built into the wall opposite them. Siegfried is standing next to the music system, facing Talulah and Taliah. There is a CD shelf behind him. Siegfried takes a CD out of the shelf. He says, '*Comfortably Numb* by Pink Floyd. My father considers Pink Floyd to be cool, and in zis one instance he iz correct.' Siegfried, turning from the CD to the twins, asks, '*Ja* or *nein*?'

'*Nein*,' say Talulah and Taliah.

Siegfried takes another CD from the shelf, spins around, and holding his half empty champagne flute to his mouth, sings, '*Heute nacht bin ich aufgewacht ich weiß, Sie hat da oben grad an uns gedacht.*'

Talulah and Taliah laugh.

Siegfried asks, 'You know who sung it?'

Talulah and Taliah shake their heads.

'David Hasselhoff. Ve Germans love Hasselhoff. Zis is regrettable.' Another CD is pulled from the shelf. It is hurled to the floor. Pointing at it, Siegfried shouts, 'I reject you Celine Dion!'

Talulah and Taliah recoil. Several drops of champagne from their flutes spill onto the sofa. They look at each other and giggle. Siegfried approaches the sofa, drops to one knee, and looking up at Talulah and Taliah with his blue eyes, he asks, 'Vhat does I reject you mean in your secret language.'

Taliah glances at Talulah.

'Come on Meme,' adds Siegfried in a soothing tone, looking up pleadingly at Talulah and Taliah.

'Meeh nuhnuh u cheline dion,' say Taliah and Talulah quietly.

'*Nein*, louder, how can I hear,' implores Siegfried.

'Meeh nuhnuh u cheline dion.'

A grinning Siegfried strides over to where the CD box is lying on the floor, stands over it and shouts, 'MEEH NUHNUH U CHELINE DION!'

Talulah shrieks with laughter, and Taliah, unable to contain herself, laughs too, wiping several tears of mirth streaming down her cheeks with the sleeve of her white cotton shirt. Siegfried selects a CD from the shelf and inserts it in the CD player. The sound of electric guitars, drums and sinister vocals fills the room.

'*Antichrist Superstar* by Marilyn Manson, you like?' says Siegfried.

A minute later Siegfried strides over to the sofa. Going down on one knee, he places a silver platter in front of Talulah, passing her a ten pound note with his other hand.

'*Fräulein* Meme, a line of MDMA?'

Without hesitation Talulah snorts up the crystals. She falls back, rubs her nose with the palm of her hand and says, 'Ouchouchi.'

Siegfried, now on two knees, looks up at Taliah, winks and purses his lips when he passes her the platter. Taliah stares at the chiselled features and piercing blue eyes, before glancing at Talulah and then peering down at the platter. She slowly picks up the ten pound note, inserts it in her nostril, and leaning over the platter, views the translucent white crystals with suspicion. She snorts the line gradually and then leans back on the sofa, rubbing her nose.

'Ow,' says Taliah. 'It hurts.'

'No pain no gain,' says Siegfried.

Taliah sneezes.

Twenty minutes later – Taliah, her eyelids fluttering, lies writhing on her back on the carpet behind the sofa. She feels lightheaded, her skin is tingling and waves of euphoria are surging through her body. Even above the frenetic drumbeat and Marilyn Manson's wails she can hear the muffled sounds of her sister and Siegfried frolicking on the sofa. Taliah sees her twin's bare legs casting shadows across the ceiling.

Taliah, her face etched with strain, sucks on her lower lip, arches her back and claws at the carpet, her breath coming in short gasps. She grimaces then cries out. Her body goes rigid. Taliah, her brow moist with sweat, lies still, the only sign of movement her breast heaving up and down. Here she remains with her eyes closed, until hearing a whispering in her ear, she opens them again. Everything is blurry. Talulah is kneeling next to her, wearing only her bra and underwear. When she feels her trousers being pulled down, Taliah reaches down to pull them up, but her grip is weak and her hands go limp. She hears her twin whisper in her ear, 'Mene ry nuhnuh meou abtary,' as she is hoisted into the air, and then lain down on the sofa on her back, in the same position as Talulah before her. Siegfried gently caresses her neck with his lips. Taliah's body relaxes.

*

The next morning – Taliah smothers a sob with the sleeve of her pyjama top, then wipes her damp cheeks. After suppressing several more sobs with her sleeve, she rolls over on to her stomach and proceeds to weep into her pillow, a torrent of tears streaming from her eyes. Talulah stirs on the bunk above. Taliah is still lying on her front, crying into her pillow when Talulah descends the bunk bed's ladder. Sensing Talulah watching her, Taliah pulls the duvet over her head and curls her body up in a tight ball. Taliah remains in this position for several hours. When she finally gets up her posture is stooped and her eyes puffy.

CHAPTER SEVEN

MONDAY MORNING – Talulah and Taliah are buttering pieces of toast when Bethany picks up the local borough newspaper from the chair beside her, then opens it and holds it out in front of her. Looking up from her toast Taliah notices an article towards the bottom of the front page with the headline, *Anarchist Arsonists Strike Again*. She swallows, glances surreptitiously at Talulah, who is oblivious to the article, and then returns her attention to the newspaper. The article states that a purposefully started fire last Friday caused considerable damage to a pharmaceutical company's office, before being extinguished by fire fighters. Mention is made of an anarchist logo, which had been spray-painted to a tree next to the building. The article mentions that this is the fourth arson attack in the borough in recent months, and in all four instances either an anarchist logo, or remnants of an anarchist logo have been discovered at the scene. Talulah is now looking at the newspaper. She is grinning.

After breakfast Talulah and Taliah set off for school. On the way to the bus stop, and when they get off the bus, Taliah falls quite some way behind Talulah. Hearing a siren, increasing in volume, Taliah bows her head and holds her breath. A police car hurtles past. Taliah exhales forcefully. Further up the pavement Talulah, her arms across her chest, is waiting. Taliah, approaching her twin, scrutinises her for any semblance of anxiety, but finds none.

At school that morning when Talulah and Taliah pass along the corridors, Talulah's chin is tilted upwards, whilst Taliah, shuffling in her wake, looks down at the floor. In class Taliah's shoulders are slumped and her eyes dull. The only time she moves is a twist of her head to gaze wistfully at Samson in biology.

It is now early afternoon. The twins are in the basement passageway. Talulah is standing about ten metres or so away from Taliah, playing a game on her mobile. Taliah is leaning against the wall of the corridor, beside Veronica.

'I'm going to make this really big animal collage for my art A level project with loads of different farm animals. It's going to be like a statement about modern farming practices and how um intensive farming is really bad for animals,' says Veronica breathlessly.

'That's a good idea,' says Taliah. 'When will you start?'

'Well,' replies Veronica. 'It will have to be next week I think.'

Taliah nods her head.

'Are you okay?' asks Veronica in a concerned tone, looking up at her friend and inspecting her searchingly.

'Yes, I am fine,' replies Taliah, standing up straight and forcing a smile.

Taliah listens half-heartedly, offering the occasional hushed word of encouragement, as an animated Veronica outlines the plans for the project. Mrs Fofana walks past, a pile of textbooks held in her arms. A scowl from Talulah sends her scurrying down the corridor. Taliah becomes aware of voices emanating from the far end of the corridor behind her. Hearing Siegfried's voice, she inhales sharply. A male voice says, 'Catch you later Siegfried.' And a female says, 'I love your Lacoste polo neck by the way, it's so you.'

Taliah watches a group of students pass by and go up the stairs, then she hears Siegfried talking to Talulah behind her. Taliah stands facing Veronica, who is now showing her a drawing of a rabbit. A moment later Veronica glances at her watch and says, 'I'm late for my psychiatry session.'

Taliah reaches out to grab Veronica. Her hand is left dangling in the air as Veronica scampers away. Taliah, her back still turned to Siegfried and Talulah, feels naked and exposed. She is considering departing discreetly when she hears the sound of approaching feet. Turning around, she feels heat rising to her cheeks.

'Saturday vas fun *ja* Meme,' says Siegfried, now standing beside Talulah facing Taliah.

Taliah takes a step back. A grinning Siegfried says, 'I have a small gift for Meme.'

Siegfried takes a red leather wallet with Che Guevara's face printed on it from his pocket. From the wallet he takes a tiny transparent plastic bag. The bag contains two small paper squares. Passing the bag to Talulah, he says in a hushed tone, 'LSD, original Timothy Leary acid.' Siegfried looks around. He leans towards Talulah. Taliah hears him says, 'One each. Put it on your tongue, let it dissolve. Zis will blow your mind.' And then, 'Do it on half term, not at school.'

Taliah senses the excitement tinged with apprehension in her twin. Talulah puts the bag in the side pocket of her jeans and then tugs at Siegfried's sleeve. She opens her mouth. Siegfried places a finger to her lips. Looking into her eyes, a wide smile enveloping his handsome face, he says, 'Can't do half term. I have to go, I vant to go, on a golf break vith my father.'

Pointing at Talulah and Taliah with the index and middle fingers of his right hand, he says, 'The LSD iz for you two to experience together. It iz crazy stuff, you'll love it.' And with that he's off, striding down the corridor, only to spin around a moment later and call out, 'Next time a threesome *ja*.'

Taliah gulps.

After school Talulah and Taliah travel home as normal, and then go up to their bedroom where they sit at their desks. Taliah, working on her biology assignment, finds it difficult to concentrate. Talulah, also with her biology books on the desk, but unopened, peers out of the window. Even though Taliah has her back to her sister she knows Talulah is not studying, and as usual expects her to complete the assignment that she will then copy. She grits her teeth in annoyance. This is the first feeling other than shame, shock and sorrow that she has felt since waking up on Sunday morning. Taliah feels anger stirring within her when she recalls the sequence of events that led to her losing her virginity. She had previously romanticised about how this life changing moment might occur, but not once had she ever envisaged her twin being in attendance. Taliah, now attempting to concentrate on her assignment, tries to block all other thoughts from her mind.

After dinner Talulah returns to the bedroom and takes her diary from the shelf. A pensive Taliah lingers in the kitchen, slowly eating her Petits Filous. When she goes upstairs, she sees Talulah writing in her diary. Taliah, sitting at her desk, hearing the pen moving across the page behind her, feels the pride and confidence emanating from her twin.

Taliah stares aimlessly at the wall in front of her for quite some time. Twisting her head slightly, she watches an oblivious Talulah out of the corner of her eye. Taliah reaches up and takes her diary from the shelf. She opens it and scans her entry from yesterday. There is no mention of the momentous event in her life that had occurred the night before, as if by not mentioning it she had not admitted to herself that it occurred. Taliah takes her biro from the desk. She writes, *Am I a puppet on a string? What will become of me? I have lost something so precious and personal, now I have nothing left that belongs to me, and not also to Meme. Nothing at all that I can think of, but this diary, this little piece of me, containing my hopes, desires and this brief summary of my ~~life~~ existence. Maybe there will be no me at all one of these days. In the not too distant future I'll*

Her feelings and fears for the future pour out onto the pages of the diary in a manner uncharacteristic of recent times. Frantically writing page after page, unburdening the emotions that have been trapped inside her, hidden from everyone, even her twin, Taliah is unaware of the watching eyes.

Taliah stops writing. She can no longer hear the sound of pen against paper behind her. On closing her diary, Taliah visualises a vast vacuous space, a vacuum like she learned about in Mr Kenton's physics class. When Taliah becomes aware that Talulah's attention is drifting away from her, she waits several minutes, then reopens the diary, inserts the strand of hair between the front cover and the first page, and then places the diary in its usual position. Then she gets up, walks out of the room, heads downstairs and goes into the sitting room. Bethany is on the sofa watching television, twirling the curls on the side of her head in her fingers. Bethany turns off the television and pats the sofa next to her with the palm of her hand. Taliah approaches the sofa and sits down beside her mother. Examining the bracelet on Bethany's wrist, Taliah says, 'That bracelet is lovely, was it one of granny's?'

Bethany smiles. She says, 'Yes it was, it's ivory.' Bethany slides her slender arm across Taliah's lap. Taliah, gently running her fingers over the smooth surface, inspects the ivory's off-white colour with a hint of yellow.

'It feels so smooth,' remarks Taliah. 'And it matches your blouse and nails perfectly.'

'Thank you,' says Bethany, looking into her daughter's eyes. 'You can borrow it sometime.'

'Really, I would like that,' says Taliah.

Bethany, studying her daughter's face, says, 'Is anything wrong, you have looked sad the last few days?'

Taliah shakes her head. Smiling wanly, she says, 'No Mum, I'm fine.'

'Dat's good,' says Bethany.

Mother and daughter remain on the sofa for quite some time.

That night Taliah dreams that Talulah has grown so large that when she cranes her neck to look up at her, she is unable to see her head, which resides above the clouds. She wakes up, her brow damp with sweat, the sound of her heartbeat resounding in her ears, only for sleep to find her again. Taliah tosses and turns when she dreams that Siegfried is laying on top of her, his raucous laughter merging with that of Talulah's.

Taliah awakens the next morning before dawn. She lies on her back, her hands placed behind her head, listening to a sleeping Talulah breathing deeply on the bunk above. To Taliah, who cannot hear her own breathing, it seems that her breathing is synchronised with that of her sleeping twin. She pulls the duvet up to her chin.

As the grey light of dawn pervades the room from beneath the blind, the dolls on the shelves become visible. From the top shelf on the opposite side of the room a clown leers at Taliah. Taliah pulls the duvet up so that it covers half her face. On the floor the Lego Architecture models are now emerging from the darkness. Peering at the replica of the Sydney Opera House, Taliah remembers constructing it when she was six-years-old, her memories of the project gaining clarity with the intensifying light. Talulah had worked at the front, she behind, Talulah barking instructions in cryptophasia, her obeying them. Taliah's focus shifts from one Lego Architecture monument to the next, remembering as she does so how the protocol had been the same with each and every project.

Taliah's large hazel eyes focus on the diary on the shelf above her desk. As she watches it transform from a dull grey to magenta, she recalls Talulah watching her writing in her diary last night. Taliah, reflecting on this, bites on her lower lip. Several minutes have passed when she stands up, tiptoes over to her desk and picks the diary off the shelf. Glancing across at the top bunk, Taliah sees the duvet moving gently up and down. Taliah opens the front cover. She blinks. Her mouth opens, her eyes scan the page, her mind searching for some other explanation as to why the strand of hair is gone. A surge of anger resonates through her. She turns to face the bed, her jaw clenched tight. Every impulse screams at Taliah to attack her sleeping twin. Still Taliah stands staring at the gently heaving mattress. She walks out of the bedroom, goes into the bathroom, washes her face under the cold tap and then looks at her reflection in the mirror above the basin. Gradually her heartbeat slows. When Taliah returns to the bedroom, she lies down on the bottom bunk and draws the duvet up to her chin. Taliah's pupils dilate as she looks upwards at the bunk above her where Talulah is sleeping.

Talulah stirs on the top bunk. Taliah holds her breath. The movement stops. The sound of lethargy fills the room once more. Taliah pulls the duvet back and rises to her feet. She tiptoes quietly over to her desk, where she picks up a pen before continuing on tiptoes across the room to Talulah's desk. There is movement on the top bunk. Taliah holds her breath and stands completely still. Talulah's blue diary is lying flat on the shelf above the desk, an anarchist logo plastered to its front cover. Taliah's heartbeat quickens and her pupils constrict as she looks across the room at the top bunk, where Talulah lies on her side, her eyes closed, the duvet moving gently up and down. Turning back to the bookshelf, Taliah places her hand on the diary. She strokes the front cover with her fingertips, feeling its textured surface. Having glanced at her sleeping twin on the top bunk, Taliah uses the thumb and index finger of her left hand to slowly open the diary at the first page. There is no strand of hair. Taliah flits through the diary until she reaches today's date. She then writes, *Meow peciooki mene crible derdand.* Taliah closes the diary, returns the pen to her desk and then goes back to the bed, where she lies down, hands placed beneath her head. Contemplating what Talulah's reaction will be on opening her diary that evening and discovering what she has written, Taliah's heartbeat quickens. Remembering the LSD that Siegfried gave them yesterday, Taliah reflects on Talulah's excitement, which she had noted was uncharacteristically tinged with apprehension.

Talulah sits up in bed and rubs her eyes. She is surprised to see that Taliah is already dressed. Talulah clambers out of bed and opens her wardrobe. She takes out her Calvin Klein jeans, a blouse and a blue jumper, an identical outfit to that chosen by Taliah, only Taliah's jumper is green. By the time Talulah is dressed, Taliah is already downstairs in the kitchen. When Talulah enters the kitchen, Bethany, looking up from the local borough newspaper, says, 'Mawnin Talulah.'

Talulah nods in acknowledgement, sits down next to her twin and pours herself a glass of orange juice, as Taliah butters a piece of toast.

'Any interesting news?' asks Taliah.

Bethany, unaccustomed to hearing her daughters say more than a few perfunctory words at breakfast time, puts the newspaper down. She says, 'Just the local elections.'

'Local elections, how interesting,' says Taliah putting emphasis on the all the s's.

Talulah returns her glass of orange juice to the table with a thud. For the remainder of breakfast Bethany and Taliah continue conversing about the news, the words pouring eloquently from Taliah. In between talking to her mother, Taliah nibbles delicately on a piece of toast and takes sips from her glass of orange juice. The only noises Talulah makes during breakfast are when she plunks her glass of orange juice back down on the table and bites into her toast.

When Taliah finishes her breakfast, she dabs her lips with her napkin, smiles at her mother, then stands up and departs the kitchen, leaving Talulah at the table alone, who moments later scrunches up her napkin, throws it on the table, and ignoring her mother, storms out of the kitchen.

Having brushed her teeth and applied a dab of rouge to her cheeks, Taliah strides up to Talulah's desk, pulls open one of her desk's drawers, takes out a tiny transparent plastic bag and places it on the desk top. Talulah looks down at the transparent bag containing the two small paper tabs that Siegfried had given them. Pointing at the window Taliah says, 'It's a sunny day, let's go outside and take these.'

Talulah, unaccustomed to being addressed at such length in English by her twin, glares at Taliah. Despite her fear of the drug Taliah feels a surge of confidence at challenging her twin. Talulah reaches towards the bag on the table, but Taliah grabs the bag before she reaches it and puts it in the side pocket of her jeans. Taliah walks out of the room and heads downstairs to the kitchen. Talulah follows her.

In the hallway the twins take their respective coats from the coat rail and head towards the front door. Taliah calls out, 'We will be back late afternoon.'

Taliah senses her sister's confusion at her confrontational stance and she feels a sense of competitiveness surging within her. On the bus Talulah nibbles on her fingernails and casts furtive glances out of the window, as Taliah in the adjoining seat, sitting upright, her gaze fixed directly ahead, savours the nervousness permeating from her sibling. Though also apprehensive about taking the LSD, Taliah, refusing to dwell on it, slows her breathing.

At the Paisley Park stop Taliah and Talulah disembark from the bus. They cross the road and turn right down the narrow asphalt path, either side of which are expansive, lush playing fields, bathed in sunshine. Taliah walks beside Talulah along the path. Talulah's pace quickens as she attempts to get ahead of

Taliah. Taliah does not fall behind Talulah in her customary fashion, but instead quickening her own pace, stays abreast of Talulah. They turn right down a narrow footpath lined with trees, whose branches form a canopy above the path. Their pace slows after taking a right turn into the playing fields. Ahead of them are the charred remains of the brick building that had been Paisley Parish Church Community Centre, the remnants of the anarchist logo that Siegfried had sprayed on the door that night now merely a curved line on a strip of blackened wood.

They stop in front of the building and sit down on the grass. Talulah fixes her hazel eyes on her sister. Taliah sees the trepidation in their depths, but feels no sympathy. Having taken the bag containing the two paper tabs out of her pocket, she inspects the small square tabs, inscribed with the outline of a man's face. Talulah edges towards Taliah and studies the tabs held aloft in her sister's hand. Taliah relishes her twin's apprehension when Talulah draws closer to her, sees the excitement mingled with fear in her dilated pupils, hears the escalated rate of her breathing and feels the pounding of Talulah's heart, as if it is resonating through her own body. Taliah remains calm, her breathing measured, a strength of purpose diffusing through her at the realisation that she is in the ascendency and that Talulah though excited by the prospect of the LSD, is fearful at its potential. Looking from the bag to her sister and back again, Taliah's eyes are expressionless, her mouth forming a thin horizontal line across her face. For quite some time she remains like this, revelling in Talulah's discomfort. Talulah wants to reach out and grab the bag from her sister's grasp, to establish her dominance over her twin, but remembering the students she had once overheard at school discussing the powerful effects of LSD, she is afraid.

Taliah opens the bag, puts her little finger in it, removes one of the tabs and places it on her tongue. Talulah snatches the bag from Taliah with a trembling hand and empties the remaining tab onto her tongue. A faint metallic taste diffuses through their mouths. Talulah and Taliah lie back on the grass, the unseasonably warm sun shining down upon them. High above them swallows, recently arrived from Africa, tweet exuberantly in the clear blue sky. The sound of children shouting mingling with applause emanates from the playing fields.

A pigeon lands on one of the blackened walls of the building. When it takes to flight Talulah and Taliah follow its flapping wings, shielding their eyes against the sun with their right hands. Little by little Taliah edges away from her sister, until separated by about three arm's lengths. Lying with her back on the ground, her head cushioned against the soft grass, Taliah looks up at the bright blue sky. Taliah's pupils dilate and her fists clench tightly by her sides when she hears Talulah shifting her body along the ground towards her. Talulah is nearly an arm's length from her sister when she stops moving. Reclining back against the grass, her chin pressed against her chest, Talulah examines the charred remnants of the building in front of her, a smirk flickering across her pretty face, as the raging flames from that night appear before her.

It occurs to Taliah that perhaps her apprehension over the LSD has been unwarranted for she feels no different than when she took it nearly forty minutes ago. Closing her eyes, she focuses on expunging all thoughts of Talulah from her mind. Talulah turns her head towards Taliah. Observing Taliah motionless in the grass, Talulah is acutely aware of her sister's animosity. Reaching out with her left arm, she stretches it through the grass towards Taliah. Talulah takes comfort from her close proximity to her twin.

Taliah watches a small, solitary cumulus cloud floating in the vast expanse of blue high above her. Out of the corner of her eye she sees a grasshopper clinging onto a blade of grass, only inches from her face. Surprised to see a grasshopper so early in the year, Taliah rotating her head towards it, marvels at the large, inquisitive dark eyes, the green armour of its thorax, the long, slender tibias, delicate wings and the thin antennae tentatively probing at the air. Talulah, lying beside her, is gaping at the blueness of the sky and the vivid green of the lush grass, shimmering in the sunlight. Having removed a 330ml bottle of Evian mineral water from the pocket of her coat, she unscrews the top and takes a gulp. Water has never tasted so cool, refreshing and pure to Talulah.

An hour later – swallows dart through the air, tweeting elatedly. Taliah, still lying with her back on the grass, giggles, as she follows the birds' flight with her eyes. Frown lines are visible across Talulah's forehead as she follows the flight of the swallows with bulging eyes, biting on her lower lip as she does so and clawing at the grass beside her. Talulah watches as the birds cease their seemingly haphazard darting in all directions and proceed to circle her, their small frames expanding in size before her eyes, casting ominous shadows on the ground, their exuberant tweeting transforming into a ghastly, relentless cawing.

A staccato burst of cryptophasia piercing the air preludes Talulah's finger prodding Taliah repeatedly in her arm, each occurrence sending a ripple of anxiety coursing through Taliah's body, that escalates into waves when her arm is shaken vigorously. Taliah feels the gentle breeze become a gale, sees the grass transform into writhing green tentacles, hears the sporadic bursts of cheering and applause emanating from the playing fields as frightful, vociferous lamentations and clamorous rolls of thunder. Overhead cawing birds circle relentlessly, their expanding frames casting shadows on the sea of green tentacles below.

'AT WAHWAH!' wails a kneeling Talulah, tugging vigorously on her sister's arm with one hand, prodding frenetically in the direction of the grass in front of her with her other. Taliah, following the direction of her twin's prodding finger, is met by the sight of a ghastly green and black-blotched, armour-plated, animate military vehicle, lurking camouflaged amongst the writhing tentacles, poised for assault. The twins stare in horror at its large, emotionless, dark compound eyes, and the two spear-like appendages probing menacingly in their direction. Discharging a diabolical clicking noise it leaps into the air before plunging down onto Talulah's shoulder. Screaming hysterically Talulah and Taliah clamber to their feet and flee across the ground, legs pumping, arms flailing and mouths shrieking bursts of cryptophasia in unison, as the circling birds high above them caw ever louder and black shapes in the distance swarm incessantly in every conceivable direction.

*

A police car is parked in Tragunter Lane. Its occupant, Sergeant Dalton, is slouched in the passenger seat, his head resting against the window. His eyes are closed and he is snoring loudly. The driver door opens. Sergeant Dalton awakens abruptly. A thin, uniformed policeman with sparse red hair clambers into the vehicle, slams the door behind him and deposits a paper bag in Sergeant Dalton's lap. Having hesitantly opened the bag, Sergeant Dalton reaches into it and takes out half a sandwich. He peels off the top piece of bread, inspects the contents, grits his teeth, and turning to his colleague, Constable Grimshaw, who is poised to take a bite of his own sandwich, enquires in a gruff voice, 'Where's the cheese?'

Constable Grimshaw, having examined the sandwich clutched in Sergeant Dalton's hand, shrugs and says, 'Ay forgot like,' before taking a large bite of his own sandwich.

Sergeant Dalton sighs. The two policemen proceed to consume their sandwiches in silence. Several minutes have passed when Constable Grimshaw, now holding a half eaten Mars Bar in one hand, stops chewing and leans forward in his seat, his nose pressed against the windscreen. He swallows, nudges Sergeant

Dalton with his shoulder, and gesturing with his head, says, 'Lewk lewk over there like.'

'What?' replies Sergeant Dalton, raising his right hand to his eyebrows and peering through the windscreen. The short-sighted Sergeant Dalton is unable to see what is causing his colleague's agitation.

'Lewk there like,' says Constable Grimshaw in animated fashion.

Sergeant Dalton, scrunching up his face, continues to peer through the windscreen. He blinks then blinks again. 'Let's go!' he exclaims, opening the door and clambering out of the car.

Sergeant Dalton races down Tragunter Lane, Constable Grimshaw following close behind. Sergeant Dalton draws to a halt by the letterbox at the corner of Paisley Park Road, a breathless Constable Grimshaw pulling up beside him. They watch the two teenage girls on the other side of the road running frantically up and down the pavement. Sergeant Dalton shakes his head when he realises that the girls running legs and manically gesturing arms are moving in exactly the same time as one another, and Constable Grimshaw, his mouth agape, is quite certain that the girls sporadic, staccato bursts of speech, are uttered not only in a language quite unlike any he has heard before, but simultaneously. Some time has passed when a grim faced Constable Grimshaw asks, 'Wa' now like?'

Sergeant Dalton, observing the peculiar pair's frantic synchronised movements, runs one hand through his thick hair. He mutters, 'Twins.'

Constable Grimshaw, glancing across at the sergeant, opens his mouth then closes it again. A salvo of loud, unfathomable language, audible even over the noise of passing cars sends a shudder coursing through his body. Talulah and Taliah stop running. They step out into the road.

'Get off the road!' shouts Sergeant Dalton.

A car horn sounds, a motorbike swerves. The twins march

across the road and onto the pavement, where Sergeant Dalton, his arms stretched out in front of him, calls, 'Stop.'

'Wo wo stop,' adds Constable Grimshaw, his hands poised on the pair of handcuffs and truncheon held at his side.

Talulah and Taliah proceed at haste up Tragunter Lane. Sergeant Dalton, dashing after them, orders, 'Stop, this is the police.'

Talulah and Taliah stop. Two pairs of identical, incognizant eyes turn towards Sergeant Dalton. He approaches them and grabs Talulah by the wrists. Constable Grimshaw walks over to Taliah and grips her wrists.

'Ucki bothigo wuthiwuthi waba meme!' they shriek in unison, pulling effortlessly away from their would-be captors and racing back down Tragunter Lane.

'Stop like!' calls out Constable Grimshaw.

Talulah steps onto Paisley Park Road, Taliah follows her. A car skids, a careening van veers to the right. Talulah and Taliah cross the road and mount the pavement. Sergeant Dalton shouts, 'Stay there!'

Talulah and Taliah stand beside each other facing the road, vacantly watching the two policemen striding towards them. Sergeant Dalton lunges forward towards Taliah.

'WUTHIWUTHI WABA MEME!' wail Talulah and Taliah as they take off again, running along the pavement, the policemen in pursuit. The twins turn right and race up the narrow asphalt path that leads to the playing fields.

'They're getting away,' says Constable Grimshaw as he surges past Sergeant Dalton.

Talulah and Taliah stop running and turn to face their pursuers. Constable Grimshaw draws to a halt. He says, 'Stay there.' Talulah darts right and scrambles under the hedge, Taliah following closely behind. 'Quick quick like,' says Constable Grimshaw, hurrying up the path and then crawling under the hedge, cursing loudly when the twigs brush against his face.

Talulah and Taliah are tearing across the playing fields,

Constable Grimshaw in pursuit. Sergeant Dalton, having inspected the hole, makes the decision to continue up the path and locate a more accessible entry point.

There is a football match in progress. The twins are heading towards it. Talulah barges into a female spectator, who squeals, 'Oh my god!'

A middle-aged male spectator shouts, 'How dare you!'

Talulah and Taliah are on the pitch now. The game's participants stop playing and gawk at the pair.

'STOP THEM!' calls out the pursuing Constable Grimshaw.

A corpulent spectator braces himself to grab the twins.

'UGI BOBOTHI!' shout Talulah and Taliah in unison, swerving away from him, Taliah to the right, Talulah to the left.

The man dives at Taliah's feet, misses. Talulah and Taliah race onwards, watched in silence by the game's stunned attendees. Constable Grimshaw crosses the pitch and hurries after them. Sergeant Dalton, who is lagging far behind, sees that the twins have veered left and are heading back towards Paisley Park Road. He radios for backup.

'WUTHIWUTHI!'

'Stop!' yells Constable Grimshaw.

On exiting the playing fields, they turn right and race along Paisley Park Road. Two teenage boys are approaching from the opposite direction. Talulah collides into one of the boys. He tumbles to the pavement. Taliah runs over the prone boy.

'Dunci waba waba meme!' shriek Talulah and Taliah.

'Stop, stop like!' calls out Constable Grimshaw, hurrying past the two boys.

Cars stop, pedestrians stare, and passengers on the top deck of a bus gape at the two identical girls careering down the pavement, pursued by a policeman, another policeman trailing far behind.

Talulah and Taliah turn into the shopping precinct. Talulah collides with a woman carrying shopping bags and Taliah crashes into an old man.

'WABA MEME!' scream the twins, as Talulah runs into a burly man, sending him falling to the ground and her falling on top of him. Taliah stops and watches her twin struggling to her feet. Constable Grimshaw rushes up and grabs Taliah around the waist with both arms.

'Wuthiwuthi wuthiwuthi,' shrieks Taliah, trying to shake him off.

A policeman and policewoman are hurrying towards the twins. The policeman leaps on Talulah's back, sending her toppling forward to the ground. Meanwhile the policewoman grips Taliah's right wrist. Taliah, squirming to free herself, screams, 'UCKI BOTHIGO WABA MEME!'

And Talulah, trying to crawl out from underneath the policeman wails 'WABA MEME UGI BOTHI!'

Taliah stops struggling, goes limp and collapses to her knees. The policewoman attaches handcuffs to Taliah's wrists, which are now held behind her back, as a panting Constable Grimshaw presses down on her shoulders to prevent her from standing up.

'BOBOTHI UCKI BIGI!' yells Talulah, fighting to free herself from beneath the policeman. She squirms away and clambers to her feet. The policeman grabs her right ankle, but she pulls free and races off, watched by the shoppers.

'NOOO!' shouts the policeman, struggling to his feet.

People stare, some gasp, others hold their hands to their heads. Talulah is racing up the shopping precinct. She barges into a teenage girl, who emits a cry as she is knocked over.

'GYAL GO!' shrieks Talulah before colliding with a lamppost and falling to the ground.

Talulah is rising groggily to her feet when the pursuing policeman rugby tackles her, sending her crashing to the ground. Sergeant Dalton, sweat pouring from his face, is racing up the precinct towards Talulah, who is now grappling with the policeman on the ground.

'WABA MEME!' screeches Talulah.

Meanwhile Taliah is being led by the policewoman and Constable Grimshaw back down the shopping precinct towards a waiting police car.

'WABA MEME!' wails Talulah.

Sergeant Dalton hurries over, bends down and grips the side of Talulah's collar with one hand. Talulah bites Sergeant Dalton's hand.

'NOOO!' he screams. Blood gushes from his hand.

The other policeman grasps one of Talulah's wrists, twists it behind her back and attempts to attach handcuffs to it.

'Help!' shouts Sergeant Dalton, trying to pull his bleeding hand from Talulah's jaws.

'Get off!' yells a watching boy.

'Someone do something,' screeches an elderly woman, looking imploringly at her fellow onlookers.

'Help!' shouts Sergeant Dalton, who then prods Talulah in her eye with his finger.

Talulah's teeth remain clamped onto Sergeant Dalton's hand. The other policeman attempts to haul Talulah by the waist away from Sergeant Dalton.

'NOOO!' screams Sergeant Dalton.

'Do something!' screeches the elderly woman.

The policewoman, who had been leading Taliah away moments ago hurries over. She says, 'Move back.'

The onlookers step back. Sergeant Dalton, still fighting to release his hand from Talulah's mouth, moans, 'Do something, quick!'

The policewoman pulls a canister from her belt and opens the top. The policeman gripping Talulah's waist closes his eyes and holds his breath. The policewoman reaches out with the canister and sprays a jet of mist into Talulah's snarling face.

'Jesus,' moans Sergeant Dalton, covering his face with one hand. Coughing fills the air. The onlookers step back. Still Talulah does not release. 'Again!' bawls Sergeant Dalton.

The policewoman sprays again. There is coughing and spluttering. Talulah releases the hand. Sergeant Dalton falls back to the pavement clutching his bloodied hand. The other policeman secures Talulah's hands behind her back.

'WABA MEME!' screams a struggling, spluttering Talulah, fighting to escape her captors.

A heavyset male ambulance worker, clad in green, is approaching.

'Hold her down,' demands the ambulance man, who then kneels beside Talulah and takes a syringe from a bag attached to his belt.

'Stand back!' orders the policewoman to the people crowding round once more.

'Waba meme waba meme.'

The syringe is inserted into Talulah's neck. She goes limp.

*

One hour later – Taliah is lying on her back on the bed's blue plastic mattress, her hands held behind her head, looking up at the strip light on the ceiling, whose incandescence appears to ripple across the whitewashed ceiling and walls. She can remember idling on the playing fields with Talulah and being taken to the police station in the car, but she has virtually no memory of what occurred in between. Taliah feels no sense of panic at being separated from her twin, nor does she find solace from her awareness that Talulah is close by. She yawns. Her eyelids flutter then close.

*

That afternoon at the police station during a lively discussion about the bizarre nature of the incident involving the twins, one of the station's staff suddenly remembers that several members of the public have reported identical, teenage, mixed-race girls behaving oddly around the time and in the vicinity of two of the arson attacks. This culminates in a search warrant being issued for Talulah and Taliah's home.

*

Bethany is sitting at the kitchen table, her head held in her hands, the occasional tear trickling down a cheek, as she tries to comprehend what course of events led to her daughters' altercation with the police. She refuses to accept that Talulah and Taliah are capable of the maniacal, violent behaviour they are accused of. Bethany is nibbling on one of, what had been perfectly manicured fingernails, when the doorbell rings.

Two policemen are standing on the front step.

'Hello,' says Bethany, viewing them suspiciously. 'Can I help you?'

One of the policemen gives her the search warrant. Bethany scowls. She is poised to launch into a passionate diatribe when she notices her neighbour peeking through partially drawn curtains. Bethany quickly ushers the policemen inside and closes the door. When the policemen leave fifteen minutes later they are carrying several large plastic bags containing Talulah and Taliah's belongings, including their diaries.

Chapter Eight

TALIAH, PLACING HER final tile on the table, says, 'Domino.'
'Well done,' says the female staff member. Her name is Debra.

'Can we play again, please?' asks Taliah, sitting up straight in her chair, a smile beautifying her pretty face.

'Okay, one more,' says Debra.

'Have you played All Fives before Debra?' asks Taliah, gathering the dominoes from the table with both arms.

'No, what's that?'

'It's a dominoes variation. I think you will like it.'

'Have you heard of All Fives Kalina?' calls out Debra.

Kalina, who is on guard duty by the door, replies sombrely, 'No, I never heard of this.'

Taliah, turning the dominoes upside down, says, 'You might like All Fives Kalina.'

Kalina, looking across the room at Taliah's cheerful countenance, smiles for the first time that day. She says, 'Maybe.'

Taliah, now leaning forward in her seat, her elbows resting on the table, says, 'The aim of the game is to be the first person to get the agreed number of points. You win points by making the exposed ends of the chain total a multiple of five. The winner...'

'Whoa, not so fast, you're losing me,' interrupts Debra.

Taliah giggles. She says, 'The winner at the end of each go...'

The door opens. A man is standing in the doorway. He says, 'Taliah, it's time to go.'

Taliah sighs, her shoulders slump, the smile vanishes.

'Cheer up,' says the man. 'You're going to see your twin.' He departs the room.

Taliah drags her feet and stares down at the floor when Debra and Kalina escort her out of the room and along the corridor. Taliah has not seen Talulah since the incident three days ago. Whilst she has been housed here in this centre for troubled teenagers, Talulah has been in a remand facility in Middlesex. Taliah has not missed her twin, and she does not feel ready to see her quite yet.

Forty minutes later – Taliah is escorted from the van by a bald, burly social worker and a petite, perky mental health nurse, who keeps a reassuring hand on Taliah's shoulder as she is led to the meeting room on the second floor of the solicitors firm Framptons. The social worker knocks on the door.

'Come in,' utters a female voice on the other side of the door that Taliah recognises to be her mother's.

Taliah opens the door and enters the room, followed by her two chaperones. Her mother and father are sitting next to each other at the rectangular table.

'Mum, Dad,' says Taliah breathlessly, hurrying over and throwing one arm around her mother's neck, the other around her father's.

'Lovely to see you. Talulah will be here soon,' says Bethany.

The door opens. A man walks in. He approaches Taliah hesitantly and says, 'Good afternoon, I'm Felix Travis your solicitor.' The grin that adorns his countenance is in stark contrast to his protuberant eyes.

'Hello, nice to meet you, I'm Taliah,' greets Taliah meekly, releasing her grip from her parents' necks.

Travis sits conversing with Colin and Bethany, casting occasional uneasy glances in Taliah's direction. Taliah sits in silence, the social worker and mental health nurse standing behind her chair. Examining her mother's puffy eyes and her father's pale, drawn appearance, she swallows. Shuffling in her seat, she puts her hands in her pockets, then places them on the table before clasping them together in her lap. She feels her twin drawing closer. Taliah wishes she were still at the centre playing dominoes with Debra.

Meanwhile Talulah is in the back of a minivan, a bulky female nurse sitting on either side of her. The road ahead is congested with traffic. Talulah tuts. She asks, 'How long?'

The nurse, swivelling to face Talulah, blurts out, 'About five minutes.'

Other than a few words uttered to her mother on the telephone, Talulah has not spoken during the three days she has been separated from her twin. She has not played dominoes, nor smiled, nor interacted with the remand centre's staff in any way. Talulah has also refused many of her meals. For the most part she has lain on her bed longing for her twin, preoccupied with this thought day and night. So concerned was the remand centre director by Talulah's unresponsive behaviour that she ordered her to be kept under twenty-four hour observation.

But now as Talulah senses her twin drawing closer, her chin is held high and a thin smile is visible on her attractive but weary face.

Six minutes later – Taliah holds her breath when Talulah enters the room.

'Talulah,' greets Bethany.

'Hi Talulah,' says Colin.

Talulah, ignoring her parents stares at Taliah.

'So you're Talulah,' greets Travis. 'My name is Travis and I'm your solicitor. Pleased to meet you.'

Talulah does not look at Travis, but continues gazing at her twin. Taliah swallows. She does not turn to face Talulah. One of the two nurses who escorted Talulah here, pulls out a chair and gestures for Talulah to sit down. Having sat down, Talulah shifts her body towards the right hand edge of the chair, so as to be as close to Taliah as possible. Still Taliah does not glance in Talulah's direction. If she were to she would notice that Talulah is slightly thinner, her hair bedraggled and her complexion less radiant than it was the last time she saw her.

During the meeting Travis discusses the forthcoming preliminary hearing at the youth court. On occasion he addresses Talulah and Taliah directly. Taliah's memory of the events of that day remain vague, and it seems to her that the three adults are discussing something that does not involve her. Talulah, inattentive to the conversation, gazes at her twin, pining for her attention. Taliah, trying to ignore Talulah, attempts to focus on her mother, father and solicitor.

Neither twin has been informed of the arson accusations. When the word arson is mentioned, Taliah gasps and looks down at the table whilst Talulah glances across the table at Travis and then at her mother and father, before returning her focus to her twin. When Bethany informs her daughters that the police have removed some of their possessions from their room, Talulah shakes her head vigorously and Taliah gasps. Taliah, assuming that the police have taken their diaries, wishes she had not alluded to the fires in her diary. Now Taliah examines Talulah. She is convinced Talulah has done more than allude to the fires. Talulah looks away from Taliah and stares impassively ahead, trying to keep her mind a blank canvass, refusing to give her prying twin any information pertaining to her diary's contents.

*

Three days later – Talulah and Taliah are in their preliminary hearing at Halmsworth Youth Court. Taliah grits her teeth, then looks up at the ceiling. She can feel Talulah pining for her from her seat, a metre or so to the left, which is making it difficult to concentrate on the proceedings.

'If you would please consider our request that Talulah and Taliah be reunited,' implores Travis. 'It has been extremely difficult for the twins to cope with being separated from one another.'

Talulah's hands adopt a praying gesture when Travis says this. Taliah glances guiltily across at Talulah and then at her mother. She has no desire to be reunited with her twin quite yet, as she is still angry with her, but she does not want Talulah or her mother knowing this. Talulah is glowering at Taliah. Taliah tries to empty her mind, to leave it devoid of thought. She closes her eyes and imagines an empty space.

'I have considered your request,' remarks the ageing male magistrate gravely. 'But considering the fact that your clients, the twins, Taliah and Talulah, have been accused of suffering from a compulsive disorder, namely pyromania, there is the real potential to reoffend.' The magistrate now addressing Talulah and Taliah directly, says, 'It pains me to say this but you two are to remain in separate facilities until the trial.'

'NOOOO!' shrieks Talulah, leaping from her seat and charging across the court towards the magistrate's bench.

'Help!' screams the magistrate.

'BOTHI BOBOTHI UGI!' yells Talulah.

A court clerk grabs Talulah. Two psychiatric nurses jump on her. Talulah is carried out of the court screaming and writhing, Bethany hurrying after her. Taliah, staring down at the floor, feels heat rising to her face. The embarrassment she is experiencing over Talulah's actions is as acute as if she had committed the act herself, but there is no sense of sadness at the magistrate's verdict.

*

Halmsworth Youth Court – Talulah and Taliah are sitting in adjacent chairs to one another, their hands held in their laps. Taliah is wearing a brown, pleated skirt that falls to just beneath her knees, a dark green cardigan, a white, collared blouse, pulled up long navy blue socks and patent, black leather loafers. Talulah's outfit is the same, only her skirt is maroon and cardigan dark blue. Bethany has chosen these outfits because she believes them to be suitably austere for such an occasion. The twins' mohawk-styled hair, having been deemed too rebellious, has been restyled. Taliah's hair has been trimmed on top, then scrunched together at the sides of her head and tied with pink hairbands to form a paltry replica of her childhood hairstyle. Talulah's headstrong temperament, curbed by antipsychotic medication and the loss of her twin, had sat limp and listless when the remand facility's hairdresser had shorn the hair on the top of her head. Tufts of hair now stick out inelegantly in all directions.

Opposite Talulah and Taliah, sitting behind a raised wooden table, are three magistrates – two women and a man, dressed in smart casual attire. To the twins' right sits a suited Felix Travis, and a few metres to his right the prosecution's lawyer. In front and to the right of Talulah and Taliah is a small table, where the clerk of the court is stationed, her head bowed, as she scribbles notes on a pad of paper. Behind Talulah and Taliah, within arm's reach of them, are two psychiatric nurses and two members of the court staff. Behind them sit Colin and Bethany, listening attentively to the proceedings.

The prosecution's lawyer Mr Bowen-Jones, a man of porcine appearance and persuasive temperament, announces that he will now show the CCTV footage of the incident to the court. Travis protests vehemently, stating that it will be disturbing for the twins to view the episode. His protests are overruled. Talulah and Taliah, neither of whom have seen any footage of the incident, and continue to have only a vague memory of what occurred after they fled the playing fields, watch themselves rampaging down the street shrieking incessantly before fighting with police. A trembling, open-mouthed Taliah, sweat glistening on her brow, grasps the edge of the table in front of her with both hands.

Talulah, leaning forward towards the screen shakes her head several times, looks across at Taliah and then back at the screen. Meanwhile Bethany covers her eyes with her hands, a pale-faced Colin holds his head in his hands, and Travis, turning from the screen to the shocked faces of the magistrates, gulps.

The recording has been playing for nearly thirty seconds when one of the magistrates orders it turned off. Then the prosecution calls to the stand Dr Tryon, a middle-aged male psychiatrist. Dr Tryon states that, having analysed the footage of the incident and evaluated both Taliah and Talulah in their respective remand facilities, he is in no doubt that they are suffering from *folie simultanée*. *Folie simultanée* he explains, is when two people either suffering from delusional psychosis or predisposed to delusional psychosis, trigger symptoms in each other, to the effect that the composition of the two person's delusions become identical. Having warned the court of the dangers posed by the twins, Dr Tryon departs.

Now the prosecution focuses on the twins' lives. In a deep, authoritative voice, Bowen-Jones outlines their *oral communication issues* and education at a special needs school. Not once does he refer to Taliah or Talulah by name. He discusses the results of the drug tests that have been conducted on Talulah and Taliah. The results showed a positive reading for both marijuana and MDMA. Whilst the prosecutor does not suggest that the drugs had caused the pair's bizarre antics, he attempts to taint the twins' characters in the eyes of the magistrates. As the prosecution discusses the results of the drug tests, Talulah looks across at Taliah, who sits, shoulders slumped, looking dejectedly at the floor. She feels the presence of her sister looming over her as if it were a shadow. Neither Taliah nor Talulah experiences any sense of relief that the LSD has not shown up in their drug tests. Their initial test did not cover LSD, and by the time a further more exhaustive test, ordered by the prosecution's psychiatrist, was conducted four days after the incident, the drug was no longer in their systems.

Next Bowen-Jones argues that there is overwhelming evidence of the twins' guilt in the form of CCTV footage placing them at the scenes of the fires, in addition to a report from a forensics lab stating that traces of lighter fluid have been found on one of the coats seized from the twins' home. He omits to mention that it was Talulah's coat. Bowen-Jones holds up a transparent evidence bag containing two books. The books are Talulah and Taliah's diaries. Taliah gasps and Talulah groans.

'Entries in these diaries emphatically prove the accused's guilt,' states Bowen-Jones severely.

Taliah wishes the ground would swallow her up as she imagines the two legal teams, cups of tea in hand, laughing and passing comment as they read about the most personal moments of her life. Bowen-Jones reads out a few brief entries, all of which are from Talulah's diary. These include: Fire is my friend – is there anything more satisfying in this world than witnessing a monument to our supression engulfed in flames. And then, The inferno has only just begun.

Taliah, twisting her head to her right, looks at Talulah and mutters, 'Mene derriii derriii dunci.'

The prosecution now asserts that as the twins have gained personal gratification from the fire starting, their crimes cannot be categorised as arson, for arson describes fires started for personal or financial gain.

'The accused,' states Bowen-Jones, 'derived gratification and a sense of euphoria from the fires because they suffer from an impulsive control disorder known as pyromania.' Having said this, he looks with disdain in the twins' direction.

Talulah glares at Bowen-Jones, her fists clenched tightly at her sides, for the love of fires that Siegfried has instilled in her remains, and to hear this symbol of authority denouncing their symbolic fire starting as merely a disorder provokes anger in her, even in her medicated state. An angry Taliah looks across at

Talulah, who ignoring her, continues to glare at Bowen-Jones.

'Only incarceration can protect the public and themselves from further attacks.' This being Bowen-Jones's final statement.

There is a break. Bethany, Colin, Travis, Talulah and Taliah file out of the room, the two psychiatric nurses and a member of the court staff following close behind. Colin, Bethany and Travis take a seat on a long bench in the foyer. Taliah sits down on the bench, Talulah parks herself next to her. Bethany, having uttered a few reassuring words to her daughters, joins Colin in a hushed conversation with Travis. Taliah stands up, walks to the opposite end of the bench and sits down. Even with three people sitting between her and Talulah, she can feel Talulah pining for her.

Peering out through the window of the foyer, Taliah is quite unsure what the best verdict could be. Whilst being unsure of her future and experiencing guilt over the strain on her parents has been difficult, still Taliah does not miss her twin. She has also appreciated the sense of identity granted to her in the centre, where she is addressed by her own name. Continuing to look out of the window, the Styrofoam cup of tea held in her hands quivering incessantly, Taliah, reflecting on how the ill-judged allegiance with Siegfried has led to her being stripped first of her innocence and she suspects soon her freedom, turns her back on Talulah, who is leaning forward, looking along the bench yearningly.

After the interval it is the turn of the defence. Due to the damning evidence provided by the CCTV footage for which no plausible alibi can be given, the defence rests on arguing that the twins though present at the fires, were only there as reluctant observers. Travis blames the arson attacks on a third party – a nameless adolescent anarchic arsonist, who had coerced the virtuous but impressionable sisters to witness his heinous crimes. The court has prohibited Siegfried's name from being mentioned due to a number of reasons, including concerns that he might be presumed guilty without having had the opportunity to defend himself. As Travis outlines his argument, Talulah averts her focus from her twin and fantasises about the day when the two of them will be reunited with Siegfried. Talulah, considering that Siegfried is far too clever to be caught, sighs contemplatively as she imagines that at this very moment he is furthering the individual anarchist cause.

Travis shows the court CCTV footage of the twins at the time and in the vicinity of two of the arson attacks, walking beside a tall male with what appears to be a mohawk hairstyle. This in addition to further CCTV footage of the alleged arsonist, as well as a witness statement, placing him at the location of another arson attack, the one in which there is little evidence suggesting that the twins were present.

Several character statements supporting Talulah and Taliah are read out in court, including one from Ms Thomas, which initially she had written in support of only Taliah, but after much pleading, had been persuaded to rephrase to include Talulah too.

As for the alleged adolescent anarchic arsonist, Siegfried, he was last seen fleeing on foot from Royston Park School the Wednesday after the incident, when rumour of the twins' arrest reached him. The sudden disappearance of Siegfried suits the defence well, as Travis is able to argue that this is a sign of his guilt, and therefore the twins' innocence. When Colin, Bethany and Travis tried to persuade the girls to blame *the German* when they were given the opportunity to make a statement in court, Talulah muttered *no* and Taliah said nothing. Taliah is now considering following their advice, going through in her mind what she will say if given the opportunity to make a statement prior to the magistrates' deliberation.

Travis now calls to the stand Dr Emily Devereaux, an eminent psychiatrist. She testifies that, having analysed the footage of the twins' bizarre rampage and evaluated Talulah and Taliah in person, that in her professional opinion they had been suffering from a condition known as *bouffée délirante*. Talulah and Taliah, both of whom have only a sketchy memory of what had occurred, give the psychiatrist their full attention. Dr Devereaux explains how *bouffée délirante* is a temporary psychotic disorder that could best be translated as a puff of madness. She states that identical twins are more susceptible to it as they are genetically the same, and often have, as in this instance, a very close relationship. She then explains how the boundaries that define us as individuals are blurred in the case of identical twins, and that in a sense they can be regarded as one person. This makes them more susceptible to a joint psychotic illness. Taliah shudders when Dr Devereaux says this.

Dr Devereaux goes on to explain that *bouffée délirante* is characterised by sudden, transient episodes that last from between a day to a month, and that the symptoms may include hallucinations, delusions, illogical behaviours and incoherent speech. She concludes by saying that *bouffée délirante* is not caused by a pre-existing condition or drug use, and in some instances might be a response to stress in the sufferer's life. When Dr Devereaux has finished Talulah looks up at the ceiling and makes a barely detectible shake of her head. Meanwhile Taliah holds a hand to her chin and looks down pensively at the floor. She then studies the magistrates' faces in turn, crossing the index and middle fingers of her right hand as she does so.

Travis goes on to argue that the *bouffée délirante* episode was a response to the pressure brought on by the malevolent influence of the adolescent, anarchist arsonist, who had forced the twins to witness the arson attacks. The morally righteous twins had felt unable to inform the authorities due to their fear of reprisals and their pre-existing issues with communication, culminating in a cry for help, in the form of the *bouffée délirante* induced episode. Talulah stifles a giggle with her sleeve when he says this. Taliah, like her mother and father behind her, considers that Travis's argument would be persuasive, were it not for Talulah's diary entries, an issue he has not addressed. Travis concludes the defence soon after.

Chapter Nine

ON EITHER SIDE of the large red brick Victorian building are long, modern, single-storey extensions constructed out of grey breezeblocks. At the front of the building is a wide lawn with a flowerbed on one side and a floodlit, AstroTurf football pitch on the other. Surrounding the perimeter of the Beddington House Hospital complex is a ten metre high security fence.

Behind the hospital's reinforced entrance door is a spacious white-walled hall with big barred windows. Two passageways lead from the hall to the various wards that house the facility's thirteen to eighteen-year-old male and female patients. A black metal door at the end of the passageway to the left of the hall leads to a narrow grey-walled, brown asphalt-floored corridor, illuminated by a thin strip light that runs the length of its ceiling. On either side of the corridor are rows of bolted doors with built-in observation holes and hatches. Behind each door is a three metre long, two metre wide rectangular padded cell, furnished with a moulded plastic bed, desk, chair, and a toilet and basin. A twenty centimetre by two centimetre slit in the far wall affords the only view of the outside world.

In Cell B Taliah is lying on the bed, one arm flopping limply over the side, a thin stream of drool hanging from the corner of her mouth. She flaps her arm feebly in the direction of a puzzle magazine on the floor, her fingers grasp the corner of the magazine, the magazine is hauled towards the bed. Taliah's arm goes limp, her eyelids flutter then close. The screaming of the self-harmer in the adjoining cell awakens Taliah. She yawns widely, rubs her eyes, rolls to her side, and props her head up with the palm of her hand.

A diminutive young woman clutching a mop is standing on tiptoes outside Cell E, peeping in through the peephole. The woman watches the teenage girl lying on the bed, her head resting against the palm of her right hand. Having leaned the mop against the frame of the door, she scampers along the corridor on the balls of her feet. Ignoring the screaming of the self-harmer in Cell C, she peers through the peephole of Cell B at the girl lying on the bed, in exactly the same position as the one in Cell E. The woman holds her breath when Taliah turns her head towards the door.

There is the sound of wheels squeaking against the asphalt floor. A trolley is approaching, pushed by a burly, black, blue uniformed female nurse. The nurse makes a tutting noise when she sees the cleaner standing outside the door of the cell. The cleaner, having backed away from the door, scampers off in the direction from whence she came. The trolley draws to a halt outside the door of Cell B. The nurse glances through the peephole and then opens the hatch.

'*Medicine!*' she calls out.

Taliah remains motionless on the bed. She does not respond to the second or third utterance of the word medicine. Though she is aware from the commotion she has heard from the adjoining cells during her five days in the facility, what happens when patients refuse to take their medicine, she does not move.

'Jaffa Cakes,' calls the nurse through the hatch.

Taliah rubs the back of her head with one hand.

'Jaffa *Cakes*,' repeats the nurse, drawing out the word cakes.

Taliah is imagining the taste of the sumptuous soft chocolate and sweet orange interior. Incarcerated in this cell, devoid of sensory stimulation, and afflicted by a craving for sweet delicacies, a side effect of the anti–psychotic medication, Taliah finds herself unable to resist the promise of the Jaffa Cakes. She rises to her feet, staggers to the door and picks up the two large capsules in one hand and the glass of water in her other, which have been passed to her through the hatch on a tray. Despite the fact that the capsules appear to her to be far too large to swallow, she puts one in her mouth. Ignoring the protestations of her throat she forces it down painfully with a gulp of water. She repeats the process with the second capsule and then returns the plastic glass to the hatch.

'Good girl,' says the nurse.

The hatch closes then opens again, revealing three Jaffa Cakes. Taliah grabs the Jaffa Cakes and stuffs one into her mouth whole. The taste of chocolate diffuses through her mouth.

'Any treat requests for later?' asks the nurse.

The nurse, unable to hear the barely audible response, says, 'Again dear?'

'Petits Filous.'

'Okay darling.'

The trolley continues down the corridor. Taliah collapses onto the bed, where she quickly devours the two remaining Jaffa Cakes. As the taste of chocolate orange dissipates the sense of despair returns. Taliah buries her face in the mattress and sobs, reflecting bitterly as she does so on the events that have led her to this dungeon, including the trial, where after the defence had concluded its arguments, Taliah had been poised to deliver a short, pre–rehearsed statement to the court on behalf of her and her twin, when Talulah, leaping to her feet, had made an anarchist salute, consisting of a raised fist, much to the chagrin of the three magistrates, who had been vociferous in their condemnation. Taliah never got the opportunity to deliver her statement.

When they were sentenced to a period of detention in a secure hospital, Taliah was relieved that they were not being treated as criminals and sent to a remand centre. On glimpsing her mother and father's grim countenances, the sense of relief evaporated. As

Talulah and Taliah were to discover, being detained under the Mental Health Act is not for a fixed term and can mean indefinitely. When one of the magistrates announced that the twins were to be confined together, Talulah hugged an unresponsive Taliah. Beddington House Hospital is to be Talulah and Taliah's home until they are deemed cured, or until they reach the age of nineteen, at which time they will be transferred to an adult secure hospital. To be eligible for release patients at Beddington House Hospital have to progress through three wards with progressively less draconian laws.

Talulah in Cell E also consumed her three Jaffa Cakes quickly, and now like her twin in Cell B, is lying on her front on the bed, sobbing. Unlike Taliah however, Talulah is not reflecting on the events that led to their confinement in these cells, but pining for her twin. Constantly during the long hours of solitude Talulah pines for Taliah. Sometimes Taliah senses Talulah's pining. This usually happens during periods of relative lucidity, in the short periods of time between the effects of a dose of medication waning and prior to the next taking effect. When Taliah senses Talulah's pining she closes her eyes and holds her hands to her ears, imagining that she is separated from Talulah not by the two thick-walled-mentally-ill-teenage-girl-occupied cells that currently separate them, but by thick-walled cells that stretch to infinity.

As the heavily medicated Talulah and Taliah languish in their respective cells, wide-eyed, head shaking, tea spilling hospital staff members are in the hospital director Dr Stevenson's office, viewing the CCTV footage of the twins' rampage. Although Beddington House's management team are used to treating teenagers with a broad range of dangerous and severe personality disorders, not one of them has ever witnessed such a bizarre and unfathomable rampage as they are now. They find the twins' synchronised actions particularly distressing. At one point in the footage Dr Stevenson, holding his hands to his head, mutters a prayer to a god he does not even believe exists. When the footage has finished it is universally agreed that treatment for the pair for now will consist of keeping them apart, heavily medicated on an array of drugs, including Symbyax, a combination drug containing the antidepressant fluoxetine and the antipsychotic olanzapine, these having been decided upon by the head doctor, Dr Vitali.

Back in the female acute ward, now that the self-harmer in Cell C has ceased moaning, the only sound is the squeaking of wheels on the asphalt floor. The trolley is being pushed by the same burly, blue uniformed nurse as before. Her name is Clara. The top tray of the trolley is laden with packets and bottles containing Zyprexa, Wellbutrin, Prozac, Zoloft, Depo Provera, Ritalin, Metadate, Concerta, Adderall, Dexedrine, Cylert, Risperdal, Symbyax, Dextrostat, and a variety of vitamins. The trolley's bottom tray is crammed with packets of Jaffa Cakes, Jelly Babies, crisps, Milky Bars, Bakewell Tarts and two Petits Filous yoghurts. The trolley is wheeled up the corridor. Pills are deposited in the cell door hatches – cells where the lights are dimmed at night but never extinguished. Only after the pills have been swallowed are the snacks placed in the hatches.

Clara, peeking through the peephole of Cell E sees Talulah in exactly the same position of repose as her twin was when she pushed the trolley up to Cell B. Clara makes the sign of the cross on her chest. She does this every time she witnesses Talulah and Taliah's mirrored postures. Then, thumping on the door with her fist, she exclaims, 'Wakey wakey T-T-T!' She checks the patient medication schedule taped to the front of the trolley. '*Talulah.*'

Talulah, rising groggily to her feet, rubs her eyes with her right hand in the same manner Taliah did in Cell B when woken moments earlier. Having placed two pills and a cup of water in the hatch, Clara closes it. Talulah looks down at the pills and then raises them slowly to her mouth before swallowing them with a gulp of water. Clara opens the hatch then closes it again. Talulah snatches the two Jaffa Cakes, the Petits Filous and the small plastic spoon. Clara stands watching Talulah spooning the Petits Filous into her mouth. Due to the risk of plastic spoons being used for self-harming, hospital rules dictate that a staff member watch acute ward patients using spoons, and collect them after use.

'Same again tomorrow?' asks Clara when Talulah deposits the spoon back in the hatch.

Talulah nods and then collapses on the bed. Clara has heard her twin in Cell B say *Petits Filous* and *Thank you* in a scarcely audible voice a number of times, but she is yet to hear a word from Talulah. She wonders if Talulah is able to speak. Clara, who only brought the Petits Filous yoghurt because her twin requested one, is happy that Talulah consumed it so readily. As she pushes the trolley back through the ward, she reflects on the two occasions when Talulah was in such a catatonic state, her breathing and heartbeat slowed, that the hospital director ordered her sent to the intensive treatment room, known as the High-Care Suite. This in contrast to Taliah, who despite being listless and evidently depressed has not yet been reduced to such a state. Clara, wondering if the twins really are as similar as they appear, hopes that they will be reunited soon, as, regardless of their illness, she considers it most unchristian and inhumane to keep them apart.

*

Day 11 – footsteps are approaching, keys are jangling. The cell door opens. Taliah, sitting up on the bed, rubs her eyes.

'Are you ready darling?'

Taliah looks up at the bulky frame of Clara standing in the doorway.

'Yes,' she says, rising slowly to her feet and walking over to the door. When Taliah steps out into the passageway a small female

Filipina nurse, a stocky male nurse and a tall male with an aquiline nose are standing there. Clara wraps a powerful arm around Taliah's left arm and Maria the Filipina nurse clasps her right with both of hers.

'Dis way darling,' says Maria.

Taliah is led along the corridor, the stocky Thomas, a large bunch of keys attached to his belt leading the way. Taliah smells the bitter stench of disinfectant that permanently pervades the airless corridor, and hears the piercing shriek of the self-harmer in Cell C. She is aware that Talulah is still in her cell.

Taliah is escorted out of the acute ward and down a long, brightly lit passageway. Taliah, turning her head from side to side looks at the framed watercolour landscapes hanging from the walls. She wishes she could stop and inspect them more closely. A male voice, emanating from a room further up the passageway, shouts, '*TEAM!*'

Taliah is steered through a large double door into a spacious pastel blue-walled room, furnished with modern sofas, chairs, a TV and a newspaper stand containing magazines. Two men are standing at the far side of the room. One of the men rushes towards Taliah, the tails of his white coat flailing behind him. Taliah gasps. The nurses' grip on her arms tightens.

'Hey Taliah how's it going? I'm Dr Nicholas Vitali you can call me Nick.'

The voice is the same one Taliah heard seconds earlier in the corridor. It occurs to her that the spectacle wearing man with the unruly mop of hair, now encroaching into her personal space, looks like a mad scientist.

'You want to play games watch television listen to music?' asks Dr Vitali breathlessly.

Taliah takes a step backwards. The grip on her arms tightens. Taliah looks at the grinning doctor, his tufts of black hair sticking out frenziedly in all directions. She says nothing.

'This way,' says Dr Vitali, lurching away and dragging an

armchair from a table. 'This way this way,' he continues, beckoning Taliah with his flapping hand.

Taliah remains stationary.

'Come on dear,' says Clara.

Taliah is led to an armchair and lowered into it. She looks up at the men and women encircling her.

'Magazines, you like reading yes?' says Dr Vitali thrusting several magazines towards Taliah, all of which have been vetted for pictures of fires prior to Taliah's arrival.

Taliah picks up one of the magazines. It is a *Country Life*. She opens it. There is an article about famous English gardens. She tries to focus on the article, ignoring the multiple sets of eyes boring down on her. Perusing the pictures of flowerbeds and lawns beneath blue skies, she feels sad.

Meanwhile Talulah is being ushered out of the acute ward and down the passageway. Talulah does not turn her head to look at the watercolours. As her pace quickens, the two female nurses at her sides tighten their grip on her arms. Taliah does not look up from the magazine when her sister enters the room.

'Welcome hi good to see you,' greets Doctor Vitali, rushing towards Talulah.

Talulah, ignoring the doctor, peers around him at her twin. As Talulah takes a step towards Taliah, the two nurses hold her arms resolutely. She too is lowered into an armchair, facing Taliah. The room is silent. Multiple pairs of eyes scrutinise the twins. Taliah focuses on a photograph of a flowerbed brimming with tulips, as Talulah watches her, her arms folded across her chest. Time passes. Doctor Vitali, bearing a maniacal grin, is pushing three magazines towards Talulah. He says, 'Want to read too yeah?'

Talulah waves the magazines away, her gaze never leaving Taliah. To Talulah it seems that Taliah is now slimmer than her, that her skin is more radiant, that her eyes have more lustre and her hair is better kept. Talulah's joy at seeing her twin dissipates. She grits her teeth and clenches her fists tightly.

'Doughnuts?' It is Caron, one of the nurses that escorted Talulah into the room who says this. She is bending down, holding a plate containing two jam doughnuts encased in sugar close to Taliah's face. Smelling the jam and sugar, Taliah tentatively licks her lips. Her hand reaches towards the doughnut then withdraws again. She says, 'No thank you.'

For the first time Taliah looks at her twin. Caron approaches Talulah.

'Doughnut?'

Talulah, staring at the doughnut, clamps down hard with her teeth. She shakes her head vigorously from side to side.

'Are you sure honey? I know your medication makes you very hungry,' says Caron.

Talulah, ignoring her, looks directly ahead at Taliah. Taliah stands up and walks over to the two large windows at the back of the room, Dr Vitali and the nurses Clara and Maria following close behind. There is a door between the windows that leads to the hospital's back garden. The tall nurse with the aquiline nose steps in front of the door as Taliah approaches. Taliah goes to the window on her left, reaches out and touches the glass with her fingertips. She feels the warmth of the sun's rays beaming through the glass, sees the green grass and two towering horse chestnut trees at the back of the garden, behind which fields and a copse are visible. Tears glisten in her eyes. Talulah is standing beside Taliah.

'Music,' orders Dr Vitali, clicking his fingers.

Enya's tranquil tones fill the room. Dr Vitali hurries over to a cupboard, takes out a fluorescent yellow hula-hoop, places it around his middle and starts spinning.

'Whoa!' he shouts. 'Check this out girls.'

Talulah and Taliah turn their backs on the doctor, Thomas shakes his bald head, Caron groans and Clara peers down at the floor.

'Table tennis?' suggests a smiling Caron, who then goes over to the table tennis table on the far side of the room.

Taliah wipes her eyes with the sleeve of her tracksuit top then goes over to the table and picks up a bat. Maria, who has followed Taliah to the table, strokes Taliah's back tenderly. Caron serves the ball meekly to Taliah. Taliah returns the ball. As the gentle rally continues, Caron encourages Taliah in a soothing voice.

Talulah strides over to the table. She takes the bat from Caron. The staff members line up on one side of the table. Taliah, ball in hand, looks across the table at Talulah for quite some time before serving gently to her. Talulah returns the ball very slightly harder than she received it. Taliah blocks the ball with her bat at a slight angle, causing the ball to swerve slightly when it lands on Talulah's side of the table. Talulah returns the ball at pace. Taliah adds topspin to her return. And so the rally continues, the ball being returned with ever increasing venom.

Nurse Thomas says, 'Good play.' Maria claps enthusiastically, Clara says 'Good shot,' and Dr Vitali puts his hands in the pockets of his white coat, extracting them a second later.

The ball is flying back and forth. Talulah, lunging to her right returns a driven shot, a panting Taliah replies with a backhand. As the watching eyes follow the ball hurtling from side to side, the lethargic feeling and weight gain is temporarily forgotten by the sweating, relentlessly battling twins, who instinctively knowing where the other will place their shot, is acutely aware that only sheer power or spin can prevent her twin's return. Talulah smashes a forehand that comes off the corner of the table, Taliah leaping through the air returns with a backhand. Talulah takes a step back and hits the ball with all her might. The ball bounces off the corner of the table. Taliah dives. The ball flies off the side of her racket and across the room. Taliah remains on the floor breathing hard.

'Are you okay darling?' asks Maria, hurrying over.

Taliah is back on her feet.

'One love,' calls out the male nurse with the aquiline nose ebulliently in an Eastern European accent.

Dr Vitali grabs him by the sleeve and, pointing at him menacingly with a wagging finger, says, 'No.'

The ball is flying back and forth again, the spectators following its rapid movement. A topspin shot from Taliah fails to make it over the net. Talulah screams 'EAAA!' as she powers a forehand that bounces off Taliah's bat onto the floor. Taliah races over to collect the ball from beside the armchair, an agitated Dr Vitali following her, says, 'Let's stay calm.'

The ball is flying to and fro. Talulah and Taliah's faces are etched in concentration. The onlookers watch transfixed. Taliah's spinning shot deceives Talulah, who misses it completely. A ferocious sliced serve makes it three two, and a despairing Taliah dive fails to prevent it becoming four two. Dr Vitali, shaking his head mutters, 'No no no not on six milligrams of olanzapine and fifty milligrams of fluoxetine.'

Dr Vitali, taking a step towards Talulah, says, 'That's enough, the game's over.'

'NO!' shouts Talulah. She is poised to serve when Aquiline Nose walks up and grabs her right arm. Caron approaches Talulah. 'Derriii derriii dunci bigi bobothi bothi!' screeches Talulah trying to pull away from the male nurse. Caron grips Talulah's left arm. Thomas rushes over and picks Talulah up by her legs. As a screaming Talulah is carried away from the room, Maria and Clara clasp Taliah's arms resolutely. A panting Taliah does not resist.

Talulah's screaming is no longer audible when Taliah is led from the room. A wild-eyed Dr Vitali, turning to the one remaining occupant says, 'Clozaril, twelve point five milligrams daily.' He then hurries from the room.

*

Three weeks later – 'How are you darling?' asks Bethany.

'I'm okay,' replies Taliah, stifling a sob.

'It must be really difficult for you,' says Bethany.

Taliah hears her mother sniffling on the other end of the line.

'I will be fine,' replies Taliah, before smothering another sob with her sleeve.

'Being kept apart from your twin most of the time is really hard.'

Taliah cups her hand over the telephone transmitter. She says, 'No Mum, that is not the problem Mum, I need to be on my own now, do you understand, I need my own space, to be free…'

'Are you still dere? I can't hear you.'

Taliah takes her hand off the transmitter. She says, 'Yes Mum, I'm still here.'

'I hope Talulah will be okay, she was very quiet on the telephone,' says Bethany, who having sniffed several times, adds, 'she is really missing you.'

'She will fine Mum, please don't worry.'

The conversation continues.

Maria is knocking on the telephone booth's door. Taliah says, 'Have to go.'

'I hope to come and visit you two soon, and your dad too of course,' says Bethany hurriedly.

'Love you Mum. Bye.'

Taliah steps out of the telephone booth. Maria and Clara are waiting for her. Clara grips Taliah's left arm and Maria clasps her right with both of hers. They escort her along the corridor, but not to the female acute ward.

Taliah shields her eyes from the rays of sun beaming through the window. Accustomed to the artificial, subdued light of her cell, where she has been detained for up to twenty-two hours a day, her only forays outside, desultorily traipsed circuits under heavy escort around the rain-sodden Astroturf football pitch, it seems to Taliah, sitting in the plastic moulded chair, in this small office, with its neutral grey painted walls, that the sun has never been so hot or bright.

Dr Singh, the psychiatrist, ceases twirling the pen and looks up from the papers on his desk. He says, 'You like art Taliah?'

Taliah makes a barely perceptible nod of her head. She says, 'Yes I like art,' in a quiet, deadpan voice.

Taliah is oblivious to Dr Singh, now studying her from the other side of the desk, for she is thinking about the telephone conversation she just had. This was the first contact Taliah has had with her mother since her arrival at the hospital. Taliah, her head lolling forwards, feels tears welling in her eyes as she thinks about her father, who she is yet to speak to. The moment passes.

'You haven't had a tour of the hospital yet, have you?' enquires Dr Singh.

Taliah shakes her head.

'Well it's about time,' he says, rising to his feet, taking the blazer from the back of his chair and putting it on.

Dr Singh opens the door and waits patiently for Taliah to get up from her chair. Clara is on sentry duty outside the door. Dr Singh says, 'We're fine thanks.'

'Okay,' replies Clara, who then departs in the direction of the female acute ward.

Taliah trudges behind Dr Singh. Dr Vitali is approaching hurriedly from the opposite direction, the tails of his white coat trailing behind him, Thomas, the nurse, jogging to keep up with him, the keys on his belt jiggling noisily.

'Hey,' calls out Dr Vitali as he draws alongside Taliah. 'What's up?'

Taliah takes a step back. Dr Vitali, tugging Dr Singh by the arm, whispers to Thomas, 'Watch her.'

Now a few metres away from Taliah, his back turned to her, Dr Vitali asks in a hushed tone, 'What're you doing Hardeep walking around unaccompanied with a psychotic patient suffering from *folie simultanée*?'

'*Relax*,' replies Dr Singh. 'You look like you've just come out of an electric chair.'

Dr Vitali casts an uneasy glance in Taliah's direction and then leaning into Dr Singh says, 'I'm increasing their Clozaril dosage by fifty milligrams next week.'

'We'll talk about that later,' replies Dr Singh in a hushed voice.

'Oh you want Depixol injections biweekly do you?' replies Dr Vitali menacingly before spinning around and calling out, 'See you later T-T.' And then he's off, hurrying down the corridor, Thomas jogging to keep up.

Taliah, her head bowed, drags her feet as she follows Dr Singh along the passageway. The psychiatrist stops outside a partially open door. He says, 'This is one of our classrooms.'

Taliah, raising her head, sees teenage boys and girls sitting at desks, a teacher, pen in hand, standing at the front of the room next to a whiteboard. These are the first patients Taliah has seen since her arrival at the hospital, other than her twin. Dr Singh continues along the corridor, Taliah following behind. They pass through the main hall and proceed up a passageway, where Dr Singh, stopping outside a room, leans his tall frame against the wall and places his hands in the pockets of his flannel trousers, as he waits for the trudging Taliah to catch up. Taliah, lifting her head, peers though the open door at the spacious brightly lit room, furnished with lilac sofas and chairs. There is a large gridded mat with different coloured squares on the floor. The room reminds her of the psychiatrist George's room at Hunter-Thornton Integrated Counselling Services. Dr Singh says, 'This is the learning and therapy centre.'

Next Taliah is shown a games room, a multi-faith room and a fitness suite, complete with an array of machines and weights.

'You ever seen these chairs before?' says Dr Singh, opening a door with one hand and beckoning Taliah to approach with the other.

Taliah, taking a timorous step forward, hears mellow music emanating from the dimly lit, unoccupied interior. Having surveyed the room's two rows of black leather armchairs, she says, 'No, I don't think I've come across chairs like these.'

'They are massage chairs,' says Dr Singh. 'Give them a try?'

Taliah lowers herself onto one of the chairs and examines the remote control attached to its arm. She presses a button and then another. The chair starts vibrating.

'How strange,' mutters Taliah to herself, and then in a slightly louder voice, 'it tickles.' She presses the plus button repeatedly until it reaches its max. The chair's massage balls press hard against Taliah's back. 'Ow, that's too much,' says Taliah, who then presses the minus button repeatedly.

Dr Singh, standing by the open door, keenly observes Taliah's interest in the chair. When he hears Taliah giggle he smiles.

After the relaxation room Dr Singh escorts Taliah to the room where she had battled with Talulah on the table tennis table. Two boys are playing table tennis while others, both female and male, recline on the sofa and chairs watching television and reading magazines. Taliah, scanning the room, notes that there are only three nurses present, in contrast to the seven staff members who were in attendance when she and Talulah were here. A brown-haired boy with sunken features is pacing relentlessly up and down one side of the room.

'Hi Robin,' says Dr Singh when the boy approaches the door.

'Hi,' says Robin, before racing off in the direction from whence he just came.

Taliah wonders why Robin is wearing white latex gloves.

'*Tracey*,' calls out Dr Singh.

'What,' says a squat, shaven-headed teenage girl, lounging on the sofa.

Gesturing with his head towards Taliah, Dr Singh says, 'Could you spare us a moment to show Taliah your room?'

'Yeah,' replies Tracey.

Dr Singh calls out, 'Caron, can you come here please.'

Caron ambles over.

'Caron, can you accompany Tracey and Taliah?' says Dr Singh. 'Tracey has kindly agreed to show Taliah her room.'

'Of course,' replies the slender nurse, smiling serenely.

Taliah looks up at Dr Singh.

'Males are not allowed in the Violet Ward,' says Dr Singh. 'I'll be waiting for you here.'

Taliah follows Caron and Tracey along a passageway. Caron takes a bunch of keys from her pocket, selects one and unlocks a door. Taliah peers into the room – furnished with a bed, chest of drawers and a desk piled high with books, its walls plastered with posters of rock stars. To Taliah's surprise there is even an en-suite bathroom. Soon after they return to the room where Dr Singh is waiting. As Taliah follows Dr Singh back to his office, she is no longer dragging her feet.

When Talulah heard the door of Cell B open and close an hour ago, she knew that her twin was leaving the ward. Talulah paced up and down her cell relentlessly, until overcome by lethargy, she collapsed onto the bed, where, lying on her side with her eyes closed, she pictured Beddington House Hospital being engulfed in flames, as she and her twin stood beside Siegfried, watching the inferno, his handsome features etched in mirth. Talulah next imagined Siegfried fighting for the individual anarchist cause, preparing for the day when the three of them would be reunited once more. In fact at that moment Siegfried was attending an all day beer festival in the German expatriate community of Pomerode, Brazil, where he has been staying since fleeing the United Kingdom. Clad in *lederhosen*, a *stein* of beer held in one hand, Siegfried preened his purple-tinted mohawk before moonwalking to the sound of Michael Jackson's *Billie Jean* towards a group of giggling teenage girls.

Talulah, feeling drowsy, a side effect of her medication, fell asleep soon after. Awakening a short while later, convinced that Taliah was still not back she recommenced pacing the cell. She felt relief when footsteps and voices preceded the opening and closing of a cell door. Talulah, feeling certain that it was Taliah returning to her cell, sat down on the bed.

Footsteps are approaching. A key is inserted into the lock. The cell door opens.

'Come to the door polease.' It is Maria the Filipina nurse who says this.

Talulah slowly gets up, yawns and stretches her arms upwards. She then walks out of the cell. Clara and Thomas are also waiting for her. Clara wraps an arm around Talulah's left arm and Maria clasps her right with both of hers. The three of them follow Thomas towards the exit. Outside Cell B Talulah stops and peers at the door.

She is escorted along passageways to the brightly lit room, furnished with lilac coloured sofas and chairs that reminded Taliah of the psychiatrist George's room at Hunter-Thornton Integrated Counselling Services.

'Good afternoon, how are you today?' greets Isabel the speech therapist, smiling widely, revealing perfectly aligned, brilliant white teeth. 'Please take a seat.'

Talulah lowers herself into one of the lilac coloured armchairs and crosses her arms across her chest. As Isabel talks, fastidiously enunciating each and every sound, especially s's, it occurs to Talulah that the therapist resembles Ms Thomas, with her blonde bob, pretty face, slender figure, upper class voice and immaculately manicured fingernails. A scowling Talulah utters not a sound as Isabel, now holding a board with the alphabet inscribed on it, prods at each letter in turn before enunciating it. Isabel's constantly prodding finger, with its impeccably manicured fingernail, seems to Talulah to mock her own uneven, non-varnished nails. But looking ahead impassively, she shows not the slightest hint of the animosity seething within her. Meanwhile Clara and Maria sit perusing magazines, as Thomas stands on duty outside the room, engaging in brief conversations with the staff members and patients who pass sporadically along the corridor.

'*Pool*,' articulates Isabel, prodding with a pink nail-varnished finger at a picture of a swimming pool on a chart on the wall. 'Please repeat after me. *Pool.*'

Talulah stares ahead, arms crossed across her chest.

'*Pizza,*' articulates Isabel, the smile never leaving her face. '*Bear,*' says Isabel prodding at a coloured in picture of a bear on a different chart.

Talulah's hands form clenched fists. She continues to look ahead.

'*Brain,*' enunciates Isabel. And then pointing at a drawing of a toad, '*Toad.*'

Talulah does not respond.

'Repeat after me, *Sun.*'

Talulah clamps down on her jaw.

'*Soldier.*'

Talulah, her breathing now harried, pictures her twin in this very room, enunciating each and every s flawlessly.

'*Fridge … flour.* Please repeat after me,' says Isabel, prodding at the pictures depicting these items as she does so. '*Fire.*'

'FIRE!' shouts Talulah. 'Fire, fire fire.'

Isabel takes a step back. She holds a hand to her mouth. She says, 'Oh my.'

At the back of the room Clara and Maria stop reading their magazines and place their hands on the arms of their chairs, poised to stand up.

Having composed herself Isabel says, 'Let us try some more,' before picking up a chart from the sofa and holding it aloft, as Talulah stares impassively ahead.

'*She sells seashells* by the *seashore,*' articulates Isabel, prodding at each word in turn.

Talulah exhales sharply.

'The *shells she sells* are *surely seashells.*'

'NUHNUH BICHI BIGI BOTHI!'

Clara and Maria drop their magazines and approach Talulah.

'That was not English,' says Isabel. Looking down at Talulah, now flanked by a sombre-faced Maria and Clara, she adds, 'You need to speak English. Can you speak English?'

'Fuck you.'

Thomas opens the door and strides over to Talulah, the bunch of keys jingling on his belt. He says, 'You know how this can play out, don't you?'

Talulah, looking ahead vacantly, does not respond.

'The session is over,' says Isabel.

'Stand up,' says Clara.

Talulah, slowly standing up, is loath to continue with any outbursts, for she does not want to be taken to the hospital's High-Care Suite, nor does she want the embarrassment of being carried back to her cell past her twin's. She goes limp when Maria clutches one of her arms with both of hers and Clara the other. Talulah's feet shuffle along the polished floors of the corridors, as she is led back to the female acute ward.

CHAPTER TEN

THE FOLLOWING WEEK Taliah goes to speech therapy. The wall chart containing the picture of the fire is removed prior to her arrival. When Taliah enters the room the smile that adorns Isabel's attractive face is in contrast to her protruding eyeballs and jerking motions. Taliah, as Talulah the week before, sits in the same lilac coloured chair looking ahead impassively, and like her twin, it also occurs to Taliah that Isabel resembles Ms Thomas, only when Taliah thinks this her eyes become moist with nostalgia. Initially, Taliah, lost in thought, does not repeat the sounds that Isabel instructs her to. As the session progresses however, Taliah vocalises them, though in a barely audible voice that Isabel has to lean towards her, a hand held to her ear in order to hear. After a while Isabel, noting the relaxed manner of Clara and Maria at the back of the room reading magazines, feels confident enough to approach Taliah and crouch down in front of her. When Isabel does this she discovers that Taliah's tongue rolls impeccably in her mouth to form refined r's, touches the roof of her mouth to make taintless t's and draws close to the front of her teeth to execute splendid s's. Towards the end of the session when Taliah utters the tongue twister – *She sells seashells by the seashore* – with consummate ease, Isabel claps ebulliently.

Talulah and Taliah have been in Beddington House Hospital for seventy-one days. If one were to ask them how long they have been here, they would not know the answer, for in the female acute ward, as in the male acute ward on the other side of the hospital, there are no time keeping devices, and as the lights are never extinguished and the medicated patients languish in their cells most of the time, days and nights merge in an intoxicated blur, punctuated by the arrival of the trolley bearing medications and treats. Treats that the twins continue to devour eagerly, so ravenous are they from their medication, particularly the Symbyax, that their concerns for their appearances are pushed aside.

Alone in their cells Talulah and Taliah, like most of the other acute ward patients, often take to imagining the taste of sugar, jam, chocolate and crisps, as they wait for the arrival of the trolley. Unlike the other patients Talulah and Taliah also sometimes take to imagining the soft textured, delicious taste of Petits Filous. Talulah only gets to imagine the taste now, as unlike Taliah she is no longer permitted to consume Petits Filous, the hospital authorities having recently banned her from using plastic spoons in her cell at snack times because of safety concerns, and they will not consider allowing her to devour them with fingers, deeming it to be the kind of unseemly practice they do not wish to encourage. At mealtimes when Talulah does use plastic cutlery, two staff members stand flanking her in the cell as she eats. There are no Petits Filous' for dessert at mealtimes because hospital regulations stipulate that fruit is served at mealtimes. Taliah is allowed to eat her meals alone in her cell; a staff member checking through the peephole every minute to check that nothing is awry.

Taliah is now spending marginally more time out of her cell, as she is gradually integrated into the therapeutic and educational activities that will take up most of her waking hours once she is promoted to the next ward. The hospital's management do not permit acute ward patients to fraternise with patients from other wards, and for this reason Taliah has her therapy sessions alone, the hospital authorities having decided that Talulah's poor behaviour regretfully exempts her from attending the odd joint session with her twin. Taliah has been having twice weekly counselling sessions with Dr Singh, the hospital's head psychiatrist, as well as various other therapeutic sessions, some one-to-one biology and physics lessons, this in addition to her daily showers and daily forty minute escorted trips in the grounds, the latter two activities being partaken in by all acute ward patients, unless their behaviour is so bad as to temporarily exclude them. As for Talulah, she also attends some therapeutic sessions, including speech therapy and psychiatry with Dr Singh, but considerably less than her twin. Talulah continues to be aloof and uncommunicative with the hospital's staff.

*

Day 79 – on the table is a pile of A3 sized drawing paper and several pallets of paint. Taliah is sitting at the table, bent forward, her pretty if rather puffy face etched in concentration. Mr Potts the art therapist, perched on a stool an arm's length behind and slightly to the side of Taliah, watches her paint, as a tall, severe looking female Eastern European contract nurse stands on duty by the door. Taliah is painting a picture of the hospital garden that incorporates all four seasons. In one part summer reigns – birds soar in a blue sky over one of the garden's densely leaved horse chestnut trees. A flowerbed running along one side of the garden is an abundance of brightly coloured flowers, whilst the flowerbed opposite it is bare, a few desultory stalks reaching out from the frost-bitten earth. In another section autumnal leaves – rich yellows, reds, browns and oranges are piled high on the ground. A rake is resting on the pile. Several trees teaming with

159

buds and birds nests represent spring. A child's scooter is leaning against the base of one of these trees. Mr Potts, contemplatively running a thumb and finger across his chin, wonders if the scooter, situated as it is in the spring section of the painting, represents Taliah's childhood. He considers it significant that there is only one scooter.

'Thinner brush please?' says Taliah.

'Okay,' says Mr Potts, standing up and walking over to a padlocked Perspex-fronted cabinet, containing several pairs of scissors and paintbrushes in a range of sizes. He unlocks the cabinet and takes out a thin paintbrush. Having passed the paintbrush to Taliah, he parks himself down on the stool again.

Mr Potts, watching Taliah put the finishing flourishes to her work, considers that although her efforts are a little amateurish, her talent is undeniable. Having run a hand through his shoulder length grey hair he concludes that this painting, incorporating all the seasons, represents Taliah's eagerness to experience everything immediately, and a fear that it could all be taken away. Mr Potts's long fingers move up and down as he reflects on Talulah's one and only art therapy session the previous week. At first Talulah sat with her arms crossed across her chest, staring ahead in an expressionless fashion, ignoring the painting supplies. Then she began eyeing the palate of paints. Soon after her fingers edged towards the palate. Her drawing, a deluge of reds, oranges and yellows, was of a great seething inferno, in which the spire of church and several buildings were visible. From one of the buildings purple plumes of smoke bellowed.

Day 83 – Talulah is in her cell, perched on the corner of her bed, a book held in her right hand. This is the exact same position that Taliah is adopting at this moment in Cell B. Taliah is reading *Sense and Sensibility* by Jane Austen while Talulah is reading *Animal Farm* by George Orwell. Both twins have been encouraged by the hospital authorities to read books from their

English A Level reading lists, in preparation for the resumption of their school studies, once they are promoted from the acute ward.

On reaching the conclusion that *Animal Farm* is nothing more than capitalist propaganda Talulah hurls the book across the cell. She did not wanted to read it in the first place, but it had been delivered to her cell along with a jam doughnut one morning, and with nothing else to do but stare at the wall, she was left with little alternative but to give it a go. Talulah wants to read books written by those of an anarchistic disposition such as John Henry McKay, Max Stirner and Josiah Warren, but she surmises correctly that the hospital library does not stock them.

At the first utterance of a demonic incantation emanating from Cell D, Talulah holds her hands to her ears, as does Taliah in Cell B. The recently arrived incumbent of Cell D, a fourteen-year-old member of a devil worshipping family, has been chanting day and night since her arrival, often for hours on end. The frightful sound is having a detrimental effect on the residents of the ward, including Talulah and Taliah. Now when Clara enters the acute ward, not only does she make the sign of the cross when she sees Talulah and Taliah adopting the same postures despite being in different cells, she does the same when she hears the frightful incantations of the new arrival in Cell D. She mutters prayers too and no doubt would have fingered the silver crucifix she wears around her neck when off duty, were it not forbidden due to it being a strangulation risk.

As the self-harmer in Cell C resumes wailing, her racket fuses with the demonic incantations to form an abominable cacophony. Talulah, now huddling on the floor against the far wall, as far from the Cell D as possible, holds her hands to her ears, tears welling in her eyes as she pines for her twin. Taliah, huddling on the floor of her cell, longs for the day when she will be promoted from the acute ward.

A key is inserted in the lock. The door opens. Maria hurries into the cell and bends down over the cowering Taliah. Tugging at her arm she says, 'Come on darling, it time to go,' in a loud voice, so as to be heard over the incantations and wailing.

Taliah clambers to her feet and leaves the cell. As Maria and Clara lead Taliah out of the acute ward, Dr Vitali and Thomas dart in from the opposite direction. Talulah, in a momentary lapse in the incantations and wailing, hearing the cell door close, is aware Taliah has left her cell. Unable to contain herself, Talulah starts beating on her cell door with both fists. Dr Vitali shouts, 'NO NOT ANOTHER ONE!' when Talulah does this.

Accosted by the two wailing girls and the banging of the cell door, Dr Vitali grips the curls on the sides of his head and stamps on the ground with both feet. The devil worshipper in Cell D is now barging against her cell door, chanting, '*Sanctus Satanas, Sanctus. Dominus DIABOLUS SABAOTH. SATANAS – VENIRE! SATANAS – VENIRE! AVE, SATANAS, AVE SATANAS. TUI SUNT CAELI, TUA EST TERRA, AVE SATANAS!*'

Thomas approaches Cell D and peers through the peephole at the crazed girl, her wild hair matted with faeces, blood gushing from one hand. As she charges the door, Thomas, reeling back, says, 'She's bitten her finger off.'

'Get the pacification squad, I'll prepare the High-Care Suite,' says Dr Vitali. 'GO, GO GO.'

Meanwhile Taliah is standing outside the telephone booths near the main hall, her hands clasped behind her head. Maria gives Taliah a Styrofoam cup of water, which she gulps down. Clara looks at Taliah concernedly while Maria strokes Taliah's back. A minute passes then another.

'Are you okay?' asks Maria, looking up at Taliah.

'Yes, I am okay,' says Taliah.

Clara opens the telephone booth and then takes out the piece of paper containing Colin's telephone number. Taliah has been granted permission to telephone her father on his birthday as a special treat because of her good behaviour, even though it is outside of scheduled family calling times. Taliah, who lost track of time shortly after arriving at the hospital, only found out what the date was when she saw a calendar during her art therapy session the other day. Taliah had asked if Talulah could join her for the telephone call, thinking her father would appreciate that, but this request was denied.

As Clara dials the number, Taliah waits with her hands held together in a praying gesture, pleading for her father to answer.

*

Colin has just returned from work. On entering the sitting room of the small rundown flat, he sweeps the kebab wrapper from the chair, at the same time waving away the joint being offered to him by his overweight, red-eyed, jobless, tracksuited flatmate, an old friend from university.

'*FIFA?*' enquires the flatmate.

Colin nods sombrely. His flatmate passes him the PlayStation controller. Colin, searching for a team to use, sighs as he reflects on how no one has remembered his birthday. The last few years have been arduous ones for Colin. He is depressed by his daughters' plight and by the failure of his relationship with Bethany, the love of his life. Despite his relatively senior accountancy job, Colin has been left permanently short of money, due to having to pay the mortgage and bills for Bethany's house, the relentless expenses for Talulah and Taliah, and large legal bills. As a result he can only afford to live here in this flat with its moth-eaten curtains and fungus-ridden walls. Colin has just selected West Ham United as his team when the mobile vibrates in his pocket.

'One second,' says Colin, noting with concern that the area code displayed on his mobile screen is the same as Beddington House Hospital.

Colin, leaving the room, prays there is no bad news. In the hallway he presses the accept button.

'Hello.'

'Happy birthday Daddy.'

'Taliah, what a surprise,' replies Colin enthusiastically, and then adopting a hesitant tone, 'is everything okay?'

'It's fine here. I had an art class two days ago, and I had some biology and physics lessons recently. Hopefully I can catch up with my studies soon, and Talulah too of course.'

'That's great news, I am pleased to hear that,' replies Colin.

'How has your birthday been so far?'

Taliah and Colin converse for quite some time, Taliah asking him about his life, work and his parents too, Colin making out that everything is fine, in the manner people do.

Although Maria, standing on the other side of the corridor, cannot hear all of Taliah's words, she hears the enthusiasm in her voice. Maria knows Taliah is not complaining about her torrid existence in the female acute ward. A tear trickles down Maria's cheek when she realises this. Meanwhile Clara paces up and down the corridor, trying to purge her tormented mind of thoughts of the new female acute ward patient.

When the conversation ends Colin returns to the sitting room feeling happier than he has for a long time.

*

Five minutes later – Dr Stevenson has just returned to his office, where he now sits, his feet resting on the desk, chewing on a biro pen, as he ponders the twins. Recently he has been hearing a great deal of praise for Taliah. When the twins first arrived here they were referred to as *The Twins*, but now the staff that have dealings with them, not only refer to them by their names, but also insist that Taliah is doing better than Talulah. Dr Stevenson does not want the twins housed in separate wards, as he believes that nature intended them to be together, but he realises he cannot promote Talulah, and he does not want to leave Taliah languishing in the acute ward longer than necessary. Dr Stevenson is all too familiar with the omnipresent grey pallor that pervades all patients, irrespective of gender, race or complexion, who dwell in the acute wards, on diets high in sugar and low on hope. He always strives to keep them there for the shortest amount of time possible, but the unexplainable nature of the CCTV coverage of the incident involving the twins weighs heavily upon him and sends a shiver down his spine every time he recollects it. And there are also the arson attacks to consider. The telephone is ringing. He picks it up.

'Calm down Nicholas … What did you say? … The new girl in Cell D of the acute ward, yes … She did what? … Jesus Christ I'm coming over right away.'

CHAPTER ELEVEN

DAY 91 – CLARA and Maria's smiling faces greet Taliah when she steps out of the cell into the corridor. The two nurses do not hold Taliah's arms as they walk her down the passageways. The tall figure of Eileen, the manager of the intermediate female ward, is waiting at the door of her ward. It is called the Violet Ward. It is named after a former patient at the hospital, who had gone on to become a well-known poet in adulthood. Clara and Maria congratulate Taliah on her promotion, they then head back to their jurisdiction.

'This way,' says Eileen, ushering Taliah with an outstretched hand.

Taliah blinks to clear her moist eyes as she is shown her new room – complete with a window, bed, chest of drawers, desk and an en-suite bathroom with a shower. On the bed are several bin liners. Taliah tentatively opens one and peers inside at her own clothes. She reaches inside, takes out her blue Benetton jumper, holds it to her nostrils and smells the familiar aroma of home. Taliah squeals with delight when she sees her sponge bag and make up set, minus the scissors.

'Time to go, it's break time,' says Eileen, who is standing in the doorway savouring Taliah's joy. 'Doors are unlocked at seven-thirty. Breakfast is served in the cafeteria,' explains Eileen as they head out of the ward. 'Therapeutic and educational programmes start at nine, there's a half hour break at eleven. Lunch is at one. Have you got all that?'

'Yes,' says Taliah. 'I think so.'

'*Voila*,' says Eileen, opening the large double doors.

Taliah looks apprehensively into the spacious, pastel blue-walled room that she has been in on two previous occasions, now bustling with teenagers and a handful of staff members standing on duty at regular intervals by the walls. Taliah's attention flits from the modern sofas and chairs on which teenagers sit watching television and devouring snacks, to the two boys and a girl standing beside the newspaper stand stuffed with magazines, and then to the table tennis table ahead of her and to her right, where two girls are playing each other, a bevy of onlookers sporadically applauding. Taliah, feeling her heart fluttering and beads of sweat forming on her forehead, supports her weight against the frame of the door. It is nearly four months since she spoke to Veronica in the basement of her school, those being the last words she uttered to anyone her own age, other than her twin.

'Come on Taliah,' says Eileen in a soothing tone, placing a reassuring hand on Taliah's back. 'They won't bite.'

Taliah is wondering if Eileen's last remark is correct. She suspects that in an institution such as this, it is likely that some of the patients do bite. She takes a step into the room, then another. Heads turn towards her. Tracey, the squat, shaven-headed teenage girl, who had shown Taliah her room, is sitting on the sofa watching a cartoon. Rotating her large frame to face Taliah, she says, 'Awight Taliah.'

'Hi Tracey,' replies Taliah meekly, who, though happy to be addressed by her own name, is still feeling apprehensive.

A grinning Dr Vitali is approaching hurriedly, the tails of his white coat flailing behind him. He says, 'Hey Taliah what's up?'

Taliah, frowning, steps around the doctor and continues into the room's interior. She passes a girl, her blonde hair drawn tightly behind her head in a pigtail. The girl is talking to herself in a language Taliah does not recognise. Taliah notices Robin, the latex-glove wearing boy she had seen here previously, scurrying to and fro. Wondering again why he wears these gloves, she inspects him nervously, before concluding he is most likely harmless.

Taliah is cautiously approaching the sofa where Tracey is lounging. Tracey makes eye contact with Taliah, then pats the seat next to her. Taliah lowers herself down onto the sofa. A small, handsome boy with black hair is also sitting on the sofa, perusing a pile of portraits laid out on the coffee table in front of him. Taliah, looking over his shoulder at the portraits, recognises the face of the actress with tumbling locks and large inquisitive eyes, but cannot remember her name. The boy, becoming aware of her presence, looks up from the drawings and offers his hand. He says, 'Hi I'm Adam.'

Taliah takes the hand. She says, 'I'm Taliah,' in a soft voice.

'I started out with charcoal but now prefer graphite, although charcoal is great for things like fabrics and hair,' says Adam, perusing the portraits once more.

Adam takes a portrait from the pile. Taliah recognises it as being the actor Willem Dafoe. Taliah, viewing the animated eyes and maniacal grin, marvels at the likeness. She considers that the picture is apt in such an environment as this.

'Art is a wonderful therapy,' says Adam, looking across at Taliah. 'It's really helped me start to come to terms with stuff.'

Taliah, holding her breath, grips tightly to the bottom of her tracksuit top, fearful that Adam is about to ask her why she is here, but instead he asks if she likes art. They have been conversing for the best part of a minute when Adam says, 'Please keep it.'

'Really?' replies Taliah, smiling widely, picking up the portrait of Willem Dafoe. 'Thank you.' Taliah considers what a wonderful day this is turning out to be.

Dr Vitali and Thomas, standing close together behind the television, are watching a gangly, pale, black-haired youth enter the room and traipse languidly towards them. Dr Vitali, leaning towards Thomas, whispers, 'Watch him like a hawk on visitors' day. He'll molest pre-pubescent boys on sight.'

Thomas nods sombrely. As the youth draws closer, Dr Vitali says, 'What's up dude, want to play table tennis?'

'No, I'm … um … feeling a little … weird today,' replies the youth, reaching out with one hand to support his weight against a chair.

'Okay Hubert,' says Dr Vitali, slapping him on the shoulder. He then strides off.

Taliah and Hubert's eyes meet. Taliah blinks then blinks again. Hubert's eyes never leave Taliah as he sluggishly approaches her. Taliah is trembling as she rises slowly to her feet. Hubert, now an arm's length away, examines her from top to toe, before leaning towards her and taking a lingering sniff.

'Oh you're the good one, T-T-T. Where's your other half?'

Taliah is trembling. She does not respond. Hubert grabs her by the shoulders and shakes her.

'Why are you in here, tell me?' orders Hubert.

'Piss off Hubert,' calls out Tracey from the sofa.

'Shut up Oompa Loompa,' replies Hubert.

Taliah stands transfixed, staring at the familiar pale face, puffier than when she last saw it. Hubert shakes Taliah again. 'What are you doing here, tell me?' he demands.

'Stand back Hubert,' orders Thomas, grabbing Hubert's arm.

'Get away from me blackie,' says Hubert, holding a clenched fist to Thomas's face.

'GO GO GO!' calls out Dr Vitali.

Two male nurses descend on Hubert, grab him, and with Thomas's assistance carry him out of the room by his arms and legs, a struggling Hubert screaming, 'I NEVER DID NOTHING TO THOSE BOYS THEY DIDN'T WANT!'

Taliah, her trembling hands clasping the picture of Willem Dafoe, her breath coming in fitful gasps, prays that none of the patients have picked up on Hubert's comment about her *other half*.

'Jaffa Cake? … Taliah, Jaffa Cake?'

Taliah becomes aware that Caron is holding a paper plate laden with Jaffa Cakes in her direction. Forcing a smile, she takes a Jaffa Cake and proceeds to timidly nibble at it.

It is now evening. Taliah enters the en-suite bathroom and creeps towards the mirror above the basin, stifling a wail with her hand when she views her evident weight gain. She screws her eyes tightly shut, opens them again – shrieks. Taliah takes a tentative step towards the mirror – gasps as she examines her unkempt hair, groans as she inspects her lustreless skin. In the washrooms used by the acute ward patients there are no mirrors, due to the hospital management's concerns about glass. Taliah has not viewed her reflection for quite some time.

Later, lying on her new bed, her hands held behind her head, the picture of Willem Dafoe stuck to the wall beside her, she sighs contemplatively. Even with the bars on the windows and the door locked at night, this room feels like hers. Taliah stretches out her arms at her sides, then places her hands behind her head again and peers out into the darkness. Reflecting on how the other patients seem not to know that she has a twin, Taliah assumes correctly that this is because hospital staff are not permitted to discuss patients with other patients. Reliving her relief that no one seemed to have overheard, or at least understood Hubert's remark about her *other half*, Taliah exhales slowly though pursed lips.

Her breathing quickens when she considers what Hubert might yet divulge. But for now at least Taliah realises that she is liberated, alone and free with her own name. She is smiling as she contemplates how her name has been uttered more times today than she can ever remember it having been in a single day. Turning her thoughts to her twin languishing in the acute ward, Taliah rolls onto her side and curls up in a ball. She feels sympathy for her twin's plight, and guilt that for the most part, she has been enjoying herself, but Taliah does not want Talulah to join her in the Violet Ward. Taliah, feeling shame, pulls the duvet over her head.

*

That morning in the acute ward when Talulah became aware that Taliah was not in her cell, she tried to ignore the fact, attempting to keep her medicated mind focused on other matters. As the afternoon progressed Talulah was to be found pacing up and down her padded cell, nibbling at her fingernails, her breathing harried, beads of sweat visible on her brow. When Clara wheeled the trolley up to her cell with her evening medication, Talulah refused it. No amount of coaxing could persuade her, not even the promise of Jaffa Cakes, Bakewell Tarts and crisps. Eventually Dr Vitali was called. When his pleas were rebuked with a scathing, staccato burst of cryptophasia, he ordered her removed to the High-Care Suite.

This is where Talulah is now, strapped to a bed in the small, square, white-walled, brightly lit room. A lethargic Talulah, pacified by tranquilisers, can make out the hazy contours of a female contract nurse and Dr Vitali, who is swaying peculiarly to the tranquil tones of Enya playing over the loud speakers. The nurse, approaching the bed, says, '*Relax,*' in a robotic sounding voice.

Dr Vitali is swaying closer. He is holding a syringe in a latex-gloved hand.

*

Day 101 – Taliah's busy timetable consists of biology, physics, maths and English lessons in the mornings, and an afternoon therapeutic schedule of one-to-one psychiatry sessions and cognitive behaviour therapy (CBT), supportive therapy and group therapy sessions with various psychotherapists, as well as voluntary aerobics and fitness training. There are so many nurses, doctors, occupational therapists, psychiatrists, psychologists, psychotherapists and counsellors, not to mention fellow patients, that Taliah finds it quite impossible to remember all their names. Although she remains shy, Taliah converses readily with some staff members and a number of patients. When the hospital's therapists and counsellors witness Taliah conversing with other patients, they tick boxes on pieces of paper next to words such as *integration, confidence* and *communication*.

It is now late afternoon. Taliah is in one of the hospital's meeting rooms waiting for the arrival of her twin. They have not seen each other since Taliah's promotion. Talulah's behaviour has declined since Taliah's departure from the acute ward. Her sullen and uncooperative demeanour has been punctuated with periodic outbursts, as well as several catatonic episodes, which on several occasions have resulted in her being secured in the High-Care Suite, tranquilised and fed on drips. The hospital director Dr Stevenson is distressed at having been compelled to separate the pair. He is keen to reunite them as soon as possible, but for now sporadic meetings such as this will have to suffice.

Taliah, sitting at the table, runs a fingertip around the rim of her Styrofoam cup of Pepsi. Prior to coming to this room she had washed the makeup off her face, ruffled her hair so it appeared unkempt, taken off her designer yellow, sorrel camo print Club Monaco jacket that Bethany had recently ordered and had delivered to the hospital; a top that accentuated her now marginally slimmer figure, a result of exercise and eating less since coming off the Symbyax. She is now taking Invega, which is not increasing her appetite. Taliah is wearing a shapeless sweatshirt with a picture of Minnie Mouse emblazoned on it and brown tracksuit bottoms. As Taliah waits, she tells herself that she has made these changes to her appearance because she does not want Talulah to feel envious, but she knows that this is not the only reason.

The door opens. Talulah enters the room followed by Clara and Maria. Talulah rushes towards Taliah and hugs her. Taliah pats her shoulder with one hand. They stay like this for several minutes before Talulah takes a seat on the opposite side of the table to Taliah. Talulah and Taliah, a Styrofoam cup of Pepsi clasped in their right hands, examine each other as Maria and Clara stand on duty outside in the passageway, observing the twins at regular intervals through the small internal window. Talulah, having felt her twin's slimmer figure when she hugged her, is now thinking that they have never looked more different from one another. Taliah, regarding her sister's tired, puffy features, unkempt hair and chipped nails, feels guilt that her twin is still languishing in a cell whilst she is living in relative freedom. When the twins take intermittent sips from their Styrofoam cups, the cups are lifted to their mouths at different times. Talulah focuses on her twin, prying for information about her new life as Taliah, looking back at her, concentrates on keeping her mind devoid of thoughts about life on the Violet Ward. Talulah feels that her mind is disconnected from her twin. She believes that this is because the hospital authorities are giving them different medication. At this moment Talulah hates the hospital authorities as much as she ever has. She has to fight to prevent herself from venting her fury, aware of the fact that if she does it will bring this meeting to an abrupt end.

'Mediichi,' says Talulah, breaking the silence.

'Medi ucki.'

'Mediew.'

'Medi nuhnuh ew.'

'Klathi tudi en ogi mathi – ooki wede crible peciooki,' says Talulah.

Taliah and Talulah continue conversing in their cryptophasia. Soon the Styrofoam cups are moving to their mouths in time with one another.

That evening after dinner, Talulah lies on her bed in her cell, staring up at the ceiling, deep in thought. With her devil-worshipping neighbour now heavily sedated and the self-harmer in Cell C silent, Talulah's pattern of thought is uninterrupted, until Clara pushes the trolley up to the cell door. Clara is surprised to see a smile illuminating Talulah's puffy visage. Having taken her medication without complaint, Clara thinks she hears Talulah say *thank you* when she passes the chocolate doughnut through the hatch. Pushing the trolley away, she assumes she must have been mistaken.

*

Mid-morning break – the recreation room – 'There's nothing like the taste of Cyprostat in the morning,' remarks Hubert before swallowing a pill with a gulp of Coca Cola.

Thomas and the intermediate male ward manager, who have been standing either side of the armchair where Hubert is reclining, depart when they see he has taken his medication. Taliah regards Hubert with concern. She is fearful of this link to her old life and her twin, whom she has still made no mention of to anyone. She is planning to, but not quite yet. Thankfully, since Hubert has returned from a stint in the male acute ward, he has shown not the slightest interest in her. She hopes this will remain the case.

'What's next?' says Hubert. '*Texas Chainsaw Massacre*?'

A large boy with acne, sitting on the sofa, laughs when Hubert says this. The room's television delivers a steady stream of educational material – arts and crafts, literacy and anger management programmes, and a twice-daily Trivial Pursuit type game show. A programme about making jewellery out of beads is starting. Taliah, mildly intrigued, takes a step towards the television, but thinking that it would be unwise to be in such close proximity to Hubert, makes her way towards the windows at the back of the room.

175

Lucy, the blonde-haired girl Taliah heard speaking in a strange language during her first mid-morning break here, is standing alone, leaning against the radiator. The large, bewildered eyes and the chin that recedes abruptly from her lower lip are now a familiar sight. Taliah, advancing towards her, considers not for the first time how Lucy seems capable of only two expressions – confusion and concern. Rarely does one establish complete dominance over the other, rather they merge, confusion temporarily getting the upper hand over concern, only for concern to gain the ascendency. At this moment confusion has precedence.

'Hello Lucy.'

'?yadot tra evah uoy oD,' asks Lucy.

Taliah, placing a perfectly manicured finger to her chin, looks up at the ceiling for quite some time before replying, 'Yes my art therapy session is this afternoon.'

'?hcnuM retsnoM a tnaw uoy oD,' asks Lucy, holding a packet of pickled onion flavoured Monster Munches in Taliah's direction.

'Yes please,' says Taliah, taking a Monster Munch from the packet.

Taliah and Lucy converse for several minutes. Each time Lucy says something, Taliah's index finger moves to her chin as she reverses Lucy's words. Lucy has spoken backwards since the tumultuous incident when she was a young child that was to change her life forever. The hospital's therapists think that the reason Lucy speaks backwards is a bizarre attempt to get further away from the incident.

'Hi Taliah,' greets Adam, as he walks across the room towards her, holding his art portfolio under one arm.

Taliah sighs contentedly. Even now several weeks into her stay on the Violet Ward, each utterance of her name brings her joy. The two teenagers, now firm friends, converse, as Robin scampers up and down the length of the table tennis table, touching one end with his latex-gloved hand and then the other, repeating this over and over again. Yesterday, Adam, noticing Taliah watching Robin's antics, explained to her that Robin wears gloves to protect his hands, because he is prone to wash the skin off them due to his obsessive-compulsive disorder.

A male contract nurse's face appears in the doorway. He calls out, 'The shop is open.'

A deluge of teenagers stampede towards the exit where, forming a disorderly queue, they wait impatiently as the nurses positioned on the door allow them to file out of the room one at a time. Taliah, observing the commotion, licks her lips, as she imagines the taste of the snacks that the shop stocks, but despite the urge to join them, a result of the diminishing yet lingering effects of her previous medication and the habits she picked up in the acute ward, she remains where she is. Tracey is waving to Taliah from the queue, a girly gesture, in stark contrast to her butch appearance. Taliah waves back. Two other girls in the queue are waving now. Taliah reciprocates. She sees the Jocular Self-Mutilator; a large, cumbersome, overweight eighteen-year-old, revealing scar-ravaged pale forearms below the sleeves of his T-shirt. He reminds Taliah of the clown who resides on the shelf in her bedroom at home what with his permanent grin, in defiance of the sad eyes that bear testimony to the self-loathing and despair lurking within.

Taliah passes no judgment on any of these hospital patients based on their illnesses, but merely on whether they are nice or not nice. She and her twin had spent their early years at a normal school with normal children being bullied, harassed and ostracised. It was only amongst those labelled by society as non–normal that Taliah has ever made friends. At Royston Park, Veronica, Emma, Ben and of course Samson were the students that she still holds close to her heart, whom she often thinks about and hopes to see again. As the sound of stampeding feet disappear into the passageway, Taliah surveys the room. Only a handful of patients remain, including Adam, a small girl standing in the corner and the scampering, latex-gloved Robin, who now makes a dash for the door.

*

Talulah raises her head and listens to the noise emanating from the passageway. She looks at Dr Singh on the other side of the desk, who is leaning forward writing on a pad.

'Why the commotion?'

The pen falls from Dr Singh's grasp, he recoils, nearly topples backwards in his chair. Staring across the desk at the previously uncommunicative twin, who in all their psychiatry sessions combined, has uttered merely a solitary burst of defiant cryptophasia, complete with a raised arm anarchist salute, Dr Singh, realising he must be exhibiting an expression of utter shock, breathes in and forces a smile. He says, 'That noise is patients going to the shop.'

'I want to go.'

'And you shall, when you are ready.'

Dr Singh braces himself.

'When will that happen?' asks Talulah.

'That's up to you,' replies Dr Singh, acknowledging that Talulah's voice is indistinguishable from that of her twin. 'Do you understand?'

Talulah nods her head.

'Are you going to behave, Talulah?'

Talulah nods again. Dr Singh takes a piece of paper containing her schedule from the desk drawer, examines it briefly and then looks up at Talulah, who is sitting up straight, looking directly ahead, simpering, in a manner quite different to her usual slumped posture during these sessions.

'Will you behave and cooperate in art therapy and speech therapy?' says Dr Singh.

Talulah nods.

'Say it Talulah, make it a reality.'

'In art therapy and in peech therapy tomorrow.'

'Good Talulah, you've done excellently today. And I hear from your ward nurses that you have been behaving well.' Dr Singh studies Talulah briefly before adding, 'I know it isn't easy in the ward, especially with everything that has been going on there recently, but we're here to help you.'

'Okay, I … comprehend.'

The session ends soon after, but not before Talulah has uttered several more comments. As Maria and Clara escort Talulah back to her ward, Dr Singh, his elbows resting on the surface of his desk, his fingertips pressing against each other in a steepling gesture, reflects on the session, playing back in his mind all that Talulah said. Several minutes have passed when he realises that Talulah never uttered a single s sound.

'Interesting, very interesting,' mutters Dr Singh, forgetting that talking to oneself is the first sign of madness.

Chapter Twelve

AFTER THE ROOMS on the Violet Ward are locked at nine-thirty, Taliah can be found at her desk or lying on her back in bed, her hands placed behind her head, the portrait of Willem Dafoe hanging on the wall beside her barely visible in the half-light. At such times Taliah often takes to thinking about what her life will be like in her fast-approaching adulthood. Prone as she always has been to romanticised notions, Taliah sometimes pictures herself living in a large country house, not dissimilar to how she imagines Kellynch Hall would look like: Kellynch Hall being the house in Jane Austen's *Persuasion*. In her mind's eye she sees herself playing on a Persian rug with her young child, as her formally dressed husband reclines in an armchair engrossed in a book, or prods with a poker at the comforting glow in the fireplace. The husband in these fantasies is always Samson.

At other times Taliah envisages that she will be a businesswoman who travels internationally and dresses impeccably. And then there are the occasions when she imagines being an artist, her skills with charcoal and graphite having brought her fame and a portrait-strewn Paris apartment with a view of the Eiffel Tower. Although Taliah's imaginings about her future vary markedly, they all share the fact that she is living independently of her twin.

Taliah is aware that Talulah will probably be promoted to her ward at some point in the future. She considers that when this occurs, she might well have been promoted again, or maybe even freed from the hospital. Taliah feels guilty when she thinks this. As for what exactly occurred on that day when she and her twin took the LSD, Taliah remains unsure. When she thinks about that day, or specifically the short clip of the CCTV footage she had seen of the incident in court, Taliah experiences fear and confusion. Unable to remember exactly what had happened, she wonders if it is a repressed memory, a term she has heard used by a number of the hospital's therapists during therapy sessions.

It is not unusual for Taliah to have the sensation that she is swallowing pills when she is not in fact swallowing anything. This always occurs at times when the medications are being distributed to those in the female acute ward. At other times Taliah is quite sure she feels the effects of the Symbyax – a sudden loss of energy, an intense craving for sugared foods, this despite the fact she stopped taking Symbyax quite some time ago, and her new medication does not have these side effects, at least not for her. Taliah keeps these experiences to herself, fearful that if she mentions them to her therapists, she might be branded delusional and returned to the acute ward.

*

Whenever the trolley is wheeled up to Cell E, Talulah is to be found standing erect and unflinching, facing her cell door. She never fails to greet Clara by name, or whichever nurse happens to be on duty that day. Fortunately for Talulah none of the nurses names have s's in them. Talulah always swallow her pills quickly and without protest. Over time Talulah notices that the prying eyes that watch her through the peephole in the door of her cell reduce in frequency and duration. And when she is escorted from her cell, the forthright grip on her arms gradually slackens.

Anarchist salutes, screamed cryptophasias and oppressive

silences in therapy sessions are a thing of the past. An attentive Talulah, having recently seen a short video in a therapy session, titled *The Power of Communication*, considers for the first time in her life the significance of body language. During the last few weeks, having studiously scrutinised her therapists' body language, she is now something of an expert on the matter. In art therapy when Mr Potts speaks to her, she sits as he does, at a slight slant on her stool, one foot crossed over the other, making eye contact only periodically with the furtive therapist. In psychiatry sessions with Dr Singh, it is not uncommon for Talulah to adopt hand on chin poses and steepling gestures too, both of which he favours. But Talulah is always subtle in her mimicry, wary of being accused of insolence. She knows exactly how to achieve the right balance, so that the therapist in question will tick the boxes on the pieces of paper next to words such as *communication*, *social skills* and *improvement*.

During the long hours of solitude in her cell, Talulah often lies on her bed or sits at the desk moulded into the floor thinking about the future, only unlike her twin, she always pictures the two of them together. Even Siegfried dominates her thoughts less now, so focused is she on her one objective.

*

In addition to classes, assignments, group therapy, art therapy, psychiatry sessions, psychotherapy sessions, aerobics and fitness training, there are a host of compulsory workshops, including Social Integration and Cultural Identity, where Taliah is encouraged to embrace her West Indian heritage. Taliah hurries down the passageways from one activity to the next, returning the greetings of those she comes across along the way. If she sees Dr Vitali or Hubert she hides in a doorway or behind other patients.

During the last few nights, in the solitude of her room, Taliah has sensed her twin, heard whispered cryptophasias, seen her in her mind's eye. Taliah is unaware that the strengthening of the unexplainable telepathic bond that connects the two of them has coincided with Talulah's Symbyax dosage having been decreased. When these episodes occurred, Taliah imagined that she was turning off a tap, at the same time concentrating all her focus on erasing her twin from her mind. This is a technique that Pamela her psychotherapist taught her a few weeks ago, as a way of purging her mind of any negative thoughts. When she tightened the imaginary tap, the cryptophasia decreased in volume, until stopping altogether, and the image of her twin in her mind faded and then disappeared. The relief Taliah felt when she did this was tinged with shame.

*

Day 123 – Taliah was called by her name on seventeen separate occasions today. She cherished every occurrence. Today she wore her hair in pigtails like she used to. The pigtails were tied with green hairbands. Some days Taliah uses other coloured hairbands, but they are never pink. She also ties her hair behind her head in a ponytail, at other times she does not tie her hair at all.

This evening Taliah was unsure whether to take the passageway to the left of the main hall which leads to the recreation room, or the passageway to the right, which leads to the library. For quite some time Taliah stood pondering this. Such dilemmas are a common occurrence for Taliah even after all this time away from her twin.

Day 125 – Talulah and Taliah met today. When Talulah entered the room, Taliah noticed how relaxed Maria and Clara were, but she did not dwell on what the ramifications of this might be. Talulah and Taliah played draughts. Talulah lost the first game, but she played the next as calmly as she had the first. Maria, watching them through the internal window, noted this.

Day 128 – In the staff room during the mid-morning break Dr Stevenson heard staff praising *The Twins*. It was the first time he could remember them being referred to collectively since their first days at the hospital.

In the afternoon Dr Vitali asked a troupe of nurses heading towards the female acute ward how Talulah was faring. Clara, Maria, Thomas and a contract nurse all told him how well she was behaving. Dr Vitali punched the air victoriously and then continued at haste down the passageway, congratulating himself as he went, not only on his decision to treat both twins with Symbyax, but also the incremental changes he had made to their daily dosages.

Talulah continues to detest the pills she is given, as she believes they are a microcosm of society's demands and expectations – subordination, conformity and dependency. But despite this she swallows them without complaint.

Day 130 – Bethany came to visit this afternoon. Taliah had been looking forward to telling her all about her life on the Violet Ward, but Bethany's initial euphoria at being reunited with her daughter soon faded, and Taliah seeing the disappointment etched across her face, knew that this was because Talulah had not been allowed to attend the meeting too, the hospital authorities having decided that acute ward patient visitor protocol was to be adhered to, even in this exceptional circumstance. Bethany would see Talulah after meeting with Taliah.

Every time Taliah started telling her mother about her lessons, friends and room, she felt guilt and shame over her absent twin, and the words trailed away, for her mother's unsaid expectation that the two of them were supposed to be together weighed heavily upon her.

In the evening, Taliah sat at her desk in her room, contemplated how if society views her as one half of a whole, as it always has, and even her own mother perceives her as such, then perhaps it is her who is insane for wanting to be viewed as an individual in her own right, for what is madness if it is not defying society's demands and expectations?

In the one-to-one psychiatry session yesterday, Dr Singh asked, not for the first time, how Taliah feels about being a twin. Taliah, as on previous occasions Dr Singh has asked her this, was not particularly forthcoming, but she did say that she had no issue with being a twin. Dr Singh then enquired if she had told her friends on the female and male intermediate wards about her twin. Taliah's response was the same as yesterday when Eileen her ward manager asked this same question. She nodded and muttered a barely audible *yes*. This was a lie. Taliah has not mentioned her twin to any of the patients. Taliah has convinced herself that Talulah will not be promoted for some time, due to her behaviour and the fact that the hospital authorities will be loath to reunite the two of them quite yet. Taliah continued to surmise that by the time Talulah is promoted to the Violet Ward, she may well have been promoted to the next ward, or possibly even released. But despite this she is considering mentioning Talulah in private to one or two patients, as she is fearful what they will think of her should she be promoted and then at a later date Talulah arrive on the Violet Ward, a twin she never told them about.

Day 132 – Yesterday in speech therapy Isabel clapped frenetically when Talulah pronounced all the sounds she asked her to repeat perfectly, in a voice indistinguishable from that of her twin, with the exception of s's, which though much improved are still a work in progress. Isabel was surprised how much Talulah's s's have improved since she first started making an effort in the sessions. She thought that this was possibly because previously Talulah was always able to depend on her twin to say s's for her, and as a result had never made a concerted effort to perfect them. Or perhaps they always had speech therapy together and Talulah was too embarrassed to enunciate s sounds when her twin's were so impeccable.

Yesterday, Pamela, Talulah's psychotherapist, was so impressed with her that she put big ticks in all the boxes on her progress report, next to words such as *improvement, comprehension* and *social skills.*

And then this afternoon in Talulah's psychiatry session, Dr Singh announced it was time for a tour of the facility. The few patients who glanced at them when the pair entered a classroom, the fitness suite, or passed them in the corridor, did not look closely enough to notice that the girl they assumed to be Taliah, was in actual fact a little chubbier, her hair rather unkempt and fingernails less than pristine.

Day 136 – Taliah is alone in the classroom sitting at a desk, peering down at her test paper. She taps the base of her pencil against the desk once then hastily draws a circle on the paper before turning the page. There is a colour photograph of a large obelisk, that Taliah recognises as the Washington Monument in Washington D.C. In the foreground is a body of water, to the left hand side of which people are congregated. Taliah, inspecting the image closely, sees that the people are evidently enjoying the sunny day. Some appear to be admiring the monument, others are cross-legged on picnic rugs, drinks clasped in their hands. Taliah notices a young couple walking hand-in-hand beside the water. Below the picture is a question. The question is – *What aspect of this picture do you feel MOST drawn towards?* There are three options – *a). The people b). The monument c). The trees/water.* Taliah swiftly draws a circle around option a, then turns the page.

There is a photograph of a grim-faced, scruffily-dressed, imposing looking, middle-aged man. Taliah looks at the question below the picture. The question is – *What would you do if this man approached you and asked for directions? a). Cross the road. b). Tell him to go away. c). Give him directions.*

Taliah taps the base of her pencil against the desk twice, then a third time. She murmurs, 'He doesn't look very friendly.'

Having tapped the base of the pencil on the desk a fourth time she draws a circle around option c. The door to the classroom opens. Eileen is standing in the doorway. She says, 'Time's up.'

Day 137 – Taliah, scanning the interior of the recreation room, is relieved that there is no sign of Hubert. Lucy is in her usual position, leaning against the radiator by the windows. Taliah wanders across the room towards her, weaving between the male and female patients. She says, 'Hi' when Tracey greets her by name and reciprocates in kind when Robin, who is relentlessly circling a chair, waves at her.

'Hello Lucy, how are you?' greets Taliah.

Confusion has precedence over concern as Lucy, her mouth hanging open, looks blankly at Taliah.

'Did you like the lasagne at lunch?' asks Taliah.

'.yako saw tI' Confusion and concern have established an approximate equilibrium when Lucy says a moment later, '.riah ruoy ekil I'

Taliah, looking up at the ceiling, mutters what Lucy has just said twice over before replying, 'Oh thank you, it was shampooed and conditioned this morning.'

Out of the corner of her eye Taliah sees Adam, perching on the corner of the table tennis table, conversing with the Jocular Self-Mutilator and the newest arrival on the Violet Ward. Taliah excuses herself and proceeds to timorously approach the trio, reflecting on her last conversation with Adam as she does so. Yesterday in a group art therapy session, Taliah confided in Adam that she has a twin. Adam responded by saying that he has an older sister and a younger brother. Taliah explained that her twin is in the hospital, languishing in the female acute ward. Adam, suspecting Taliah to be delusional or suffering from schizophrenia, pooh-poohed the notion. Their conversation was interrupted shortly after, and Taliah has not had a chance to speak to Adam again until now.

Taliah, drawing closer, listens to the hoarse voice of the girl talking to Adam. There is something familiar about the tone. Taliah suspects the girl might be her wailing, self-harming former neighbour from Cell C in the acute ward. The girl and the Jocular Self-Mutilator are walking away from Adam.

'Hello Adam.'

'Hi Taliah, I wanted to talk to you,' says Adam, gesturing with his head towards the unoccupied space between the other side of the table tennis table and the wall.

'BRU!' shouts a booming voice. And then, 'Bru, three sets of ten, twenty-eight kilo dumbbell bicep curls.'

Taliah sighs, and Adam, gritting his teeth, says, 'Congratulations,' to Cornelius, the eighteen-year-old South African patient gallivanting towards them.

Cornelius is wearing a skintight Canterbury training top, which accentuates his heavily-muscled frame and substantial paunch. Taliah and Adam wait impatiently as Cornelius recounts his recent weightlifting exploits, whilst simultaneously devouring a packet of pickled onion flavoured Monster Munches. Taliah observes Cornelius's sanguine complexion and small smudge-like nose, turned up at the end, which gives the burly teenager a porcine aspect. Cornelius throws a powerful arm around Taliah's shoulder. Taliah, trying to peel it off with both hands, says, 'Let go of me.'

'Lovely *griekwa* yah,' remarks Cornelius, strengthening his grip around Taliah's neck.

'*Griekwa*,' says Adam.

'A half-breed bru.'

'Go away,' orders Adam, as Taliah continues to try and pry the powerful arm off her.

'Make me bru, you little pussy,' responds a smirking Cornelius.

'Let go,' says Taliah. 'Please go away.'

Eileen and Thomas are hurrying over.

'Release her now,' orders Eileen. 'Or your gym privileges will be removed.'

'Relax antie,' replies Cornelius, releasing the arm and backing away, muttering in Afrikaans as he does so.

Taliah is becoming increasingly annoyed by Cornelius's unwanted attention since his demotion from the Sunshine Ward last week. The bell is ringing.

'See you later,' says Adam, joining the other patients heading towards the door.

With her group therapy session not due to start for another twenty minutes, Taliah asks Eileen if she can go outside. Eileen agrees. As Taliah walks towards the back of the recreation room, the female contract nurse standing on duty by the door makes eye contact with Eileen. Eileen nods and mouths, 'Yes.' The nurse unlocks both locks and opens the door. Taliah goes through into the garden. The nurse follows. Having locked the door behind her, the nurse sits down on the wooden bench overlooking the garden.

The rays of the warm autumnal sun beam down upon the garden and a breeze rustles the branches of the trees and gently sways the lush green grass at her feet. Taliah looks with wonder at the flowerbeds, an abundance of crocuses, dahlias and nerines. She inhales the aromas swirling in the breeze and listens to the chirping of the birds and the lethargic buzzing of a bumblebee. Ambling around the garden, allowing the sights, scents and sounds to diffuse through her, she sighs contemplatively, then bends down to inspect a crocus.

A dark shadow is cast across the ground. Gazing upwards, she sees a large grey cloud blocking out the sun. The birds stop chirping, the bee ceases buzzing. The garden is silent. To Taliah the dark shadow seems to be bearing down upon her, squashing her. Black, sinister eyes are watching Taliah from the flowerbed.

Taliah, staring back at the grasshopper, gasps. She flees across the long grass, now a surging mass of tentacles, the diabolical clicking of the grasshopper reverberating in her ears. Her clammy hand reaches for the doorknob and pulls it. The door is locked. The contract nurse, fiddling with her bunch of keys, asks in a loud voice, 'Is everything alright?'

'Yes fine,' says Taliah, who then mutters, 'come on come on.'

The door opens. Taliah hurries inside, and then through the recreation room and down the corridor to the women's toilets where she dabs her face with cold water and then stands looking at her reflection in the mirror. Ten minutes later, feeling marginally calmer, she walks into her group therapy session. Pamela, the hospital's head psychotherapist, greets Taliah by name when she enters the room. Taliah takes a seat next to a sixteen-year-old patient called Dwayne.

'Well, where were we?' says Pamela. And then, 'Oh yes, pass the ball please Ishmael.'

Ishmael passes the blue beach ball he is holding to a brown-haired girl. The girl says, 'Therapy has really helped me overcome my drug addiction.'

Taliah, listening to the girl, at the same time observing Robin gnawing on his pencil as if he were a beaver, knows that the person holding the ball is expected to discuss details of their problems and how therapy is helping to overcome them. She wants to get as far away from the ball as possible. Scanning the faces of the teenagers, she mutters their conditions to herself, 'ADD with complications, self-harm, drug addiction, narcissism, abuse at home, schizophrenia.' Taliah is unable to categorise herself.

Dwayne, slouching in the adjoining chair, masticating on a piece of chewing gum, is passed the ball.

'Anything you'd like to share with the group, Dwayne?' ask Pamela in a reassuring voice.

'Yeah awight,' says Dwayne.

Pamela says, 'Please take out the chewing gum.'

Dwayne removes the chewing gum and then looks at the group. He blinks several times.

'Well Dwayne?' asks Pamela.

Attentions turn to Dwayne.

'It started bout four.' Dwayne counts his fingers, then says, 'Nah five years ago innit.'

Pamela nods.

'I was in the garden with me brother playing football and that. Mum was putting clothes on the line.' Dwayne falls momentarily silent before continuing. 'It was hot like, cause it was summertime. Mum was wearing a vest thing innit, and on her shoulder like, she had this big fuckoff swastika.'

'A what?' asks Pamela.

'*Swastika.*'

'Oh,' says Pamela.

'Neighbour seen it, started screaming about the war and that. Then Social Services come innit.'

As Dwayne explains how this event culminated in his family being torn apart, and a descent into a life of abuse and self-harm, he has the room's attention, even Robin, who is holding the chewed remnants of his pencil in his quivering hand. Taliah, nibbling on the nail of her little finger, listens too, at the same time trying to decide what she will say.

Dwayne dabs his eyes with a tissue, his voice now trembling as he outlines the abuse he had endured whilst in care. One of the nurses standing guard at the back of the room approaches Dwayne and places a reassuring hand on his shoulder. Taliah stares at the blue ball poised to be passed to her. She holds her breath. Robin starts arguing with a boy sitting behind him. A fracas ensues. By the time the fracas has been pacified and Robin carried off in the direction of the male acute ward, the session is over. Taliah emits a sigh of relief.

Talulah is in her cell, lying on her back on the bed, looking up at the ceiling. All is quiet on the ward, the self-harmer having recently been promoted to the Violet Ward and the devil worshipper in the neighbouring cell having been successfully sedated. With the quiet and the recent decrease in her Symbyax dose, Talulah finds her thoughts are gaining clarity. In her mind's eye she pictures all the rooms and facilities she was shown on Dr Singh's tour of the hospital. Talulah imagines herself being in all these places with her twin.

Footsteps are approaching. A key turns in the lock. The door opens. Clara and Maria are standing in the doorway. They are smiling.

'Are you ready darling?' It is Clara who asks this.

Talulah, standing up, says, 'I am ready.'

The two nurses walk alongside Talulah out of the ward and down the corridors. Eileen is waiting at the door of the Violet Ward. When Talulah approaches, she says, 'Hello Talulah,' and then, 'quick quick.'

Eileen ushers Talulah to her new room. Her possessions are stacked in bags on the bed. Eileen closes the blind. She says, 'Hide behind the bed, I'll turn the lights out.'

Talulah crouches on the floor behind the bed. A minute passes, then another. Faint voices are audible from the passageway outside. The door opens slightly, then a little more. Taliah's head appears in the gap. The lights turn on. Eileen, who is standing behind Taliah, shouts 'SURPRISE!'

Taliah blinks several times. She sees a chubbier version of herself with unkempt hair, looking back at her with hazel eyes identical to her own.

'Congratulations,' says Eileen, 'you're reunited.'

Taliah edges towards Talulah, assisted by Eileen's hand pushing her lower back. Maria, Clara and two other nurses enter the room. They congratulate Talulah and Taliah on their reunion. Taliah swallows. She feels a tear stream down her cheek, then another.

'Tears of joy,' remarks one of the nurses.

'Dey need time together,' says Maria.

'Of course, everyone out,' orders Eileen, who then says, 'your mother is going to be so happy.'

Talulah and Taliah are alone in the room. Talulah says, 'Mene oomi ucki go meme geda – urrie.'

Chapter Thirteen

TWO WEEKS LATER – 'Pepa mene im,' says Talulah.

Taliah reaches across the table, picks up the pepper mill and passes it to Talulah, who says, 'Fow umi bage ucki.'

Taliah nods. Noticing that her glass is empty, she says, 'Pass me the water please?'

Talulah pushes the plastic jug of water further along the table, away from Taliah.

Taliah says, 'Oter drinki meou im.'

Talulah picks up the jug of water and placing it gently down beside her twin, says, 'Oter dinki – ango budbud wedi.'

Talulah and Taliah sit alone at the table, raising their dessert spoons to their mouths and tentatively nibbling on the pieces of mango at the exact same time as one another. Lucy is sitting on her own at the table directly in front, her back to the twins. Taliah, watching Lucy spooning mango into her mouth, knows that prior to Talulah's arrival two weeks ago, Lucy would have sat down on the same table as her. Now when Taliah wanders over to the radiator in the recreation room, she finds that Lucy is no longer talkative, offering only terse, concise statements, concern dominating confusion, as she casts nervous glances at Talulah, who is usually standing next to her sister.

Robin, the solitary occupant of the table in front of Lucy's, is spooning mango into his mouth at such a frenetic pace, pieces are spilling onto his tracksuit top. Even from where they sit Taliah can hear the metal spoon colliding with his teeth. Ten days ago, Robin, five minutes removed from his stint on the male acute ward, had scurried into the recreation room at mid-morning break. He had screamed when he saw a carbon copy of Taliah standing next to her. So hysterical had Robin become that he was returned to the acute ward. Taliah notices Robin casting frequent agitated glances over his shoulder in her and her twin's direction.

At the table nearest the door, Adam is in animated conversation with Tracey and Sunita, a recent arrival on the ward. Taliah longs to explain to Adam why she only mentioned her twin the day before Talulah's arrival, but this has proven difficult as she is nearly always chaperoned by the shadow that is Talulah. Having finished her mango, she peers down at the liquid in the base of her bowl, as if somewhere in its murky depths lurks a solution to her woes.

Roberta, one of the contract nurses, is strolling through the canteen. As she approaches the twins' table, Talulah says, 'Good evening Roberta, how are you?'

'Evening T-T,' replies Roberta, checking the colour of the hairband securing Talulah's ponytail, worn in the exact same fashion as Taliah, only Talulah's hairband is blue, Taliah's pink. 'T-Ta-*lulah*, I'm good thanks. How's the mango?'

'We like it,' says Talulah.

'That's good. See you later.'

When Roberta has departed, Talulah spits out, 'Ucki bobothi gyal bothi.'

Dinner ends soon after and the teenagers, one at a time, file through the metal detector and out of the canteen. Taliah follows Talulah through to the recreation room, where they sit on the sofa watching the Trivial Pursuit type game show on the television.

A few minutes have passed when Talulah stands up, crosses the room and starts a conversation with Betty, a seventeen-year-old fetishist, whose fetishisms society has deemed to be not conducive with liberty. Taliah remains on the sofa. Observing the two of them, Taliah is certain that Talulah has uttered more words in English in the two weeks since she was released from the acute ward than in her whole life prior to that. It has not escaped Taliah's notice that the vast majority of this talking has taken place with the most unfortunate patients, and always when there are staff members within earshot.

Taliah can feel the tension between her and Talulah even now, sitting some metres away from her. On the outside the tension between them was always broken by an argument, but in here, where any such behaviour could result in a return to the acute ward, it only builds. Taliah, watching Talulah, knows all their unresolved issues will come to a head only on their release from the hospital. It occurs to her that Talulah is still not aware that she knows she read her diary. And then there are all the other unresolved issues – Siegfried, anarchism, the fires and above all, the direction their lives are to take.

The door opens. Hubert enters the room. Several patients clap. Tracey and the Jocular Self-Mutilator stop playing table tennis and chant, 'Paedo, paedo.'

Hubert's cadaverous cheeks are tinged with red. He takes a deep bow. The chanting continues. Thomas, who is standing on duty by the door, calls out, 'Tracey, Jerome, stop.'

The pair stop chanting. Taliah watches Hubert traipse languidly across the room, sees him look right at her and then left at Talulah. He bends forward, holds his knees and laughs. Hubert then stands up straight, sweeping the lank locks of greasy black hair from his face as he does so. Having only been released from his latest stint on the male acute ward earlier today, Hubert has not seen Talulah until now. Talulah, having noticed Hubert, is walking back towards her twin. Hubert approaches Talulah, leans towards her, sniffs and says, 'Good evening Miss Sucky Sucky.'

Talulah, crossing her arms across her chest, scowls at Hubert. Hubert backs away. Talulah whispers in Taliah's ear, 'Meou hubert inna derdand.'

'Ea,' replies Taliah.

'Fidla kiddi.'

'Ea.'

Taliah is walking away from Talulah. Talulah, sensing that the events Hubert alluded to have angered her twin, resists the urge to follow her.

*

In class Taliah sits at the desk behind Talulah as she always did in school. Sometimes Taliah answers questions in class. When she does, Talulah's hand invariably shoots up in the air the moment the teacher asks the next question, regardless of whether she knows the answer. Talulah always attempts to avoid s sounds in her responses, but with her continued improvements in speech therapy, she is confident enough to utter relatively well-formed s's as and when the occasion demands. Taliah often senses Talulah's anticipation that they could be released from the hospital in the not too distant future. This anticipation does not permeate Taliah, but rather hangs in the air between them, as if it were mist or a cloud.

Taliah relishes the solitude of her room at night. She does not want to return home to share a room with her twin again. Sometimes she considers confronting Talulah about this, but she feels powerless to prevent the ominous sense of fate that has enveloped her. At other times it occurs to her that she might feign insanity in order to remain here in the hospital, but reflecting on her previous existence in the acute ward, she is loath to. And she is only too aware that Talulah would follow her, choosing incarceration alongside her in the hospital, ahead of freedom alone in the outside world.

*

It is now mid-afternoon and Talulah and Taliah are in the hospital library, seated in adjoining chairs, each clasping a book in their right hand. Taliah's book is *Mansfield Park* by Jane Austen, Talulah's is *The 7 Habits of Highly Effective People: Powerful Lessons in Personal Change* by Stephen R. Covey. Pamela, the psychotherapist, is walking through the library, holding a precariously high pile of books. Talulah tilts her book towards the approaching Pamela, so that she is able to see what she is reading.

'Hello girls,' greets Pamela as she passes them.

'Hello Pamela,' respond Talulah and Taliah in unison, looking up from their respective books at exactly the same time.

'I'll get the door,' says Taliah, standing up, going over to the door and opening it.

'Thank you, Ta.'

'Taliah.'

'Thank you Taliah.'

When Taliah sits down, Talulah frowns. The door opens. Cornelius enters the library. Noticing the sisters, he comes gallivanting towards them. He says, 'Greetings *griekwa* twins.'

Cornelius, having been demoted again, after another short stint on the Sunshine Ward, has already seen Talulah and Taliah together a number of times, but has not until now had the opportunity to get close and personal. Cornelius throws a powerful arm around each of their necks and pulls them to him. Talulah, twisting her head glares at Cornelius. She says, 'Ugly piggy.'

Cornelius's sanguine complexion pales. He recoils, collides with a bookshelf. A male patient points at him and laughs. Cornelius, now retreating at a trot, is muttering about his latest weight lifting exploits, but his voice is hesitant and carries none of its usual certainty. The bell is ringing.

Taliah follows Talulah out of the library and along the corridor to the art centre, where they have a scheduled group art therapy session. Talulah sits down at the table and Taliah goes over to the pigeonholes on the other side of the room where the students store their artwork. Taliah pulls out her pile of pictures from her pigeonhole. One of the pictures falls to the ground. She quickly bends down and picks it up, then glances at Talulah, who is sitting in her chair staring impassively ahead at the wall in front of her. Turning her back to Talulah, Taliah wistfully examines the charcoal drawing she is holding. The outline of two girls are standing side by side, the sun beaming down on one of them, a grey storm cloud poised above the other, discharging its burden upon her. Taliah reflects on the previous occasion she had drawn such a picture. It was when she was a little girl. She had given the picture to her father.

'Nothing's changed,' mutters Taliah to herself. 'I was crying out for understanding back then too.'

The picture is inserted back into the pigeonhole. Taliah, clasping her remaining pictures, makes her way over to the table. Adam is sitting at the far end bent over his drawing, a graphite pencil held in his hand. Taliah takes a seat next to Adam. Even from here she can feel her twin's contempt. Taliah watches Adam putting the finishing touches to a portrait of a gun-toting Willem Dafoe. Taliah thinks the drawing is a scene from *Platoon*, a film she had seen with Talulah a few years ago.

Nearly half an hour has passed when there is the shrill of a ringing telephone. A moment later Mr Potts calls out, '*Talulah.*' He then looks from Taliah to Talulah and back again. Talulah lifts her hand in the air. Mr Potts strides over to her and crouching down, says in a quiet voice, 'It is time for your speech therapy session.'

Talulah gets up and leaves the room. Several minutes have passed when Adam says to Taliah, 'You want to escape from her don't you?'

Taliah makes a barely perceptible nod of her head.

*

The following month – Talulah and Taliah are standing next to each other watching the disorderly queue of patients, waiting impatiently to gain admission to the shop. Talulah, thinking about roast beef flavoured Monster Munch crisps, Bakewell Tarts, jam doughnuts and Jaffa Cakes, all of which are stocked by the shop, licks her lips, imagining that she is tasting these treats and not the lip gloss that adorns them. The shop does not sell Petits Filous. Talulah does not join the queue for she knows that Taliah will not follow her. The same food items are also tempting Taliah, but her tongue does not emerge from her mouth and the temptation is only fleeting. Ignoring Talulah's lingering snack infatuation, Taliah examines the queuing patients. After all this time in the hospital Taliah is able to recognise the characteristics of those who are destined to spend their adult lives in institutions – the perpetual grey pallor of the dependent, those revealing scar and abscess ridden forearms, and the fat entombed.

'I don't want to be like them,' mutters Taliah to herself, before abruptly turning her head to the left and looking through the windows at the far end of the room, at the garden, bathed in the meek early winter sunlight. Talulah is watching Taliah.

Eileen, tall and elegant, is striding across the room.

'Morning,' greets Eileen enthusiastically. 'Ta-lulah, are you okay to see Dr Singh now, I know it's ten minutes earlier than scheduled, but something has come up and he has to finish early.'

Eileen looks from Taliah to Talulah and back again.

Talulah says, 'Okay fine, I will go there now.'

'Great,' says Eileen. 'I'm sorry to split you two up during your break time.'

And then Eileen is walking away, Talulah ambling behind her towards the door. Even now Talulah is gone, Tracey, Lucy and Robin, who are in the queue for the shop, do not acknowledge Taliah. Taliah wonders if they even know that it is her standing here and not her twin.

In his office, Dr Singh observes Talulah, sitting upright in her chair, hands clasped in her lap, her mouth forming a perfect horizontal line across her attractive, oval-shaped face, in the exact same manner Taliah does when she has her psychiatry sessions here. Talulah's lips are painted with pink lip gloss, there is a dab of rouge on her high cheekbones, her long eyelashes have been tinted, her hair, now highlighted, has been brushed straight and tied behind her head. She is wearing tight blue Calvin Klein jeans and a pink, cotton, long sleeve top that accentuate her now slim figure, a result of the changes in her medication, avoidance of the snack shop and regular aerobics and gym sessions, accompanied by her twin. Talulah's nails are impeccably manicured, painted with pink nail varnish and decorated with tiny silver hearts. It occurs to Dr Singh that Talulah and Taliah have never looked so alike. The only visible difference between the two of them now is that Talulah's hair is tied with a blue hairband, while Taliah's, since the arrival of her twin on the Violet Ward, is always secured with a pink hairband or hairbands, depending on how they are wearing their hair that day.

'Would you read this please Talulah?' says Dr Singh, passing a small booklet across the desk. 'Read it to yourself and I'll ask you about it in a bit. I'd be interested to hear what you think. It's about community awareness.'

Talulah, picking the booklet up says, 'Okay, I will do.'

'Did you enjoy the badminton yesterday?' asks Dr Singh, studying Talulah from the other side of the desk.

'I enjoyed the badminton.'

'Yes, I enjoyed the badminton.'

'Ye-s I enjoyed the badminton,' repeats Talulah.

'That's good,' says Dr Singh.

Yesterday Dr Singh had seen Talulah and Taliah engaged in a fierce badminton match in the garden. Talulah turns her attention to the booklet and Dr Singh makes notes on a pad on the desk in front of him, surreptitiously watching Talulah out of the corner of his eye. Like many of the other hospital staff he had begun to inadvertently view Talulah and Taliah as being two parts of a whole, but now as he leans forward at his desk making notes, he reflects on the markedly different results in their perception tests. A number of Talulah's responses had shown an emotional detachment and there was insecurity evident in others, this in contrast to Taliah, whose answers were empathetic and consistent. When taken in conjunction with Talulah's left slanted handwriting – handwriting analysts deem left slanting writing as signifying insecurity, a lack of spontaneity and emotional distance – Dr Singh deems the test results to be revealing. Noticing the smirk making a fleeting appearance on Talulah's face, the psychiatrist wonders if it is a manifestation of genuine amusement or scorn. He suspects the latter.

*

Half an hour later – the car draws to a halt outside the hospital entrance. The eminent psychiatrist, Dr Hunter-Thornton, takes a comb from the inside pocket of his blazer and proceeds to comb the long, sparse hairs on the top of his head to one side, examining his reflection in the rear view mirror as he does so. He then disembarks from the car, locks the door behind him and treads slowly towards the entrance. At the entrance he takes a deep breath as he waits for the reinforced door to be opened. Once inside he hands his briefcase to one of the two security guards who places it on the x-ray machine's conveyor belt. Then, having stepped through the metal detector, he grabs the briefcase the moment it emerges from the machine. The guard who took his briefcase says, 'Thank you.'

Hunter-Thornton, now scanning the empty interior of the hall with bloodshot, heavily bagged eyes, comes to Beddington House Hospital from time to time to lead training sessions for the hospital's psychiatric team. The ageing psychiatrist is acutely aware that his former charges, The Silent Twins, are patients here.

He has not visited the hospital since their incarceration. Hunter-Thornton has not laid eyes on the twins since suffering his heart attack in their presence all those years ago, but he had taken a keen interest in their court case. Having studied his file on Talulah and Taliah, Hunter-Thornton has reached the conclusion that the prosecution's diagnosis of *folie simultanée* had been incorrect. Footsteps are approaching. Hunter-Thornton holds his breath, the briefcase trembles in his hand. Pamela, the head psychotherapist, emerging from the passageway to the right of the hall, calls out, 'Dr Hunter-Thornton! Welcome, how are you?'

'Middling my dear.'

The pair walk through the hall and then turn left. Pamela, noticing Hunter-Thornton looking agitatedly around, stifles a giggle. She never ceases to be amused by the peculiar, pompous antics of the ageing psychiatrist, but is careful not to show her amusement, wary of his notoriously short temper.

'I hear you met Felix, our trainee therapist, at one of your seminars,' says Pamela, turning her smiling countenance towards her guest. 'He's nice isn't he?'

'Polite, presentable, punctilious,' responds Hunter-Thornton before glancing over his shoulder.

Two female patients are approaching from the opposite direction. Hunter-Thornton stops, holds a hand up to his eyebrows and peers down the corridor at them.

'Is everything alright?' asks Pamela, waiting for the flagging psychiatrist to catch up with her.

'Splendiferous,' he replies sarcastically.

They have only gone a short way along the passage when Hunter-Thornton stops, lifts a hand to his eyebrows again and scrutinises the boy and girl approaching along the corridor towards him. His bloodshot eyes open wide and his mouth too, revealing a filling-clustered interior. Hunter-Thornton turns and walks away at haste in the direction from whence he came.

'Wherever are you going?' asks a bemused Pamela, who thinks

she hears him muttering something French sounding as he breaks into a trot. Adam and Taliah are passing her when she calls out, 'Come back.'

Hunter-Thornton, breathing heavily, his jowls quivering, hurries on. A few metres in front of him to his right a door opens. Talulah emerges into the corridor. A crimson-faced Hunter-Thornton, a hand held to his heart, lurches to his left and rushes towards the hall, calling out, '*Folie à deux,*' as he goes. He slips on the hall's marble floor, crashes forward to the ground – a tasselled loafer flies off his foot, the briefcase slides along the floor. Having hauled himself off the ground, he grabs the briefcase, turns in the opposite direction to collect the shoe, sees Talulah enter the hall behind him, abandons the shoe and rushes for the exit, screaming, '*FOLIE á DEUX!*'

Taliah, Pamela and Adam enter the hall. The psychiatrist jumps up and down as he waits for the security guard to unbolt and unlock the door.

'*FOLIE á DEUX!*' he shouts as he flees from the hospital.

Talulah and Taliah join the security guards looking through the big barred window at the one-shoed psychiatrist scrambling towards his car, then clambering into it and accelerating away.

As the amused security guards return to their positions and a bemused Pamela and Robin depart the hall, Taliah, turning to her sister, opens her mouth to speak. Talulah, pre–empting what she is going to say, says, 'Wuthiwuthi derriii ugi bothi baldi hunter thornton.'

Talulah laughs and Taliah too, the shrill sound reverberating through the hall. It is quite some time before they have composed themselves enough to walk away. When they do their arms and legs move in time with one another. In the corridor they commence giggling at the exact same moment, giggling that escalates into raucous, unrestrained laughter. Although they compose themselves, they are convulsed in mirth once more on entering the classroom. The room's occupants watch the laughing pair wiping the tears from their eyes with their sleeves. Thomas, who is on sentry duty, leaning against the whiteboard, chuckles aloud, his soul for so long weighed down by the plight of his troubled charges, temporarily lightened. Beneath his furrowed forehead, Hubert's dark eyes dart from one twin to the other, bewildered by the peculiar pair, whom he has been acquainted with for all these years, now immersed in unrestrained mirth for no apparent reason. Robin, having ceased his frenetic scampering, stands still as a statue, gawping at the twins, whilst Tracey sits at her desk, her doughnut-crammed mouth agape.

It is only when the maths teacher enters the room that the amusement over the Hunter-Thornton episode and the memories it has evoked begin to subside. Sitting at her desk behind her twin, listening to the maths teacher at the front of the class, and Robin at the desk beside her gnawing on his pencil, Taliah contemplates the words the psychiatrist was screaming so vehemently – *folie à deux*. Remembering the prosecution's *folie simultanée* argument during their trial, she assumes that Hunter-Thornton's words must be his explanation for the events that culminated in her and Talulah's rampage that day, an event that she continues to have only a vague memory of. Talulah does not dwell on Hunter-Thornton's words, assuming them to be nothing more than his customary pomposities, she and her twin had become so accustomed to during their visits to Hunter-Thornton Integrated Counselling Services all those years ago.

It is now dinner time and Talulah and Taliah are in the canteen, alone at a table, inserting forkfuls of stodgy sweet and sour pork balls and rice into their mouths. It occurs to both of them that their dinner is probably not beneficial for their svelte figures, but they try not to dwell on this. Taliah, observing her twin on the other side of the table, prodding at a sweet and sour pork ball with her fork, and now making an unctuous comment to a passing staff member, feels quite certain that Hunter-Thornton's words have not even registered with her. Taliah hides the *folie à deux* thought in the deepest recesses of her mind, wary not to alert Talulah to it. For though Taliah does not know what *folie à deux* is, she does not want her twin to think that she is considering that mental illness did lead to their detainment here, and specifically that she is considering that it was Talulah's mental illness.

That night lying on their backs in their beds in their respective rooms, their hands clasped behind their heads, Talulah and Taliah are in pensive frames of mind. Talulah, reflecting briefly on the Hunter-Thornton episode earlier that day giggles. She does not think about the words he uttered. Next she ponders what life will be like in Serenity, this being the name of the hospital's third female ward. Soon after she falls asleep.

Taliah, inspecting the contours of the portrait of Willem Dafoe, finds herself contemplating Hunter-Thornton's words again. Although she views the psychiatrist as an object of ridicule, she remains keen to explore anything that might shed light on the events of the day that culminated in her and her twin's detention. Even here, removed from her twin by several thick walls, she is fearful that Talulah might somehow discover her thought. Taliah is aware from her French studies that *folie à deux* means something to the effect of madness of two, but she knows nothing more, and in the absence of the internet, which is permitted only in Serenity, she cannot discover the definition of the term.

*

Bethany is the first to pass through the metal detector. She grabs her handbag from the conveyor belt, rushes over to her daughters and pulls them to her.

'It's so good to see you,' she says, her eyes moist with tears.

'Hello Mum,' respond Talulah and Taliah in unison, as Bethany, clutching their necks, delivers kisses to their cheeks.

'Here at last. It's been a while. How are you?' says Colin, kissing first Taliah on the cheek and then Talulah.

'We're fine,' say Talulah and Taliah at the same time as one another.

'It's so good to see you both together again,' says Bethany. 'You look great, you've lost weight.'

Colin nods in agreement. Eileen enters the hall, greets the family and then leads them down a passageway to the right of the hall, to a small room, where she informs them that they have half an hour together. She then leaves the room. The family cluster around the table, sipping tea from Styrofoam cups and nibbling on digestive biscuits and custard creams. Although Bethany and Colin have visited the hospital before, this is the first time they have been permitted to see Talulah and Taliah together.

'I can't wait for you to come home, your room is just as you left it,' says Bethany.

'Really, that-s good, we're ec-s-tatic to hear it,' says Talulah.

Bethany starts clapping. She says, 'Your s's Talulah, dey're … *amazing.*'

Talulah is grinning. Colin says, 'I'm very impressed Talulah. Evidently the speech therapists in here are better than the ones I spent thousands on.'

Bethany's hazel eyes fix on Colin, who lowering his cup to the table, says, 'So, anything new?'

Taliah opens her mouth to speak, but before she is able to utter any words, Talulah says, 'Art, therapy and trying to catch up with our A level s-ubject-s.'

Taliah, taking a gulp of tea, watches her mother clap, and now her father too. Talulah is grinning again. Several minutes have passed when Colin, making eye contact with Taliah, says, 'How are your friends here getting along?'

'They are fine,' replies Taliah. 'Adam, Lucy and…'

'They are not important,' intrudes Talulah forcefully. 'We are together again, which i-s the main thing.'

'Yes it's wonderful,' says Bethany, reaching across the table and clasping Talulah's left hand and Taliah's right.

Bethany and Talulah are looking at Taliah. Taliah forces a smile.

And so the meeting continues with Bethany and Colin repeatedly congratulating Talulah on her s's and impressive vocal output, and Talulah speaking before Taliah has a chance to, or on the few occasions she doesn't, finishing her sentences for her. Taliah, feeling dominated by her twin, wishes she were alone in her room on the Violet Ward.

Chapter Fourteen

THE FOLLOWING WEEK – as the kitchen staff scurry from table to table checking that the same number of knives, forks and spoons are on the tables as at the start of breakfast, the queuing teenagers, waiting to pass through the metal detector, chatter amongst themselves, several to themselves.

Lucy joins the queue. Taliah, turning to her, says, 'Morning Lucy.'

'.hailaT gninroM'

Taliah is about to ask Lucy about her forthcoming day when Talulah, pulling at her sleeve, says, 'Gyal ucki dunci.'

To Taliah, waiting behind Talulah in the queue, it seems that Talulah is taller than she has even been before and stronger too, that her fierce temperament, temporarily dulled by medication, is re–inflating as her medication is reduced.

Doctor Vitali is dashing up and down the queue greeting patients in an enthusiastic tone.

'Morning Sam, like the T-shirt. Hello Lucy. Hubert hey, what's up? Ahmed, hi. Cornelius you've been working out again dude.' And then striding up to the most recent arrival on the male intermediate ward, Taran, he says, 'Hey what's up?'

'Get out of my personal space bruv,' replies Taran.

Dr Vitali steps back. Taliah sees him whispering something in Thomas's ear that she cannot hear, but she suspects is an order for a change to be made to Taran's medication. Dr Vitali approaches Talulah and Taliah, frenzied eyes flitting from one to the other.

'Morning twi, um girls,' he says, and then leaning forward towards them, he adds in a quiet voice, 'you're doing great, promotion coming soon.'

Taliah tries to smile, fails.

'Thank you, have a wonderful day,' says Talulah.

'Ingratiating bitch,' utters a female voice from the back of the queue.

Talulah passes through the metal detector, followed by Taliah. Eileen walks over. She says, 'Ta-liah, you remember your psychiatry session is now. Afterwards, please come back to the ward. I'll be waiting for you.'

Taliah says, 'I will do.'

'It's so hard to tell you two apart sometimes,' says Eileen before walking away.

Taliah leaves Talulah and goes to Dr Singh's office, where she sits upright in her chair, her hands clasped in her lap, the psychiatrist on the other side of the desk inspecting her studiously, a biro protruding from his mouth. The only sounds are the ticking of the wall clock and the intermittent footsteps emanating from the passageway outside.

'How are you getting on with your medication?' asks Dr Singh.

'Fine thank you.'

'We'll be looking to reduce them soon.'

Taliah nods.

'And how are things with your twin?'

'Okay.'

Dr Singh, noting the hesitation in her tone, asks in a reassuring voice, 'Your relationship with Talulah, is it … good?'

Taliah nods again, smiles faintly.

Dr Singh scrutinises Taliah, tapping the index finger of his right hand against the surface of his desk as he does so. He is becoming increasingly convinced that Taliah and Talulah's symbiotic relationship is a strained one, the details of which are a secret between them.

'Are you sure everything is fine between you? Now is the time to resolve any issues … we're here to help.'

Taliah opens her mouth then closes it again.

'Would you like a lollipop?' asks Dr Singh, breaking the silence.

'Yes please.'

Dr Singh pushes the pot of lollipops at the end of his desk towards Taliah. He watches intrigued as she selects a lemon-flavoured one, this being the same flavour that her twin selected in her last session here. Taliah delicately unwraps the lollipop and puts it in her mouth. Dr Singh leans back in his chair. He says, 'You must be really looking forward to being promoted to Serenity.'

Normally when Dr Singh mentions the prospect of promotion to his patients they appear excited, but Taliah merely bows her head and looks down at the floor, the lollipop gripped between her teeth.

'In Serenity you have your own room key. There's internet, games consoles, films and a kitchen,' says Dr Singh.

Taliah is now looking straight ahead, her eyes expressionless, her mouth forming a horizontal line. Dr Singh considers it significant that this is in stark contrast to Talulah, who seemed excited about the prospect of promotion. He rotates his biro in his fingertips and then out of habit, asks, 'Any questions?' Taliah never asks questions.

'What does *folie à deux* mean?'

'*Folie à* what?' says Dr Singh.

'*Folie à deux.*'

Dr Singh wonders not only why Taliah is asking this, but also where she has come across the term, when even he, an experienced psychiatrist, has only heard mention of this extremely rare psychiatric syndrome on a handful of occasions.

Drumming his fingers against the desk, he ponders where Taliah might have come across the term. Then he remembers that when Talulah had left his office after a session not so long ago, that sanctimonious old psychiatrist, who occasionally comes to lead training sessions, had shouted out something French sounding starting with *folie*. Dr Singh hadn't been able to make out the rest. He assumes this must be where Taliah heard it. Dr Singh says, 'Well it is a um, it sort of translates into English as a … madness of two.'

Dr Singh, unsure as to exactly how to phrase the rest of his response, reaches for his keyboard, opens his internet browser and types the term into *Google*. He knows he should not be discussing things of this nature with a patient but, looking across the desk at Taliah's pretty face and pleading eyes, he feels obliged to at least answer her question in part, this being the only question she has ever asked. He sighs then looks at the screen. There is a pause.

'*Folie à deux* can be translated as a madness shared by two. It is an extremely rare condition, in which an individual suffering from a … a mental illness, gives, well infects, their partner, with, the … delusional beliefs.'

Dr Singh is about to read the next bit aloud, which states how identical twins are likely to be particularly susceptible to this due to their uniquely close relationship, but stops himself just in time. The session draws to a speedy conclusion.

As soon as Taliah leaves, Dr Singh rushes back to the computer. When he finishes reading the article about *folie à deux*, he surmises that it appears to provide a more adequate explanation for the twins' bizarre rampage than the *folie simultanée* diagnosis presented by the prosecution at Talulah and Taliah's trial, a diagnosis he had thought to be correct. But now in the context of his dealings with the twins, and the differing results in their perception tests, he considers that *folie à deux* makes more sense. He feels quite certain which twin was and maybe still is suffering from the delusional beliefs. On reaching this conclusion Dr Singh hits his forehead with the palm of his hand.

After the session Taliah traipses up and down the hospital corridors, deep in thought about what Dr Singh has just told her. Twenty minutes have now passed and Taliah is still pensively traipsing up and down. Eileen is hurrying down the corridor towards her.

'There you are, I've been looking everywhere for you. You forgot you were to supposed to meet me after your psychiatry session in the ward.'

A minute later – there is a granite effect, kitchen utensil laden worktop running the length of one side of the small, windowless room. The worktop has two gas rings and two basins built into it. Prior to being escorted here Talulah was told that she was having an impromptu home economics class, home economics being an integral part in preparing the hospital's teenage charges for their eventual release. Unlike the other home economics classes Talulah has attended, there are no other patients present. There are however three staff members – Thomas, Roberta and another female nurse, whose name she does not know. Roberta is nibbling furtively on a fingernail whilst the other female nurse shifts her weight continuously from one foot to the other. Talulah is suspicious. Before she came here she was preoccupied with thinking about what her twin was up to in her one-to-one psychiatry session, but now her current situation has her full attention.

The door opens. Eileen enters the room, followed by Taliah, who puts all thoughts of *folie à deux* out of her mind the moment she sees Talulah. Taliah senses Talulah's perplexity. Having scanned the room she appreciates why. Eileen departs. Colleen, the hospital's part-time home economics teacher, enters the room.

'Hello twins,' greets Colleen in characteristic jovial fashion. 'Okay, so today we're going to make pasta. Do you know any of the steps for making pasta?'

'We don't know how to make handmade pas-ta.' It is Talulah who says this.

'Oh now let's not get ahead of ourselves,' says Colleen. 'We are going to be making pasta out of a packet. Do you have any idea how to do that?'

'Boil a pan of water with s-alt in it,' says Talulah.

'Put the pasta in the boiling water,' adds Taliah.

'Read back of packet for cooking in-s-truction-s,' says Talulah.

'Periodically taste pasta. When okay turn off heat and put pasta in a sieve, over a sink of course,' adds Taliah.

'*Voila*, pa-s-ta ready,' says Talulah.

Colleen claps enthusiastically. She says, 'Wonderful, you must really like pasta.'

'No, it-s a carbohydrate. Carbohydrate i-s fattening, if you eat it you retain water and look fat,' says Talulah gravely.

Taliah thinks that her twin should not have said this, considering Colleen's physique. But Colleen's chubby visage shows no sign of discomfort.

'As you can see there are two stoves so you can both make your own pasta,' says Colleen.

'No, we want to do it together,' says Talulah.

'It's important that we know you can both do it,' says Colleen in a patronising tone. She then instructs the twins to go to the fridge in the corner of the room and take out a jar of tomato pasta sauce. Talulah goes to the fridge first and takes out the required item, after which Taliah does the same. Talulah and Taliah place their jars of sauce on the worktop. Colleen says, 'Okay are ready? You have fifteen minutes.'

Talulah and Taliah nod in unison with one another.

'Go,' says Colleen.

Talulah and Taliah fill their saucepans with water. Colleen passes a box of matches to each of them with a trembling hand. Indicating with a quivering, tubby finger, she says, 'Turn on the gas there and then hold the match to it.'

Talulah hurriedly extracts a match and strikes it.

'You're going to burn your finger,' remarks Colleen.

Talulah, ogling the flame, is oblivious to her words.

'T-T-Ta...' says Colleen.

'Talulah,' interjects Thomas from the other side of the room.

Talulah blows out the flame, puts the burnt remnant on the worktop, strikes another match, turns on the gas and holds it to the ring.

Only now does Taliah strike a match. She hears someone gasp behind her. Having turned on the gas she holds the match to the gas ring. Instantaneously there is a circle of bluish fire. Neither twin has seen fire since their arrival at Beddington House. As the water comes slowly to the boil, Taliah reads the instructions on the back of her packet of pasta and then inspects some of the kitchen utensils on the worktop. Talulah's gaze never leaves the ring of flame.

Thirteen minutes later – Colleen, chewing on a piece of Taliah's pasta, remarks, 'I like *al dente*.' And then, '*Al dente* means that it is still firm. It is Italian.' Colleen goes over to Talulah, impales a piece of pasta with her fork and puts it in her mouth. She chews on it for quite some time. Her jovial expression evaporates. She says, 'A bit squidgy.'

Talulah was gazing so intently at the blue flame that she lost track of time and overcooked her pasta.

'Oh,' says Colleen in a loud voice, 'we just have to go outside, we'll be back in a minute.'

Colleen and the three nurses leave the room. Exactly a minute has passed when they come back in. The class ends soon after and Talulah and Taliah leave the room and head downstairs for their scheduled biology class. The moment the door closes behind them, Colleen seizes the box of matches from beside the gas ring Taliah had been using and hurriedly counts the contents. She then does the same with Talulah's box. After which she exclaims jubilantly, 'They're all here!'

The door opens. Eileen walks in followed by Dr Vitali.

'Well, how did it go?' It is Eileen who says this.

'Fine,' replies Colleen. 'They passed.'

'I told you they would pass,' says Eileen.

'Did you count the matches?' asks Dr Vitali.

'Yes,' says Colleen.

'Twice?' says Dr Vitali.

'Twice,' says Colleen.

Thomas and Roberta glance at each other. It did not escape their notice that Talulah appeared mesmerised by the flaming gas ring.

Chapter Fifteen

SERENITY IS ON the hospital's second floor. Its female residents share their facilities with their male contemporaries in the Sunshine Ward. The inhabitants of Serenity and Sunshine have their own keys to their rooms. The rooms have thinner bars on the windows than those in the Violet Ward and the male equivalent. There is a kitchen boasting a kettle, toaster and metal cutlery, though the knives are of the type one finds on aeroplanes – small and rather blunt. The recreation room has a television and several internet booths. Here teenagers are to be found slumped in front of the television, PlayStation controller in hand, munching on crisps and chocolate, conversing with one another, and perusing magazines and books, in a manner no different than their contemporaries on the outside, only here alcohol and smoking are prohibited, and the only drugs to be found are those prescribed by Dr Vitali.

There is no relentless scampering here, no speech uttered in reverse, and no obvious sign of patients afflicted by paraphilias or other severe personality disorders. This is not to say that these teenage boys and girls do not have their idiosyncrasies, but nothing that would cause more than a raised eyebrow on the other side of the perimeter fence.

Taliah is in the recreation room. She is sitting at a coffee table opposite Fraser. They are playing chess. Fraser is being flirtatious.

Taliah, appreciating the attention from one of the hospital's best looking patients, giggles intermittently. The door opens. Talulah walks through it. She strides across the room, ticking behavioural virtues as she goes — confidence, emotional balance, friendliness, and now empathy, as she crouches down to converse with Magnus, a seventeen-year-old whose torment over his physical disabilities led to a mental breakdown and his detention here. The two staff members present observe Talulah do this, as they did the other virtues she has just displayed.

Striding over to the coffee table, Talulah draws up a stool and sits down next to her twin, pressing her body against hers. Fraser, holding a hand to his chiselled chin, briefly ponders his next move before pushing his bishop diagonally three spaces to the left. Taliah responds rather unwisely by moving a pawn forward. When she does this Fraser compliments her nails. Taliah appreciates the compliment, as does Talulah, for she believes that it is directed at her too, for how could it not be when her fingernails are also immaculately manicured, and like her twin's painted pink and decorated with silver hearts. The game progresses. Fraser, continuing to flirt with Taliah offers sporadic compliments.

Like any heterosexual teenage male, Fraser would usually relish the prospect of being with attractive female twins, especially now that he is no longer taking the testosterone suppressant Cyprostat. However, he finds something disconcerting about the twin with the blue hairbands. Having analysed the board and deduced that he is in an advantageous position, Fraser, having checked his watch says, 'Got to go, promised Tyrone a game of *FIFA* before physical therapy. Call it a draw.'

Talulah and Taliah watch Fraser go over to the sofa, where Tyrone, reclining, PlayStation controller in hand, says, 'Ready to get schooled again bruv?'

'Tyrone, I'm going to rip you a new asshole,' says Fraser, picking up the other controller and collapsing onto the sofa beside him.

'No,' calls out a female nurse.

'Come on,' says Fraser theatrically. 'It's just friendly banter.'

'Just *no*,' adds the nurse.

'Sorry, *sorry*,' says Fraser.

Talulah and Taliah turn their attention to the chessboard.

'Meme wedi bordi,' whispers Talulah to Taliah.

'Yes let's play,' says Taliah.

'Ea wedi bordi,' whispers Talulah, wary of being overheard speaking in her cryptophasia.

Talulah stands up, goes to the other side of the coffee table and plonks herself down. Talulah and Taliah, who have little interest in chess, have not played against each other since they were small children. The contemplative nature of the game makes it too easy for one to predict what the other will do, but in this instance Talulah has surmised that the half-played game favours her.

They have played but a short time when Serenity's ward manager, Rakesha, comes into the room and hurries over.

'What're you doing Talulah, your one-to-one psychotherapy session started one minute ago,' says Rakesha sternly, looking from one twin to the other and back again.

'I know, I'm coming,' replies Talulah, who grabbing hold of her bishop is poised to take Taliah's rook when Rakesha says, 'Go!'

Talulah gets up and heads off at a jog towards the door. Now alone, Taliah reflects on her innermost thoughts. Three weeks ago, shortly after her arrival on the ward, while Talulah was in speech therapy, Taliah read an article about the psychotic disorder *folie à deux* on the internet, expanding on what little Dr Singh had told her. That night she dreamt she was lying on the grass with her twin, watching swallows darting through the blue sky above. A staccato burst of cryptophasia preceded a finger prodding her repeatedly in the arm, each occurrence sending a ripple of anxiety coursing through her body. Taliah felt the gentle breeze become a gale, saw the grass transform into writhing green tentacles and heard frightful wailing lamentations and clamorous rolls of thunder. Overhead cawing birds circled relentlessly. Beside her was a green and black-blotched, animate military vehicle with dark compound eyes and two spear-like appendages that probed menacingly in her direction.

When Taliah awoke abruptly, she lay in bed with the duvet pulled up to her chin. It was quite some time before the pounding of her heart subsided. Taliah realised that her dream was a repressed memory. She became quite certain then that Hunter-Thornton's *folie à deux* diagnosis had been correct, and that it was her twin, who had been suffering from the delusional disorder, brought on by paranoia, aggravated by drug use.

Now, perched on the stool in the recreation room in front of the chessboard, Taliah places a fingernail in her mouth, then extracts it again. She takes a handkerchief from her pocket and wipes her damp brow. A tear trickles down her cheek when she concludes that she has been merely a puppet on a string, controlled by the puppeteer, Talulah. And she sighs as she considers that her impending adulthood will either be a pitched battle for supremacy, or surrendering her birthright to her dominant twin.

Taliah, wiping another tear from her cheek with the handkerchief, realises that despite everything she still loves the person who is closer to her than anyone else in the world. Her only desire is that when they are released they can live more independent lives. Taliah closes her eyes and pictures herself going to university alone, having her own friends and making her own choices. Now, as she fantasises about a future with Samson, she smiles. The smile vanishes the moment it occurs to Taliah that these hopes are implausible, and she frowns on contemplating that Talulah's delusions and anarchist inclinations could easily return the both of them to a mental institution, or prison. Next she reflects on her mother's joy when she and her twin had been reunited on the Violet Ward. Taliah feels guilty when she thinks about this.

While Taliah continues to ruminate on her predicament, Dr Singh and Dr Vitali are with the hospital's director Dr Stevenson in his office.

'My choice of Symbyax and Invega have proven effective. They are now cured – the anarchy arson non–communication stuff is a thing of the past, do you understand?' says an agitated Dr Vitali, jabbing at Dr Singh with his index finger.

'Leave us,' orders Dr Stevenson.

'The fluoxetine and olanzapine ratios…'

'Now,' says Dr Stevenson, interrupting Dr Vitali mid-sentence.

Dr Vitali leaves the room.

'The state of that man. I could swear he's been raiding our drug supplies,' says Dr Stevenson, adjusting his spectacles and then swivelling in his revolving chair to face Dr Singh. 'Now what did you want to speak to me about?'

Doctor Singh takes a deep breath.

'As you know I have my reservations about one of the twins. I think that Talulah is not only controlling Taliah but also manipulating the hospital, so we think she's recovered.'

Dr Stevenson grimaces.

'I am convinced that their rampage,' continues Dr Singh, 'was due to what I mentioned the other day … *folie á deux…*'

'*Folie á deux*, it seems pretty farfetched to me,' intrudes Dr Stevenson. 'Now look, we've seen the footage of the incident. And though its impossible to comprehend how it happened, it seems that yes, there was some sort of malignant, symbiotic binary thing going on between the two of them, as we saw from the coetaneous actions.' Dr Stevenson shudders. 'But to claim that one is a parasitic twin who is to blame for everything, now that's something else entirely.'

'So you've read about the syndrome since we last spoke then?'

Dr Stevenson nods his white-haired head sombrely.

'All I am suggesting is we keep Talulah here for a little longer for observation,' says Dr Singh.

'Preposterous,' says Dr Stevenson. 'We wouldn't cut a patient in half, keep half here and send half home now would we?'

'No, but…'

The telephone on Dr Stevenson's desk is ringing.

'Forget this *folie à* nonsense old bean,' says Dr Stevenson. And then, 'The poker game recommences here at six-thirty.' He then picks up the telephone receiver.

Traipsing down the corridor back to his office Dr Singh is convinced that Hunter-Thornton had made the correct diagnosis. That beneath the veneer of pomposity and preposterousness there still lurks the profound insight that had made the young Hunter-Thornton the preeminent psychiatrist of his generation.

*

A month later – 'Keep up the good work girls and you'll be going home in no time,' calls out Pamela to Talulah and Taliah, who are standing by the door, poised to leave. Talulah smiles when she hears this, Taliah does not.

Taliah follows Talulah along the corridor, destination: the classroom where they have biology in five minutes.

Hubert passes a member of the hospital's security team on sentry duty in the corridor. He turns left. Talulah and Taliah are coming in the opposite direction. There are no hospital staff in this short passageway. Hubert has been fuming for weeks about the twins being promoted to Serenity, whilst he has been left oscillating between the acute ward and the male equivalent of the Violet ward. Hubert stands in the middle of the passageway.

'Hello dumb twins, long time no see.'

'Go away Hubert,' respond Talulah and Taliah in unison.

'Or should I say chatterbox twins,' adds Hubert caustically, wiping a greasy lock of black hair off his pale face. He then holds out his arms at his sides to stop Talulah and Taliah passing. 'Uh uh ah ah ahhh,' utters Hubert in a high-pitched voice. 'Do you know what that is?'

Talulah and Taliah, now standing side by side facing Hubert, shake their heads.

'That's your mum with Samson and Siegfried.' And then having looked at them each in turn, 'Oh, you didn't even know did you. Ha ha haha.'

Talulah turns left and Taliah right. Hubert again prevents them from passing with his arms. They take a step back.

'Ah ah ah oh bap bapbap.' And then putting on a German accent, '*Nein* Samson *arsch*.' And now in a high-pitched voice, 'Now Samson now.' Then in a very deep voice, 'Okay.' This followed by a, 'Suuurp.'

Talulah's pupils contract as she glares at Hubert, who staggers backwards, but determined to provoke a reaction, lurches forward.

'Bapbapbap suuurp ah ah.' And then in a deep voice, 'How do you like that?' And now in a German accent, 'She can't answer vith her mouth full, *ja*.'

Taliah places a reassuring hand on Talulah's forearm. Hubert is scurrying from side to side across the width of the passageway in crab-like fashion, going, 'Oh ah ahah, harder, bap bap suuuurp, *ja*,' changing the tone of his voice constantly to imitate the three imagined parties.

Still Talulah glares at Hubert and still Taliah's reassuring hand remains on her forearm. Hubert, his gangly frame scuttling back and forth across the width of the passageway, thrusting his hips forward obscenely when he reaches the passageway's walls, is in a trance-like state now, jerking frenziedly from side to side, repeating the actions again and again, going 'Bap bapbap ah ah suurp suuuurp *ja*,' over and over. 'Bap bapbap ah ah suurp suuuurp *ja*. Bap bapbap ah ah suurp suuuurp *ja*.'

Taliah takes her hand off Talulah's arm.

'Bap bapbap ah ah suurp suuuurp *ja*. Bap bapbap ah ah suurp suuuurp *ja*.'

Talulah continues to glare at Hubert.

'Bap bapbap ah ah suurp suuuurp *ja*. Bap bapbap ah ah suurp suuuurp *ja*. Bap bapbap ah ah suurp suuuurp *ja*.'

Taliah is willing Talulah to accost Hubert.

'Bap bapbap ah ah suurp suuuurp *ja*. Bap bapbap ah ah suurp suuuurp *ja*. Bap bapbap ah ah suurp suuuurp *ja*.'

Talulah clenches her fists at her sides.

'Bap bapbap ah ah suurp suuuurp *ja*. Bap bapbap ah ah suurp suuuurp *ja*. Bap bapbap ah ah suurp suuuurp *ja*.'

Taliah screws her eyes shut, holds her breath and tenses every muscle in her body, as she wills Talulah to attack,

'Bap bapbap ah ah suurp suuuurp *ja*. Bap bapbap ah ah suurp suuuurp *ja*. Bap bapbap ah ah suurp suuuurp *ja*.'

Talulah is trembling.

'Bap bapbap ah ah suurp suuuurp *ja*. Bap bapbap ah ah suurp suuuurp *ja*. Bap bapbap ah ah suurp suuuurp *ja*.'

Talulah rushes towards Hubert. Running footsteps are approaching. Talulah jumps back.

'ON THE FLOOR NOW!' It is a security guard who shouts this.

A delirious, oblivious Hubert, jerking relentlessly as if he were a puppet on a string, calls out, 'Bap bapbap ah ah suurp suuuurp *ja*. Bap bapbap ah ah suurp suuuurp *ja*. Bap bapbap ah ah suurp suuuurp *ja*. Bap bapbap ah ah suurp suuuurp *ja*.'

Thomas races around the corner. The security guard and Thomas rush towards Hubert and hurl themselves on top of him.

'RAHHHHH!' screams Hubert.

Dr Vitali, the tails of white coat floundering behind him, skids into the passageway, calling out, 'To the High-Care Suite, GO GO GO.'

Talulah and Taliah step around the commotion and continue on their way.

CHAPTER SIXTEEN

TALULAH AND TALIAH are eating breakfast in their ward's kitchen. Peering up from her bowl of Rice Krispies, Taliah watches Talulah's spoon moving from her mouth to the bowl and back again at the exact same time as hers. Taliah delays the raising of her spoon to her mouth, so the action is out of kilter with that of her twin. Talulah, looking across the table at her twin, says, 'Klathi geda abta unigo.'

Taliah opens her mouth then closes it again and stares down at the few remaining Rice Krispies floating in the milk at the bottom of her bowl.

'Ogi enit mathi,' says Talulah.

Taliah shrugs.

'Ogi enit mathi,' says Talulah again.

'I am not sure yet.'

Talulah glowers at Taliah, whose spoon is rattling against the side of her bowl.

'Ogi enit mathi,' repeats Talulah for the third time.

'Uni nuhnuh,' says Taliah quietly.

'Uni ea – ogi mathi dah – hoppi beddi bibta,' says Talulah. 'Bothi bobothi vitali bibta – ugi rake bibta – ucki medi bibta.' She then stands up.

Taliah rises slowly to her feet and follows Talulah out of the kitchen. The twins go to their bathrooms where, having flossed and brushed their teeth, they inspect their flawless whiteness in their respective mirrors.

'Bibta ugi ucki hoppi,' mutters Talulah, throwing her toothbrush in the bin and then striding out of the bathroom. But Taliah remains in her bathroom, viewing her reflection. She gasps, clutches the sides of the basin with both hands and peers down at the toothpaste-streaked water disappearing down the plughole. Spinning around, she scours the bathroom, before grabbing the tiny pair of hospital-issue nail scissors from the ledge by the shower. Having turned back to the basin, she snips hesitantly at a lock of hair and then observes the miniscule lengths drifting downwards. She takes a second snip, now a third. Taliah is snipping faster, again and again, the tiny lengths of hair drifting downwards becoming a cascade. Still faster Taliah snips, over and over again.

Taliah's eyes well with tears when she grabs a handful of hair on the side of her head, scrunches it up and ties it with a hairband. Having repeated the exercise with the hair on the other side of her head, Taliah stands gazing at her reflection in the bathroom mirror for quite some time. She then wipes her eyes with a tissue. Now standing in the doorway to her bedroom, Taliah surveys the interior, her attention shifting from the bed to the chest of drawers, to the desk, the barred window and the wall beside the bed, where the picture of Willem Dafoe Adam had given her was hung. Taliah takes one last lingering look at her bedroom, the only room she has ever called her own. She then turns her back on it for the last time and traipses slowly downstairs.

In the entrance hall Talulah glares at Taliah's hair, which is now not only slightly shorter than her own, but tied at the sides of her head in pigtails, this in contrast to Talulah's ponytail. Feeling the scathing glare as intensely as if it were a screamed burst of irate cryptophasia, Taliah swallows. Congratulatory staff members are descending upon Talulah and Taliah, beaming smiles upon their countenances.

'Oh, you've changed your hair,' says one. 'I can't remember seeing you with different hairstyles,' says another. 'Now everyone will be able to tell you apart,' remarks a third.

'Well done girls, congratulations!' the jubilant staff members exclaim. 'We're so happy for you.' 'Have a wonderful life together.' 'We'll miss you.' 'You will be just fine.'

Encircled by excitement and expectation, Taliah is questioning her own sanity, when Dr Vitali, his hair sticking out haphazardly in all directions, races into the hall.

'Yeah you've done it!' he shouts.

And here comes Dr Singh. He addresses Taliah by name, and Talulah too, though in a more reserved tone. Thomas is leading a small group of patients into the hall. Tracey, hurrying over, says, 'Your hair's different.' And then having checked the colour of Talulah and Taliah's hairbands, she hugs Taliah tightly to her, tears now streaming down her cheeks. 'Enjoy yourself, have a good time and don't forget me, promise,' she says.

'I won't forget you, I promise,' says Taliah, struggling to breathe in Tracey's tight embrace.

When Tracey releases her grip, Lucy ambles forward and hugs Taliah.

'.hailaT eybdooG,' she says.

'Goodbye Lucy,' says Taliah. 'Thank you for being my friend.'

Adam is approaching.

'This is for you Taliah,' he says, handing Taliah an A6 sized card.

Taliah turns the card over. It is a portrait of her with her name in the bottom corner. Taliah smiles. She embraces her closest friend in the hospital, knowing nothing about the events that brought him here, and vice versa. Adam says, 'I know you don't want to stay with her.'

'I have to, she's a part of me,' whispers Taliah in Adam's ear.

'Does one keep a tumour because it is part of you?' replies Adam.

Talulah, standing several metres away, is glowering at Adam and Taliah.

'Time to go girls,' says Thomas, waving the set of car keys held in his hand.

Taliah, pressing her damp cheek to Adam's, kisses him. Having placed the portrait in the pocket of her Puffa coat, she says, 'Goodbye Adam, I will miss you.' She then follows Talulah out of Beddington House Hospital.

Thomas opens the door of the minivan. Talulah and Taliah clamber in and sit down, Taliah in the row of seats immediately behind Talulah. Thomas turns the keys in the ignition. The minivan pulls away. They are nearing the end of the long drive when Taliah turns around in her seat and takes one last look at Beddington House Hospital, her home for the last twelve months. Talulah does not look back.

On either side of the road are lush green meadows, peppered with patches of buttercups and dandelions, where cows and horses graze contentedly. Scattered across the vast expanse of blue high above, the cumulus clouds are billowy balls of mist. The breeze gushing into the minivan's interior is tinged with the scent of fresh grass and flowers.

'The aroma of liberation, isn't it wonderful,' remarks Thomas.

'Ye-s,' says Talulah.

Taliah says nothing. Talulah looks impassively ahead, whilst in the seat behind, Taliah's attention flits from the front to the view through the side window. She can see no liberation here, nor can she smell it. The green grass and blue sky through which swallows dart, tweeting elatedly, are bringing memories flooding back of her last day of freedom on the playing fields. Taliah, her breath coming in agitated gasps, takes a handkerchief from the pocket of her jeans and dabs her damp forehead. High above a cloud blocking out the sun casts a shadow across the land. Talulah, her face expressionless, continues to look directly ahead, her derisive thoughts focusing on her twin's hair. Taliah, aware of this, wishes she could turn around and return to her friends and her room at the hospital, leaving her twin to experience her liberation alone.

Houses and shops replace the rural scene. The minivan is slowing now, drawing to a halt in Fordham Park Station's car park. Talulah quickly disembarks, Taliah remains momentarily in her seat, then stands up and leaves the van, her blue mini-rucksack, like Talulah's, slung over her right shoulder.

'Good luck girls,' says Thomas in the ticket hall. 'Here are your tickets.' Talulah grabs both tickets. Having examined the electronic train timetable, Thomas says, 'It's platform three.' And then, 'The courier service will deliver your belongings to your home tomorrow morning between seven-thirty and eight-thirty. All the best, goodbye.' And with that he is off.

Taliah, through no conscious decision of her own, falls into line behind Talulah, as she always has. Multiple pairs of eyes watch as they make their way through the station, in what has been a rite of passage for Beddington House's freed patients since the hospital's opening in 1863.

The train is pulling into the platform. Talulah and Taliah are waiting in the middle of the platform. When the train stops, Talulah presses the open button. The door opens. Talulah enters the train. Taliah exhales sharply, looks left and right and then follows her twin. Two girls around Talulah and Taliah's age are sitting halfway down the carriage, chattering animatedly to each other. Talulah strides past them, but Taliah stops and gazes at the two girls. She unslings the mini-rucksack from her shoulder and prepares to sit down in the row behind them.

'Meou nuhnuh hine gyal ung,' says Talulah.

The two girls spin around and gawp at Talulah. Taliah follows Talulah to the last row of seats at the back of the carriage.

'Mene ha ithe waba,' remarks Talulah, glowering at Taliah's hair.

'*Ea.*'

'Meou odeh ha mene.'

Taliah, looking out of the window, does not respond. The train is moving. Ten minutes have passed when Talulah, noting that the train is travelling slowly, says, 'Ooow ra – kloki bibta ra.'

'Dreety,' says Taliah.

'Meme ata geda outhe a oomi – gego dowi bordi – eain abta tudi ramp crible wede.'

Taliah watches a buzzard soaring in circles high above the track.

'Bizzi dehabta dehad,' says Talulah, nudging Taliah in the side with her elbow.

'Ea,' mutters Taliah.

Talulah, leaning into Taliah, whispers, 'Dehabta dinki dunki.'

'Nuhnuh,' replies Taliah.

'Odeh eain, breddi budud a ango.'

Talulah and Taliah sit in silence, Talulah looking ahead at the seat in front of her, Taliah out of the window. Further up the carriage the two teenage girls chatter contentedly. Taliah listens wistfully to them discussing their plans for this evening. A man wearing a suit is ambling down the aisle, talking on his phone. Taliah notices that the mobile the man is talking into is different to any that she had seen prior to her detention. It occurs to her that she never once saw a mobile phone during her stay at Beddington House Hospital. Talulah glowers periodically at Taliah's hair. When she does so her mouth turns downwards at the ends. Sensing her twin's simmering animosity, Taliah undoes the top button of her blouse.

Taliah, viewing the passing fields, woods, buildings, cars and people on the other side of the window, becomes aware that Talulah has ceased scrutinising her. Glancing across at the adjoining seat, she sees Talulah's eyelids flicker. Taliah returns her attention to the view afforded through the window. When she glances across at Talulah several minutes later, Talulah's eyes are closed and her chin is resting on her chest. Feeling Talulah's lethargy pervading her, Taliah stifles a yawn, then edges across her seat away from her.

Now free to think her own thoughts, Taliah reflects on her and her twin's life together, the memories darting through her mind as quickly as the countryside on the other side of the window. She pictures the two of them as children constructing Lego Architecture monuments, Talulah telling her what to do, she following her commands. In her mind's eye Taliah sees Talulah and herself in speech therapy, swapping seats when the speech therapist turns her back to them. Taliah grits her teeth as she recalls her twin's betrayal over Samson, and exhales forcefully through her nose when she reflects on how Talulah had read her diary. Taliah, wondering if their diaries have been returned, places the nail of her little finger in her mouth, exerts downward pressure, then quickly extracts it again. Remembering that Talulah still does not know that she wrote in her diary the morning of their arrest, Taliah hopes the diaries have not been returned, for she does not want Talulah discovering this. She rotates her head and watches Talulah's breasts moving gently up and down before turning back to the window.

Taliah's pupils dilate and her hands form clenched fists in her lap as she ponders the arson attacks, her loss of innocence at the hands of Siegfried, her trial and incarceration. The pleasurable moments of twinship are forgotten now. All that remains is the continual cycle of domination, followed by fighting and isolation from the outside world. At the hospital, the various therapists emphasised the importance of patients making a fresh start when they are released. Their words now weigh heavily upon Taliah. Talulah's hazel eyes open wide. She scowls at Taliah, frown lines visible on her brow, her hands clenched balls in her lap. Taliah holds her breath. The train is slowing. It pulls to a halt. Talulah and Taliah put on their Puffa coats, sling their identical mini-rucksacks over their right shoulders and get off the train.

Taliah is not following behind Talulah, but walking abreast of her, their feet moving in time with one another as they march through the station and then outside. High above them grey rain clouds obscure the sun, beside them the traffic hurtles past.

'Ooow aak hine,' says Talulah.

Taliah does not fall into line behind her twin.

'OOOW AAK HINE!' repeats Talulah.

Passers-by stare at the twins, several point. Talulah quickens her pace. Taliah, speeding up, her feet moving in time with Talulah's, stays level with her. It begins to rain.

'WABA DERRIII MENE HA ITHE – AAK HINE!' shouts Talulah.

Every impulse screams at Taliah to fall in line behind her twin as she always has, but she does not. Talulah starts to jog, Taliah too.

'OOOW AAK HINE!'

'NO!' shouts Taliah.

They are sprinting now, Taliah remaining alongside Talulah, on her left. Two children are approaching from the opposite direction. Talulah swerves right to avoid them and Taliah left. Now they are in familiar terrain, merely ten minutes or so from their home. Ten minutes away from their shared room, waiting for them as it has always been. Cars stop, pedestrians stare and passengers on the top deck of a bus gawp at the two identical girls careering down the pavement, one shouting at the other in an unfathomable language. Talulah barges into Taliah, knocking her into a woman carrying shopping bags, but Taliah, surging forward, catches up again. Still they race down the rain-drenched street, traffic accelerating past on the road beside them. Taliah, glancing over her shoulder, sees an articulated lorry surging along the road towards them. Talulah has one foot on the pavement, one in mid-air, when Taliah shoves her in the side.

'Meou!' shrieks Talulah, toppling sideways, teetering on the verge, her arms flapping wildly at her sides. She falls into the road. The beeping lorry, skidding across the wet tarmac, crushes Talulah's lower body beneath its front wheel. 'Meou,' she whimpers, reaching out to her twin. Taliah stands on the pavement for quite some time watching her, before stepping onto the road, bending down and clasping Talulah's hand in hers.

Taliah feels Talulah's grip weakening, sees her eyelids flutter then close. Still Taliah clasps her twin's hand in hers, even as the warmth drains from Talulah's flesh. Beside Taliah is the ashen-faced lorry driver, and behind him a long trail of beeping cars. Taliah continues to hold Talulah's hand in hers, even as the wailing ambulance and police car screech to a halt on the rain-sodden road. And she is still clasping her hand as Talulah is carried on the stretcher to the ambulance, and then hoisted into it. Taliah's fingers are gently pried away. And now the ambulance is racing away without her, its siren blaring, its blue light flashing.

The policewoman, wrapping an anorak around Taliah's shoulders, asks what her name is, and she replies, 'Taliah.' Two policemen are approaching. When they lead Taliah to the police car and help her inside, they use her name.

As the police car pulls away, Taliah turns her head and looks back at the lorry on the side of the road, growing ever smaller, until it disappears altogether in the grey mist.

Chapter Seventeen

ONE YEAR LATER – on the shelves are several Barbie Dolls, a rag doll, a nineteen-eighties Cabbage Patch Doll, a toy clown with dark mournful eyes and an array of small felt covered animals, dressed as humans. Arranged on the floor are various Lego Architecture monuments. Pressed against the near wall is a bunk bed. On either side of the room is a desk. Above the desk on the right hand side of the room is a shelf, on which are several books, one of which is a blue diary.

Taliah is sitting at her desk, brushing her hair. On the desk in front of her is a silver picture frame, containing a photograph of Talulah, taken when she was a small child. A smile adorns her pretty, dimpled-cheeked, cherubic face. Her hair is worn in pigtails tied with bright blue ribbons. Taliah glances at the photograph. She says, 'Ha wuthiwuthi – odeh da eain breddi budud umi.'

Taliah continues brushing her hair, which is now shoulder length and highlighted. She is tying her hair in a ponytail with a blue hairband when she says, 'Ha abta urrie treki – wethiwethi dunki nana danci – jahdeh tudi en.'

Bethany is standing in the doorway to the bedroom, listening to her daughter. She wipes the tear trickling down her cheek with the sleeve of her blouse. Bethany often witnesses her daughter speaking to her beloved twin, so cruelly taken away by the freak accident a year ago today. From downstairs Taliah hears her father call, 'Come down and help me.'

Taliah, gazing at Talulah's photograph, says, 'Fa eh – go meou ha wuthiwuthi wedi.' She then stands up and walks out onto the landing, where Bethany is waiting for her. At the bottom of the stairs Taliah sees her father leaning on a chest of drawers. Colin looks up the stairs. He is smiling. He says, 'Come and help me move this to the living room.'

Colin moved back in several months ago. Taliah goes down the stairs. She is poised to pick up one end of the chest of drawers when the doorbell rings.

'One second Dad,' says Taliah, who then approaches the front door and peers through the peephole. Standing on the doorstep are her friends, Veronica, Ben and Samson. Taliah opens the door.

*Please consider leaving a short review for
Symbiosis on Amazon.*

*Reviews are vital to us authors for
finding new readers.*